INTERMEZZO
For
SOLO VIOLA

Copyright © 2008 by Henriette Mendels

ISBN: 0-9801510-0-7

978-0-9801510-0-8

Library of Congress Control Number:

2008900108

Printed in the United States of America.

Editor: Carole Glickfeld

Design: Steve Montiglio

Cover Painting: Hartwell Ayles 1964

All rights reserved. No part of this book may be transmitted in any form or by any means, electronic or mechanical including photocopying , recording or by any information storage or retrieval system without the written permission of the author except where permitted by law.

Requests for such permissions should be addressed to:

Zeeland Publishing

an imprint of Tigress Publsihing

4831 Fauntleroy Way SW # 103

Seattle, WA 98116

206-683-5554

This is a work of fiction. Names, characters, and incidents, (with the exception of actual historical events which occurred during World War II), either are the product of the author's imagination or are used fictitiously. Any resemblence to actual persons, living or dead, business establishemts, other events or locales is entirely coincidental.

Dedicated

to the

Memory of My Prescient,

Sephardic Grandfather

Pierre Abas,

Who Died in Sobibor to Save Our Lives

3/31/08

Dear Pauline —

Thank you for all you do and all you are!

Love!
Harriet

Part One
OPENING THEME

SEATTLE

The few moments of sunlight were welcomed by both students and faculty after three months of rain, a deluge so relentless the usually optimistic inhabitants of Seattle were wondering if it would ever cease or, whether due to the exuberant economy and its resulting hedonistic lifestyles, this was a (probably deserved) re-enactment of the Biblical flood.

"Good afternoon," called the bespectacled instructor, who had the office next to hers, "there's fresh coffee. I'm late for class. See you later." She rushed outside and down the circular metal staircase, clutching books, a briefcase and an assortment of untidy papers.

Petra let her pass, then looked down at the steps, surprised by the changes she had not noticed earlier, too engrossed in her own thoughts, the tasks ahead, the ones completed, to realize that time had not stopped.

On the contrary, it had raced, created and destroyed, on its journey.

When she came here to teach more than twenty years ago, the college was new, the buildings recently completed, the same staircase spotless and still smelling faintly of galvanized paint, which was supposed to keep the steel from corroding.

Indeed, it had held up fairly well, but now the steps, which had initially gleamed bright orange, were darkened with rust and thick ridges of mud.

She trudged upstairs and into her office to resume the task she had begun earlier, ferreting through a mishmash of papers, academic trivia, student test results, outdated grade records.

Most would go into the recycling bins, but it was also a necessary opportunity to donate no longer used textbooks to needy students.

The publishing house representatives, ubiquitous on campus insured an endless supply of gratis publications to faculty members. After a year, the office shelves resembled local libraries.

Her collection badly needed winnowing.

She made stacks of eight or ten on the floor, until she was trapped by a series of multi-colored Pisas, which threatened to topple momentarily. Laughing at her self-imposed prison, she redistributed the books until there were ultimately many more towers but they were stable.

Three hours later, she was finished, the discarded copies were placed in a box to be claimed by new owners, and her workspace was manageable and restful.

She took down a textbook of Shakespeare's works from a nearly empty shelf, its once blue cover frayed and graying. It opened as she knew it would to "Antony and Cleopatra," and there, still hidden safely where it was placed in 1959, lay the crumpled, faded half of a ten-dollar bill.

For an instant, she gazed at an underlined passage and mused, as the memories of so long ago resurfaced, and instead of leaving the book in her office, decided to take it home.

Chapter 1

The gentle aureole of Indian summer glowed across the somber Upper West Side tenements and around Grant's Tomb, transforming their cold grayness into sparkling whites and golds, while myriad particles of light rose from the heated concrete sidewalks like tiny prismatic jewels.

Beyond the templed monument, Riverside Park, leafed and still fertile, stretched into the city, while beyond it the Hudson River gleamed, silver blue, wedded forever to the dark green hills of Palisades Park its lovely forested mystery unblemished except for the huge, red neon ALCOA sign which constantly raped it.

A young woman holding a suitcase descended from a stopped bus, glanced at the apartment house numbers, found the correct address immediately, entered and gave the elevator operator the floor she needed. The ancient golden cage stopped and, with a leer, he pointed down the hall.

"You going to move in here?" he asked insolently.

"Maybe," she murmured and left him.

The door opened immediately, even before she had a chance to ring the bell, as if the landlady had been listening for the elevator creaking its journey to the fifth floor. She glanced at the girl quickly, noticed she was clean, looked trustworthy and would probably be an honest tenant.

"So," she said, "you must be Petra. You had no trouble finding the place?" Then she gestured and preceded the visitor through a long, gloomy corridor covered with the classically cheap, striped runner, its colors muddled together with age and accumulated dirt, stopped before a closed door, produced a key and stood aside to show the room.

"Eleven dollars a week, you do your own cleaning up. I'll supply fresh sheets when you need them. Toilet's down the hall. You can use the bathtub whenever you like, except on Sunday mornings. That's when Mister takes his bath."

Her tongue was thick in her mouth, as if after all these years in New York she still had difficulty speaking English, more at home always in her native German, her accent as awkward as the heavy-weighted body leaning assertively against the door, forcing an agreement to all terms.

The girl sighed, placed her solitary suitcase on the floor and nodded, tired but sensing she would be safe here. She reached into her purse, pulled out a ten and a single, took the key and waited while the landlady wrote out a receipt.

"Everything has to be in order," she announced. "Do you know the lousy I.R.S. insists on making me pay taxes on these few dollars?"

The new tenant mumbled some inane reply, not willing to begin a long conversation, and the woman soon turned around and lumbered crookedly back down the dark hallway.

Petra took a long breath and perused her new home. A dark, heavily stained dresser pushed against grey-stripe papered walls, a hard little folding cot that could never have supported its owner's own weight, a wooden mirrored armoire leaning in a corner, and a checkered-clothed card table with one metal chair facing a window lacking a river view.

It certainly wasn't Park Avenue, but it was New York. Finally...New York, and that was a victory in itself!

She frowned, heard people shouting outside, and with trepidation glanced down through the solitary window expecting to see an inner courtyard filled with city detritus. Instead, to her astonishment, directly beneath her sunlight streamed onto a clay tennis court where an immaculately white-dressed woman with glasses and blonde hair was instructing a young Asian man also in tennis whites.

"Play closer to the net!" she commanded, her voice rising slightly.

Her student ran forward trying to obey, leaped high in the air, lashed furiously at the oncoming ball, and watched in bewilderment as it flew, untouched, right past him.

Grimacing, he threw his racket on the ground, and then shrugged. "Let's just forget it for today, Jopie. I've got to study for a bio midterm. I guess that's why I can't concentrate!"

They disappeared through an archway leading into an adjoining building.

For a few moments the court was deserted and quiet, but soon a doubles match began. Petra heard again the staccato bouncing of the ball, the humming of the strings as it hit the tennis rackets, and the triumphant laughter or shouts of frustration which invariably followed.

Above her the tower of Riverside Church rose, its pure Gothic lines incongruous among the semi-tenements it neighbored. At that moment the carillons began to chime. Delighted, she chose to consider their song a personal welcome from the city she had always loved and could finally again call "home."

Chapter 2

Unpacking and hanging up jeans, sweaters and skirts didn't require more than fifteen minutes. The rest of her clothes, black dupioni silk cocktail dresses, peau de soie and chiffon pastel evening gowns, elegant high-heeled gold and silver sandals with narrow straps, remained behind in Washington.

And could rot there for all she cared!

After all, wasn't she now residing in the garment center of the world? A world she had known since childhood?

And though Bergdorf's was within her mental capacity, it was not yet in her newly independent financial one. But she vowed that as soon as she had a decent job, when New York recognized her talent and rewarded her accordingly, the boringly conservative, work-related wools she now needed would be replaced with the most expensive, luxuriant cashmeres.

She owned one "job-search" garment, an olive green, mohair Hattie Carnegie suit, silk-lined, purchased on sale at Saks Fifth during a last winter weekend, mini-vacation-after-finals-trip. It was simple and beautiful, showing off her unusual coloring admirably.

That coloring helped her play a defensive but usually effective game with men she knew who were trying to flatter her into doing what they wanted. Which might not be what she wanted! Lowering her eyes and head demurely as they gazed lust-eyed at her nose and scalp, she would ask innocently, "You say you love me. Well, then, flatter me, tell me how much you admire my hair and my eyes. What color are they?"

Almost invariably the laughing, immediate response would be a confident variation of, "Hey, I'm not blind! A blue-eyed, honest-to-God blonde!"

They were partially correct; after all, they were gazing right at her hair, roots and all. And she was a natural blonde. But still, their ardent suits were lost as she smiled back at them with eyes that were hazel, usually green, but never, ever blue. And the olive green Hattie Carnegie brought their color out as if they were jade cactus leaves.

She hung it up carefully, grateful it had helped her find a new job, aware the very low salary it paid would permit few shopping trips for a while. And none to Saks Fifth!

In June she had graduated from college and during the following summer months worked at a large department store, intending to save up enough to finance a move to New York. She was assigned to the perfume department and delightedly swabbed Cabochard and Chanel No. 5 behind her ears and on her wrists. The salesgirls were encouraged to heavily push a new fragrance just released by a famous cosmetics firm (and as an extra incentive they would receive a small commission for every bottle sold). Unfortunately, the perfume wasn't very successful because, as customers soon discovered (and she agreed), instead of enhancing the sexuality of its wearers, the stuff stank like underarm perspiration.

Which might have been considered an aphrodisiac in France, but not in America!

In mid-September she purchased a train ticket, rented a room in a cheap, midtown Manhattan hotel and tried to get interviews at numerous publishing houses and advertising agencies, diploma-with-honors in hand, confidence in her heart.

The closest she got to actual interviews was to leave unread résumés at the receptionists' front desks, which were tossed into the nearest circular files even before she left the offices. Desperate her money would evaporate before she found work, she went to an employment agency and was offered an entry level job at one of the most prestigious advertising agencies in the city, packed her one suitcase and went looking for more appropriate living quarters. This room would suffice for now.

The hormone-heavy males who had unsuccessfully wooed her, she left forgotten behind, home in Washington.

Suddenly Petra frowned. Memories of Washington D.C. as "home" until a few days ago had not been particularly joyous. In fact, she wasn't even really sure what defined the word "home."

As a child, hand-held by her parents, she had been brought to New York, wide-eyed, unable to speak a word of English, uncertain about the future.

The great city held out its arms in welcome and compassion. She grew up knowing it intimately, feeling it was "home," its parks her playground, its fountains replacing the canals of that other home, its museums free and accessible, allowing her to wander and explore, its public schools with their traumatic Regents Exams universally hated and feared by all students, forcing her to learn, even when she didn't feel like it.

Then, just after the first half of her senior year in high school ended, her father accepted a position at The Netherlands Embassy in the nation's capital. Soon afterwards the family moved south.

She detested it, its maudlin eternal tombstone pageantry, scoffed mutely towards the tourists, awed at how their taxes forever honored the dead in frozen marble edifice after edifice, while she who had to live in it viewed the city as an enormous white-washed cemetery. Worse yet, the capital of the United States, already the greatest country on earth, was a cultural wasteland, a backwater not worthy of its historical rank, which possessed one ill-supported symphony orchestra, no permanent concert hall for performances (with the exception of the unfortunately named Constitution Hall belonging to the DAR, whose members continued to deal with their deservedly sullied reputations as racists), had absolutely no interest in forming its own professional theater or ballet companies (although there were amateur groups which performed both), and considered the possibility of a resident opera house as simply preposterous.

Foreign diplomats, who might have considered postings to the city as major promotions and arrived expecting the same cultural sophistication to which they were accustomed, were quickly disillusioned and learned to look for such amenities elsewhere or do without.

Students at the local universities crammed into whatever things had wheels and spent weekends in New York whenever wallets and indulgent parents allowed, away from their culturally deprived city of idealized death.

Even before graduation Petra informed her parents that although she had no friends who lived there anymore, would have to struggle to re-learn its rhythms and its patterns, and entirely pay all her own expenses, nevertheless, she was moving home as soon as possible.

Home to New York.

Starved for good music, ballet and theater, she arrived at Penn Station, in love with the great city even before she had a job, or acquired the basic little room which temporarily, would shelter her. And so now, as she heard the lovely ringing of the church bells, she knew they were a good omen and listened, entranced, and imagined they sang just for her.

Chapter 3

With clothes put away she gazed silently at the tennis players below the window, vowing to buy a radio soon so she could listen to WQXR, the classical music station, and another previously deeply missed link to this amazing city.

Suddenly there was a knock at a connecting door to her left.

"How do you take your coffee?" asked a tall, grey-haired woman peeking around the room. "It's instant. But I have sugar. No milk though. Figured you didn't own a hot plate yet." She held a mug of black liquid in one hand, turned aside to reach for another and entered without being invited, apparently not doubting for a second she would be welcomed.

The uninvited visitor was beautiful. Not at first glance; rather, her beauty grew with familiarity. She was imposing, almost six feet tall and perfectly proportioned. Grey hair framed large blue eyes above a perfect nose. It was impossible to guess her actual age because despite the ashen hair, her face was almost devoid of lines. She could have been forty or perhaps more.

"I'm Ellen Douglas. Who are you?"

"Petra Fresco," she replied, searching for a non-existent seat, finally perching on the cot while her visitor sat in the single chair at the little table.

"New to New York?"

"No, I was raised here but have been gone for many years."

"I see."

The coffee tasted terrible but Petra could have kissed the woman who brought it to her. New York, the most exciting city in the world for which she had longed so desperately, could also be the loneliest.

Ellen had unexpectedly taken control of that problem. "Where are you eating dinner?" she asked gruffly lighting a cigarette.

"Can you recommend a place?"

"Most of us eat at the International House. The food's pretty good, geared towards the non-existent budgets of starving foreign students. Usually a real bargain. The toast is free, the coffee's cheap and the cups are refillable." Ellen spoke confidently, a deep voice, smoke-tinged with a distinct New England accent. "It's the big building next door with the double wings. The tennis courts also belong to it."

"Can I use their dining room whenever I want to?"

"No. You have to be a member or going for an advanced degree. I'm at Columbia, working towards a Master's in Sociology. What's your field?"

"I majored in Comparative Lit and just graduated. I came here to work. Not to study right now."

"Don't count on a high level job! Your chances of landing one are infinitesimal."

Petra protested immediately. Her grades had earned her a place on the Dean's List for four years and she had no doubt she would succeed.

"Ha!" sneered her neighbor, who had quickly assessed the humbling results Petra's job search would bring, "Here a diploma is worth remarkably little. As a woman you have a choice of two jobs, secretary or junior-secretary. Which one are you?"

Petra scowled and answered her, "But don't think I'm staying at that level! I hate office work. It's not what I was trained to do."

"Ever worked before?"

"Sure. I was a cashier during the summer."

"Doesn't count. So consider yourself as unskilled and inexperienced labor. In fact, the ideal junior-secretary."

She took another sip of coffee and continued, "I can picture the men discussing your future in the Board Room. Fresco? Smart girl. Attractive, too. That's a negative. Doubt if she'll stay. Soon as we've spent the time and money to train her she'll meet some guy, marry him and be knocked up within the year. And there goes our investment in the diaper pail. The trouble with broads is, you trust them, teach them, they're gravid, they're gone!"

Petra frowned. The one argument that would keep women in the basement, irrevocably, unchangeably, eternally, lay imbedded in their bodies. Possession of a more than healthy set of brains could not absolve the potential sin of ever-imminent germination.

Ellen was absolutely right.

And it hurt like hell.

Petra felt a distressing rtssss against her leg and watched helplessly as a huge run in one nylon stocking slithered past her knee and stopped just below the ankle, then wondered if she could afford to buy a new pair, or if she dared to wear them once more and pretend she didn't know.

"I'm sorry to have been so hard on you," Ellen said. "Come on, I'll show you around the I. House. Dinner's on me. Ever traveled abroad? Or have an interest in international relations? With a little encouragement and some luck, we might be able to get you an Associate Membership even if you're not a student."

"Does being born in Europe qualify for being abroad?" Petra retorted sweetly.

"Hurray! You're in! I am relieved. I was having visions of you walking up to Broadway alone every night. Summers are no big problem but winter is coming and it gets dark early. It's cold and lonely, and there are some real creeps hanging around. Not really healthy for young women in this part of town. But now you can probably use the facilities next door."

She went to her room, grabbed her purse and together they entered the building next door.

Chapter 4

The main entrance to the International House faced a small park adjacent to 123rd Street. As Ellen opened the massive lobby doors, Petra's first impression was pure amazement. They were in an enormous room, marble walled, luxurious, with easy chairs and coffee tables placed in nooks, or close to arched floor-to-ceiling windows. People were seated in small groups talking, studying, or sleeping. Every spot was occupied but it did not even appear crowded.

They rushed down a flight of stairs and into the cafeteria.

"Welcome to the Waffle Wing. Grab a tray and help yourself."

Wall paneled and furnished in maple, its soft golden veneer the predominant color, the restaurant consisted of two large areas; the first, where the two women chose to eat, held the kitchen and main dining area and was connected via French doors to the adjoining larger room, which faced the river and contained additional maple booths, tables and chairs. Now in mid- October, it was dark and deserted as the river gleamed beyond it.

Supper (chopped steak, mashed potatoes and salad) was healthy, uncomplicated and quite edible. Not Chambord or Pavilion, but infinitely more suited to the budgets of needy students.

Or junior-secretaries.

During the apple pie dessert (no hard sauce or ice cream), two Turkish graduate students joined them.

"They're my friends," whispered Ellen quickly, as the taller, self-assured and arrogant, took possession of a chair next to her. His features were regular and his eyes, slightly tipped upward, hinted at an exotic Asian gene pool. He might have been quite handsome except for the sardonic sneer lurking around his mouth, dominating any other emotions behind even his most innocent remarks.

He looked at Petra and she at him and both came to an immediate conclusion: It was hate at first sight.

His companion was short, fat, with the soft-eyed tolerance and forbearance of a beast of burden. He plumped himself into the other chair and listened to the words of wisdom pompousing continually from the mouth of his countryman.

Because she was a guest and a newcomer, Petra aped for a few minutes the wide-eyed acclamation for the Turkish guru. Ultimately she learned nothing from him, but enough about him to ascertain he was Ellen's current moment. Her roommate was gazing at him with tolerant, hypnotized eyes, nodding wordlessly in accord with every inanity he babbled, her face turned with full attention towards him.

But suddenly absorbing what he was in fact saying, not simply listening to it, she exclaimed in pure Bostonian, "You damned Turks! You haven't any idea what's actually going on around you in the rest of the world! You're at least a century behind the times socially, and economically you're still in the Middle Ages!"

Then smiling sweetly she continued, "But mind you, we'll drag you kicking and screaming into the modern world whether you like it or not!"

For an instant everyone looked at her in shock, waiting for her demon lover to react, but he burst out laughing, and instead turned to Petra."You. How old are you?"

"Salmi!" Ellen gasped, "that's none of your business!" But he ignored her. "You sit, observe, and say nothing. Where do you come from?"

"Boor," Petra thought but answered, "I'm twenty-two." A quick pause and then, "So, my turn. How old are you?"

Instead of answering he grumbled, "Where in America are you from?"

"D.C. Any more questions?"

Salmi growled something unintelligible, hatred snapshotted all over his face. To her surprise Kerim was staring at her. "You are that old? I thought you much younger. Like a little girl you still look. In Turkey you would be long married, have children!"

"Long live the good old U.S.A." Petra exclaimed. "That kind of *tsouris* I don't need!"

"What is it you don't need?" he asked.

She smiled back at him innocently, cruelly, ignoring his request for clarification and the questioning frowns of the others. Then decided not to respond. There are some words that defy translation. They'd have to discover the meaning for themselves.

But Salmi, quicker, angrier, unwilling to allow a mere woman to challenge his male omniscience snarled, "There is nothing wrong with marrying young. You Western women are so proud of your independence, and what do you do after you have finished screaming about equality? You fall desperately in love, cannot wait for a ring on your fingers, and are never heard from again. Except as reflections of your husbands or asinine allusions in the society pages about your unimportant, silly, charitable doings."

"In other words," he continued, sarcasm dripping like brilliantine from his words, "your lives are the same as those of Turkish women. Only the inevitable occurs when you are older, perhaps a bit more sophisticated and far more dissatisfied because of it. And," he postulated, "all this waiting is unhealthy, resulting only in unnecessary sexual suppression and frustration."

He slurped his coffee loudly for effect, wiped his mouth with the back of his hand.

"Yes, Salmi dear. You are absolutely right," Ellen assured him.

Recognizing she was humoring him he started to retort but rather suddenly decided to stop preaching, as if he really weren't interested in the subject any longer.

Ellen had pushed her chair very close to his and placed one aristocratic hand beneath the table. (Although the upper arm was still clearly visible and moved almost imperceptibly up and down.) Salmi was clearly touched by her support of his position!

The angry furrows on his forehead began to soften and the sneer around his mouth weakened to an imbecilic grin. For a moment he attempted to maintain his composure but failed completely. Clearly in distress, the over-confident sage mumbled something about taking Ellen to a movie.

Kerim, typically oblivious and foolish, immediately invited himself along. Salmi grabbed his coat, buttoned it quickly, effectively covering any obvious physical embarrassments and stumbled painfully out of the Waffle Wing, followed by his countryman and a jubilant Ellen.

Chapter 5

And then Petra was sitting alone on a Friday evening in the most exciting, wide-awake city in the world. She looked at her half-filled coffee cup feeling lonely, and, yes, missing the company of a special man. She was aware not all of Salmi's chauvinistic sermon had been garbage. But she would rather die an old maid than let him know it.

She drank the last of the coffee and went upstairs to explore the rest of the International House, tried to appear casual and ambled to the far end of the lobby, found an empty chair and curled up in it. A door nearby opened and closed continually, and she heard music coming from the interior but didn't know if she was allowed to enter. Shy, but more bored than frightened, she sauntered in behind someone, pretending she knew exactly what to expect, and assumed if she was unwelcome she would find out soon enough.

No one protested or even noticed her.

Before her lay one of the most exquisite rooms she had ever seen. Wood, seasoned and dark, paneled the walls; fern green leather sofas and matching overstuffed chairs rested on thick patterned Persian carpets; massive Gothic tables held shaded lamps whose soft light supplemented the brilliance of the great crystal chandelier which hung in the center of the ceiling.

In a far corner several people were shuffling records into and out of albums, whispering, until suddenly the music began again. The Bach "B Minor Mass!" Petra had always loved it and now thought, "This Friday night will not be wasted. I've found a haven!"

But soon the music ended, the room emptied, and the friendly, beautiful shelter that had embraced her so completely suddenly emerged as a labyrinthian cavern, engendered with numerous dark and menacing corners.

Dejected, she considered the remainder of the evening. It was only 9 o'clock.

She decided to make one more trip to the Waffle Wing, get one coffee refill, then...what alternative was there?...a chilly stroll back to the impersonal little room with its hard bed, cheap furnishings and miserable lighting.

She took the cup to an empty table, nursing its contents into lukewarmness, already having drunk more today than she usually did in a week, while the coffee's aftertaste hung in her mouth, bitter and unpleasant. Even so, she tried to sip, stared at the ground, did not want to submit to the loneliness creeping over her, forcing her to wish she was already safely next door in her own shelter, awful though it might be, where darkness would insulate her against this conspicuous, unnerving sense of public newness and unworthiness, which was very successfully devouring her. Although she tried to fight them back tears were very—

"Pardon me, please. May I join you?" came a very quiet voice directly behind her. Startled she looked up from the spot on the ground where she had been focused and saw a bespectacled man standing there, teacup in hand. It was obvious he was from India, and even the expensive, custom-tailored suit he wore could not for an instant actually hide or enlarge the fragile, bone-thin body beneath it. But his eyes behind silver-rimmed glasses were gentle, and he smiled shyly as he gestured towards one of the three empty chairs next to her.

He was around thirty-five or perhaps older, with both intelligence and sensitivity deeply sketched on his face: But even more, she also perceived honesty and humor, the certain recognition, he would never harm her, and trusted him immediately. "Of course. Please sit down," she replied softly.

He seated himself, arranged the beverage carefully before him on the tabletop and said, "You are a newcomer, are you not?"

She nodded.

"I know everyone here and when a lovely young lady arrives I am always the first to notice. Unfortunately noticing her is usually all I can manage." The grin was pure mischief.

"He's got a great line," she thought. What could be more effective than the truth? If it was!

His voice, low, the words deliberate, was very sweet, accented with the peculiar musicality which Indians give to the English language, enhancing and softening it simultaneously.

"My name is Baboo. Not really, certainly. But the actual is very long and completely unpronounceable to Western tongues. This nickname suffices."

She said nothing, nodded in affirmation.

He sipped again and then said, "I am finishing a dissertation in electrical engineering. I hope the committee will find it acceptable, and then I will be on my way either back home or somewhere else. Do not be afraid of me, my child. I only want to be friends with you. Nothing more."

Still, she did not know how to respond and remained silent.

"Perhaps you will trust me more if I tell you I am engaged to an Indian lady. I do not even want another woman. Soon she will be joining me here in New York and we will be married. At that time our dearest wishes will be fulfilled."

"Congratulations!" she said then. "How long have you been engaged?"

"Only eight years. Do you think we know each other well enough?" Again, that impish grin conquering his entire face.

She fell back in her chair and laughed, now completely at ease with him.

Suddenly he leaned towards her and looked deeply into her face. "I have approached you because you are sitting here by yourself. A pretty girl should never, under any circumstances be allowed to do that. In an institution such as this one, geared primarily towards friendship and international understanding, it is the one sin unforgivable."

He took another sip and continued, "With your permission I shall take care to remedy this deplorable situation at once." Again his dark eyes behind the wire rims peered solemnly at her. "Do you understand, my child?"

"Yes," she answered but not actually sure what he meant.

"So, I have told you my name and a little about myself. Will you do the same?"

When she had revealed as much as she felt was appropriate he asked, "And you have friends here?"

"No, not anymore," she answered, quickly becoming defensive.

"You have come here by yourself and you are not afraid?"

She shook her head again, suddenly hurled into silent thoughts which she would not reveal. Memories of long ago when she was just a child. Memories closer here in this city than anywhere else on earth. Sorrow? Yes, and perpetual. But fear? None! It was far too late for that!

But she said none of this to him, not willing to be questioned further, to expose more. He sensed it instantly.

"Such a situation must be rectified. May some of my friends join us?" A slight pause, "Only be very wary of the Indian men. When they see a blonde they become instantly hyper-excited."

He grinned again, an enormous smile practically obliterating the smallness of his face. "I am no different."

She consented. Baboo gestured behind her and immediately the chairs at her table were occupied, more were being added and quickly, the table became the focal point of intense discussions, primarily she noticed, involving controversial political issues, which led to several emotional outbursts.

Still no one remained angry, and no one left.

A young Pakistani, smooth haired, with a thin mustache just beginning to pencil his upper lip, argued noisily with another man apparently from India. Their faces were unsmiling, each transformed with anger.

"Jinnah was a great man. A patriot who recognized there was only one way. He had no choice but to take it!"

"Mohammed Ali Jinnah? Great? A fanatic, devoid of even a tiny bit of conscience who coldly urged the displacement and murder of millions of innocent people just to satisfy his own ego!"

"He founded a nation!"

"He divided a nation!"

Baboo interceded quietly, "Remember where you are, gentlemen. Please."

They glanced at him and the Pakistani held out his hand. "I apologize," he said.

"So do I," answered the Indian, taking it.

Petra stared in fascination as the two, only moments ago deadly enemies, were now discussing the symptoms of an exotic, tropical disease.

The miracle of the I. House manifested itself. Its concept—international understanding—was the basis. That established, friendship and tolerance were poured unconsciously with sugar and cream into the never-empty coffee and tea cups.

It became difficult to continue hating an entire nation, religion, race, culture, once students learned to appreciate each other as individuals, rather than unknown and uncounted members of a group. Here, friendship and perhaps peace, were formed, one person at a time.

Towards 1 a.m. Baboo announced without even consulting her, "I shall take my daughter home. It is not seemly for a lady to be out alone this late." He picked up her coat, waved goodbye to the others and escorted her into the autumn night.

At the door he said, "Realize, Petra, what has happened. I shall watch over you, and no one shall ever harm you. My friends, some of whom you have met, will do the same."

"But why, Baboo? Why do you care what happens to me? Before tonight you didn't even know me and now you are taking my safety on your neck. I don't understand it!"

"There is nothing to understand, Petra. You are open, still very young," he almost whispered, "And while you laugh with your mouth there is pain in your eyes. I see it now, although you appear indifferent. I will not ask you about it. But if you choose to tell me, I will listen."

He gazed at her tenderly, his thin face becoming almost luminous.

She did not want a stranger to know her so well, or this quickly. It made her feel discomfited, transparent, and she sneered, "You're being damned presumptuous!"

He was not insulted. "Yes, I believe I am. But we will watch over you nevertheless. Now, enough of serious nonsense and on to more important subjects.

Have you ever had a homemade Indian dinner?" The small dark eyes danced behind his glasses, their intelligence modified only slightly with amusement. "Next Friday night some of us will prepare several authentic South Indian dishes. Can you join us? I promise you won't have to wash dishes since you are a newcomer."

In fact, Petra had tried Indian food several times in Washington and winced, remembering the inadvertent tears which rolled down her face to everyone else's laughter.

"Will it be very hot?" she asked dubiously.

"Very, I suspect," he pronounced, "but do not fear. I shall personally prepare for you. Then maybe you will not get curry cramps."

"Thank you, Baboo. I would love to come."

Chapter 6

The following Monday morning Petra dressed as Madison Avenueishly as her wardrobe allowed, boarded the bus on Riverside Drive and entered the skyscraper that housed McNeil-Smith Advertising, prepared to begin the first day of her poverty-salaried-but-bound-to-get-better-in-the-immediate-future junior-secretarial position.

A redheaded personnel assistant escorted her into the presence of the great man for whom she was destined to become flunky and machine. But instead of taking her to the beautifully decorated, high windowed offices visible directly behind her, they took an elevator down to a lower floor. She opened a door, which led into a tiny office with a dark foyer where a desk with a typewriter on it stood. A man waited at the threshold.

"Hello, Wilson. This is your new secretary."

"Petra, Wilson Burken is one of our most important and upcoming young executives. I'm sure you'll enjoy working for him."

Wilson Burken saw a thin, blonde personage whose "how do you do" was said in a soft voice tinged with a slight Southern accent, and fittingly (as her superior) acknowledged her existence from an enormous distance by nodding wordlessly at her. But when the redhead turned to leave them alone—together—horrified lest the Personnel Department had misunderstood his explicit requests, he raced after her, a child desperate for reassurance, and whispered loudly while Petra heard every word, "Maureen, wait! You can't leave yet. You promised me a bi-lingual one. Is she?"

Petra raised each eyebrow individually (a trick she had learned from a classmate at P.S. 69 many years ago), heard herself sigh involuntarily (or was it?), and judiciously decided to let them fight it out. Obviously both of them considered her a thing, a commodity, mindless, opinionless and apparently incapable of auricular sensitivity, since neither even bothered to lower their voices.

Somehow "Maureen" must have convinced him to "keep her for the time being" because when he returned from their impromptu liaison in the hallway he was trying to be boyishly charming. "Miss Barret tells me you speak French," he wheedled.

"Yes," she responded.

"And perhaps another language also?" sweetly, hopefully, "in addition to French?"

Petra nodded affirmatively and decided to torture him a little longer, "English."

He gulped audibly, a sound she had never heard from a grown man. "Well, yes, that was to be expected, wasn't it?" noted patiently, accompanied by a superior, yet kindly and only fleetingly patronizing smile.

Now she had him figured out. "Why? I had to learn it."

"Yes, of course, we all did, didn't we? But it's your mother tongue, so it doesn't really count. We all learned English when we were children." Again that sickening smile, a genius attempting to teach the ABCs to an idiot.

"It's not my mother tongue."

His eyes lit up for an instant and then he frowned, "It's not? What is?"

Close to giving him an instant full-blown illustration, she answered, "I curse in Dutch."

His response elicited a reaction she had not expected. His pseudo-sophisticated veneer dropped for an instant while he tottered on the verge of some unseen, infantile ecstasy. "I've got her," he mumbled, "I've got her!"

Then still assuming she could not hear him he babbled, "A jewel. A real jewel! French and Dutch. Both of them! And me with the Belgian government account. I'll make a fortune for the agency...in no time they'll make me Chairman of the Board!"

"Don't forget I know some English, too," she fumed silently and glared with a now-mirrored simpering smile on her own face. Instinctively she detested this man, contempt for him immediate, absolute. Irreversible.

After just having met Burken she knew him completely. What one saw at first glance, she recognized, was all there was. A tall man in his early thirties, tending towards extreme plumpness, Brooks Brothers *de rigueur* charcoal greys with the necessary vest, brown curly hair enshrining a round-via-fatness face, which was probably actually square, a regular nose, and small, set close together dark eyes. Nothing extraordinary.

Except for one feature.

His mouth was unusual. Petra had never paid much attention to anyone's mouth before, not as an independent organ. Behinds, waists, eyes, noses. Not mouths.

What was special about Wilson Burken's mouth? Those two pink pieces of tissue opening and closing in response to nervous stimuli even when at rest screamed his entire life's history. Infant-sized and thick, formed in the shape of a Cupid's bow, his lips tattled brazenly that, although a grown man, he was still his mommy and daddy's darling, to be cherished and bankrolled by them forever. And entitled to be spoiled by everyone else!

To her horror, in time she learned the expression on his tattle tale mouth was truthful.

In the next few minutes he notified her that he would refer to her as "Petra," while she, however, as a mere underling, would address him only as "Mr. Burken." Then apropos of nothing, he haughtily informed her he was a graduate of Harvard. She was immediately tempted to ask him if Harvard was as proud of him as he was of Harvard. And if so, in God's name, why?

That rosy little mouth, with its indulged, recalcitrant preciousness told the entire story.

And so from Wilson Burken, Petra learned to understand how mouths can speak lies, but can also, without the use of words, reveal truths.

In dismay she looked around at the grey walls, the grey metal furniture, the grey typewriters reflecting additional greyness from the ugly grey laminated floors. "Oh shit!" she screamed silently, "get me out of here!"

And then Ellen's cynical comments made sense. She had a glamour job on starvation pay, accepted with the promised bait of advancement. But no guarantee the promise would be kept. To make it even worse, she had drawn an arrogant charlatan as her boss. Her boss! The word made her want to vomit. Boss, indeed! The man was a whining boor!

In time she would learn to know him better.

Or simply longer.

Knowing him better was physiologically and psychologically redundant.

Chapter 7

Eight hours later she returned home, having typed innumerable letters, corrected Burken's spelling and grammar—both of which were deplorable despite his Harvard-boasted education—and brain-washed herself into thinking it was a first step towards success and wasn't it wonderful to have a job.

Actually she felt miserable, terrified her future might consist only of the same, robot-like existence. She crept into her cold, stereotypical little room and sat on the bed, wondering how she would survive.

Suddenly Ellen emerged through the connecting door holding a bottle of gin in one hand and two glasses in the other. "Catch, "she yelled. "Let's celebrate your new job!"

Petra scowled at her, "I don't want to celebrate. It's boring, my boss is a pompous idiot and I hate it!"

"Cheer up, youngster. First days are always like that. Once you're broken in, know what to expect, you'll feel better."

Petra stared back at her, not replying.

"Of course, just like the horse, your spirit will be broken. But also like the horse, you'll have a few oats to eat occasionally and water to drink. The quality of those will depend, obviously, on the rider, uh, owner, you get."

Although true, the comment did not help.

"Smile," Ellen continued, "By next week you won't even realize you're a slave. Meanwhile, have a swig of this stuff. Salmi presented me with a bottle all my own. He's not known for his generosity so when he offered I accepted. Let's finish it quickly and inspire him to repeat the gesture."

"You're trying to make a goddamned lush out of me. Shame on you! So, why are you hesitating? Pour!"

"Just remember. If you end up lying in the gutter singing bawdy ballads on Christopher Street, I will personally instruct Bellevue to send the wagon to pick you up. See what a good friend I am?"

Petra gulped. It was like swallowing eau de cologne. The alcohol burned her stomach, and the only flush she got was from trying to force more of the stuff down under protests from her intestines. "Ugh," she muttered and involuntarily dry-heaved.

Ellen began to laugh, then suggested they go to a Cantonese restaurant on Broadway. Salmi had to work on a research project and not only did Ellen hate drinking alone, she also hated eating alone.

"Oh, by the way," she interpolated suddenly as they walked towards 125th Street, "I won't have to worry about paying my tuition. I've been offered a job at Mt. Sinai Hospital. Part-time. Means I can still finish at Columbia."

"How wonderful! What will you be doing?"

"Statistical follow-ups on coronary disease. They have the best cardiology department in New York. Maybe even the world."

"Statistics?" Petra replied thoughtfully. "So you're going to be a glorified file clerk."

Ellen frowned, then grimaced. She knew it.

Petra began to giggle. "I wonder how all those sensuous Jewish doctors are going to react to you, an honest-to -God, alive-and-ready-to-be-discriminated-against WASP. Should be interesting for everyone concerned. I can hardly wait to hear the stories you'll bring home!"

"Damned little brat! Hurry up! I'm hungry," she retorted and led the way to the restaurant.

Chapter 8

Hoping she would not be dependent on the vagaries of Burken's social inadequacies for more months than was bearable, Petra drudged through the initiation week. By Friday afternoon she was routinely writing press releases supposedly authored by him. Her name appeared nowhere on them but she kept copies. Perhaps someday...

She bought a chrysanthemum plant for Baboo, arrived two minutes late, apologized and was immediately teased.

"In India," he pronounced solemnly, "we are always on time. Never late, not even one minute. Let alone two." Then realizing she did not know if he was serious or not, he laughed and led her into the living room while the exotic perfumes of Indian cuisine escaped from the kitchen. Flowers were everywhere, huge vases of orange tiger lilies, multi-hued zinnias and primroses, budding pink and purple cyclamens in terra cotta pots.

She placed her gift on the sideboard next to a copper tea samovar and an exquisite ivory carving of a deity.

"This is Krishna, ruler of the world," Baboo said somberly, then winked, incapable of remaining solemn very long; "only Radha rules him. It is no different with the gods. One beautiful woman can make heaven and earth an eternal happiness. Or not."

"Come now and meet the other guests," he said, leading her into the adjoining room where people were seated on pillow-covered carpets. Most appeared to be from India but one saried woman was from South America.

In the tiny kitchen a blue suited and green-striped aproned-businessman, apparently designated chef-for-the-day, was assiduously stirring something bubbling in a large pot.

"Oh, do hurry, Alan," admonished the host. "Put the chickpeas in now. At this rate we shall not be eating in time for classes next week!"

"Go away, you silly Gujerati. Just get out of my way and let me teach you how to prepare a proper curry. You cannot hurry it. Now go on. Out!" and Baboo retreated, shrugging and laughing.

The ad hoc chef gave the food one more educated stir, threw the chickpeas in the mixture and inhaled. With a final peek and a satisfied "hmmmm" he ran into the living room and shouted jubilantly that dinner was now ready. Did you hear? Now! Immediately! At once please, before it spoils. Ladies and gentlemen!"

Baboo guided Petra to a place at the end of a long table and said, "Come daughter, let me help you," then carefully filled her plate, choosing, selecting, rejecting, returning. Although his intentions and choices were cognizant of and sensitive to the blandness of her Northern European palate, tears still managed to blind her and she found herself laughing and crying at the same time. Of course he noticed.

Finally himself able to enjoy the food he had prepared, the cook, gleaming with pride after unanimous plaudits for his efforts, turned to Baboo and asked, "Who is this pretty blonde lady you have invited? And whatever will Gita say when she hears about it?"

"Gita will most certainly say nothing at all," answered Baboo calmly. "First of all she knows her future husband completely and is confident of his love. And in the second place I am sure Gita and she will immediately like each other."

Then he continued, "Petra, this is my friend Alan. He also has one of those long, complicated Indian names but this one will suffice. Not only is he a superb chef as you have noticed, but he is also the richest man I know. Don't ask me where he gets his money, I have no idea, but we all pray fervently he earns it legally."

Alan glared at him.

But Petra was staring at Baboo. "Is Gita your fiancée's name?" she asked.

"Yes. It means 'song' in Hindi. Do you like it?"

"It's my name also. Jewish children are given two sets of names, one in the language of the country where they live, the other is their Jewish name. Mine is Gita."

Alan and Baboo both frowned.

A woman's voice sing-songed from the other end of the table, "Come, with your silly chatter your dinners are getting cold."

"That is Eila, the best surgeon in the world and a woman I adore," grinned Baboo pointing towards her.

"You will learn, Petra, that Baboo has many women he adores," she retorted very quickly. "So I will spare him from making further allusions to his present coronary status and introduce you to the rest of the people here."

Between curry tears and laughter, Petra met the other guests, all of whom were either graduate or post-graduate students or well established in business.

It was impossible for her to remember them all but she was drawn to Parvati, tall, slender, completing a residency in pediatrics at Columbia Presbyterian Hospital, imbued with a sweet quietness. When she smiled to acknowledge Petra's handshake, she revealed front teeth so protuberant and unfortunately spaced that they instantly made her sad, intelligent face grotesquely ugly.

Eila, who was her elder sister, was well into her forties, tall and plump beneath a pink sari, radiating confidence and good humor. Both women spoke fluent, lovely English. One, shyly, an introvert; the other, with great verve and exuberance.

And Chedda, a massive middle-aged Parsi attorney, whose charm and warm-heartedness bubbled over the guests, making them laugh raucously at his wit, grounded frequently in risqué and accurate perceptions.

Maria, a translator at the United Nations, was from Uruguay and reputed to be more than just a friend of Alan's (although neither mentioned it and no one asked). A lavender silk sari was wrapped around her slender body and her black hair was coiled into a thick chignon encircled with white freesias. She missed being beautiful but her sexual attraction was overwhelming, as obvious as heavy perfume.

Alan pretended to be casual but never took his dark eyes away from her, guarding, watching, jealousy lurking close to the surface, desire etched around his mouth even as he carried on conversations with everyone else. She laughed, smoked, chatted, was gracious to everyone, occasionally nodded at him and smiled subtly.

Next to her sat Thalia, a Greek law student who wore thick glasses and appeared totally nondescript, saying little, fidgeting with her napkin, her eating utensils, apparently ill at ease among this cheerful crowd, contributing nothing to the party atmosphere, and simply observing without absorbing.

Petra murmured to Parvati, "Your saris are so feminine and beautiful compared to our clothes," and glanced at her own wool sweater and skirt, while admiring the fragile green gown shot through with gold.

Parvati whispered a shy "thank you" and then, "If you should ever care to borrow anything, my entire wardrobe is at your disposal."

Having met the woman only moments earlier, Petra was startled by the offer. "Thank you," she stammered. "Perhaps one day I can try one on. But I could never wear it as you do, with such elegance. Besides, my coloring is all wrong. Saris and blondes are contradictions."

She had intended it as a cultural comparison and no more, but Parvati flinched.

But after an instant, the doctor realized that no insult was intended or even intimated. She then bowed her head slightly and said, "I will teach you how to wrap, wear and walk in it."

Again that instantaneous shocking generosity. Petra felt she needed to reciprocate. "I have warm sweaters, skirts, clothes you will need for the New York winter. You're welcome to borrow them."

This time Parvati stiffened and lifted her head proudly. "Thank you, but it will never be necessary. Indeed, I do own such clothing. If you like I will present it to you. I have been here for two years and am well aware of the inadequacies of silk. Nevertheless I shall not wear those heavy things ever again."

"Why are you so angry? We're only discussing clothing, not politics or religion." asked a puzzled Maria.

"Are we, indeed!" retorted Parvati. "The first and last time I wore your graceless western garb someone called me a filthy nigger."

Maria gasped and the others stared in horrified silence.

Then Petra recalled the saried women on the streets of Washington, D.C., shivering in their robes, sloshing through the sleet-snowed streets in flimsy leather sandals. How many, she now wondered, clung to their splattered, inadequate silks and cottons for precisely the same reason?

"Ah you," chided Eila, "you are so sensitive!"

"It's true!" her sister rejoined immediately. "You know it too. With all your loud love for modern things and Europeans ways, look at you. Still wearing the sari too! You have bobbed your hair but that is the only thing you've really given up. How dare you try to deny it," she screamed wildly, her dark eyes staring furiously at her sister.

Eila accepted the attack but remained silent while Parvati's face contorted with anguish.

Alan dropped his fork and bitterly spoke up, "I too have been called names. Why should color...anyone's color... be a criterion for anything?" Softly he answered his own questions, "We are all people, human beings, the same."

Parvati, hysterical an instant ago, was now totally silent, all emotions drained away. Dumbly, she retired from any conversations, veiled in her own unhappiness for the rest of the evening.

But Eila, ever exuberant, wasn't going to let her sister's moody outpourings destroy the festivities. She also wanted to rebuke her a little. She waited until everyone seemed to have absorbed the ugliness of a few minutes ago, and safely changed the subject. "Good god, child. When are you going to remove that horrible chignon? Mine gave me the worst headaches. The first thing I did after leaving India was to get rid of it. Wonderfully light this way. Much easier to keep my hair clean, too! Now, pet, what do you say? Shall we go together to the beauty parlor next week and have the filthy thing cut off?" She gazed with disdain at the heavy, shining ebony coil at the base of her sister's head.

With envy, Petra admired it. So clean and smooth, adorned with jewels and flowers, it remained the one truly positive feature this ugly woman possessed and she hoped Parvati would reject her sister's suggestion."It's beautiful," she said then, fearing the strong-willed Eila would eventually overrule her shy sister. "It suits you."

Parvati smiled her disfigured gratitude but remained silent, the green-gold veil of silk covering her body and thoughts as if she were no longer present.

"Alan, come now and cheer up!" Eila began again. "Do be a good boy and put some decent music on. None of the Indian classics, please. Some Bach would be nice. She turned to Petra and said, "I don't understand why Indian music has survived as long as it has. It is uninspiring and long-winded. You cannot sing it. You cannot move to it. And it just goes on and on. When I was in medical school I was first exposed to western music and have become addicted to it. Do you like Bach?"

"Yes, he is one of my gods."

"Good. Then I shall order tickets, and if you agree, please be my guest at the Bach Festival Series next week."

Again, that spontaneous gesture of friendship. Was this something typically Indian, Petra asked herself?

Then she stopped analyzing and looked around.

A week ago she had been sitting alone, lost, feeling conspicuous and miserable in the International House Waffle Wing, questioning if she would be able to absorb the city's expected initial reticence towards newcomers. And now she had a roomful of friends.

She took another bite of food and saw Alan and Baboo both staring at her while the curry tears poured over her cheeks and gleamed silver on her sweater.

She took out a handkerchief and wiped her face. Then picked up her fork and reached for another mouthful.

Chapter 9

The next day Petra applied for I. House membership, a procedure enhanced because an African prince clerked at the front desk. He handed her a form, glanced at it, took her check, handed her a membership card, welcomed her, and turned away to assist the next person.

"Why does he have to work?" she asked Ellen.

"Who knows? Maybe his mother wasn't an official wife. But his half-brother, who doesn't resemble him at all, seems to have no shortage of money, lives in an apartment on Park Avenue, never does an iota of anything, no work, no school, nothing... His name is Solomon and he has a dramatic henna-haired mistress we have nicknamed..."

"Ha, ha," interrupted Petra, "The Queen of Sheba?"

"An 'A' for you!" responded her roommate.

Petra found a sign-up sheet for private tennis lessons, saw there was an opening and immediately entered her name.

Saturday, finally, she thought! Time to experience the Upper West Side neighborhood before daylight disappeared again. Each weekday morning she boarded the bus to work, passed by Riverside Park aching to walk there, to inhale the fresh autumn air, to dream while she watched the Hudson as it meandered between the shores and palisades of New Jersey and New York.

Autumn and its glorious rust, gold, green ephemeral renaissance, which would soon yield to grim leaflessness, had always been her favorite season. This year the pageantry seemed even more magnificent, and she tramped delighted, child-innocent, through beds of maple and oak strewn on the moss covered earth, a blazing mattress of passionate hues and shades, textures and resilience.

"New York," she sighed, "how I have longed for you! How I love you!"

Later she attended the tennis lesson and found her teacher was the same woman she had seen from her window, a fourth-year medical student named Jopie van Dijk from Rotterdam, who was delighted that her new student was Dutch also.

But no matter how hard she tried to obey instructions, Petra and tennis found little in common. The more she struggled, the worse it got. Valiantly she tried to chase balls already whizzing past her and bouncing on the ground, leapt high in the air for sure retrievals when she should have bent lower to scoop them up, heard the often shouted admonishment, "Play closer to the net."

She did, watched the ball zoom above her, reached up, lunged at it, heard it connect with the racket and simultaneously felt a muscle in her neck protest so badly it tingled every cell in her lower skull. She leaned down, grimacing with pain and rubbed the painful area.

"Well, guess that's all for today," called her mentor. "Let's get a cold drink."

Still bent over, Petra wiped her face with an immediately sooty tissue, and gratefully followed...

Jopie found a table, threw her racket casually on a chair and brought a pitcher of iced tea and two glasses. Petra gulped greedily (a parched wanderer rescued after three waterless months alone in the Sahara) and slowly began to breathe normally again as the stabbing pain in her head subsided.

"The tennis lessons are to defray tuition?" she asked.

Jopie nodded. "In Holland I was a nurse. Lifting grumpy men on and off urinals and trying to soothe hysterical women was not enough. I wanted to do the real stuff, make diagnoses, try to heal the patients. I applied here, was accepted and, in two years, I hope I can start my residency."

She smiled cynically. "I shall also be forty years old and just starting my life. But if I must spend it alone, then I prefer it this way. Much better, I think than being an old-maid cockroach, or a flunky forever dependent on a meager salary doled out by a crabby doctor."

Petra listened silently, her face still burning from the exercise, clothes clinging uncomfortably to her body, black sweat marks on her arms and hands. She felt filthy next to the composed, immaculately dressed woman sitting across the table.

"Hello. How are you? May I join you?" a young man said to Jopie.

She nodded, motioned to an empty chair and began an animated conversation with him. Petra sipped her drink and watched them interacting.

The aging, brilliant woman, fair, rail-thin and muscular, was hypnotized by the boy's words, her eyes behind the glasses focused on him, her blonde head inclined towards him as she listened. Their interchange was easy, unrestrained, based on an obviously well-established friendship.

Neither of them bothered to include Petra or to make an introduction. She guessed him to be about six feet tall, broad-shouldered, athletic, and assumed he was also one of her tennis students. Then during a break in their conversation he leaned back on two legs of his chair and for the first time looked directly at her.

She gasped.

He was the most beautiful creature she had ever seen, male or female. His hair and eyes were dark brown, the skin pale olive. Yet his face was absolutely masculine, with a small, straight nose, white even teeth over full lips grinning at some Dutch earthiness coming from Jopie, while laugh wrinkles deepened around his mouth and cleft chin. She assumed he was from the Mediterranean but couldn't identify his accent. Or perhaps she wasn't even listening to what he was saying, just staring at him helplessly.

Then he asked, "And what is your name? Are you an American?"

She blurted out, "Petra. Raised here," and was too flustered to say more except, "And you?"

"My name is Dev," he answered slowly; "I am from India."

"Well," she thought, "that's the end of that. I wonder if Jopie realizes it!"

From Baboo she had learned that most male Indian students were engaged and the ones who weren't had taken vows of non-involvement or even celibacy. But this man seemed in no hurry to end his comfortable friendship with Jopie, questioning her about her studies, laughing with and at her and often succeeded in making the formidable Dutch woman blush.

Petra watched and listened, too uncomfortable to join in. Her iced tea had become cold water and she felt increasingly aware of how dirty she was.

"Time for me to go home and make dinner," Jopie announced after a while. Petra followed her, while the boy disappeared.

"Obscenely handsome, don't you think? How long have you known him?"

Bewildered, Petra turned to her, "I? I don't know him at all. I thought he was your friend!"

"To my regret I have to admit I have never met him before today," replied her countrywoman.

"But, but he seemed so comfortable with you. The way you were talking, as if you were old friends. And yet you don't know him?"

"Guess we met in a former life or something like that. Anyway, believe me, he would be hard to forget! Why would I lie about it?"

Petra stopped walking and looked up at Jopie. "Just like that. Cold. No one to introduce him. Just plunked himself down at your table. Like he'd known you for years? Even assumed you knew his name!"

"But I didn't," Jopie said.

"Hmm, I wonder what prompted him to do that." Petra puzzled.

Jopie smiled at her. "Indeed. I wonder, too." But gave no further clarification. Then she seemed to remember something. "Petra, soon it will be time for the annual Halloween Festival. Would you like to take part in the Dutch skit?"

"Each year there's a huge celebration," she explained. "Every nation with more than five I. House members decorates a booth, prepares a fifteen-minute program and sells native handicrafts and food. The consulates take care of getting donated goods. Proceeds benefit the House Scholarship Fund. People from all over New York come! It's very profitable and great fun."

"We're selling cheese and a special shipment of tulip bulbs is coming from Lisse, just in time for autumn planting. And we're going to perform some typical Dutch dances. Do you know how to do the *klompendans*? We can always use another person."

"I've never done it. Halloween is only a few days away, not really enough time to learn it, I'm afraid. Besides I don't own a Dutch costume."

"Oh, neither does anyone else! The Netherlands Consulate provides them. Tomorrow night there's a rehearsal in the gym. Nettie de Vos, who's studied ballet, is leading us. She even taught me and I cannot dance at all."

When she noticed Petra hesitating she pleaded, "Please, do come. It's for a good cause and we need you!"

"Well, all right, I guess."

When she arrived the following evening, everyone else was already occupied, either practicing dance steps or hammering and sawing. There was a lot of commotion and much laughing and chattering as the sawers sawed, the hammerers hammered and the dancers attempted to ignore them both and concentrate on some recorded music.

A dark haired young woman was shouting in accentless English, "Okay, everyone. Pay attention. We've only got two more rehearsals. Come on, people. Just ignore the noise. Right now we have to practice."

Jopie introduced Petra. Nettie de Vos stared coldly at her, then pointed to a couple who were rehearsing the *klompendans*.

"Can you do that?" she asked.

"It doesn't look difficult. Let me try." Petra did a quick waltz step, added a hop and another waltz step and stopped.

Nettie watched. "No, no, not that way. It's step, hop, step, step, step. Like this," and she whirled away to demonstrate.

Petra aped her exactly.

"No, I said not that way!" Nettie grimaced, taking Petra's arm and stopping her from continuing. "This way!" Once more she solo-danced and Petra duplicated her movements perfectly.

"For God's sakes, this is ridiculous! You're going to ruin the whole thing. Jopie, why did you invite her? We were doing fine without her. Now we're going to make a mess of it!"

Petra felt her face burn and turned away.

"She's trying her best. I'm sure she'll catch on."

"We don't have time! When will she know it, on Sunday afternoon when the festival is over?"

Petra didn't understand what prompted the temper tantrum but decided she would not bear its brunt again. "You're right. I'll just watch and you go ahead without me." No performance was worth such humiliation in front of strangers. She wanted out!

"Damn it! The steps are easy. Any idiot can do them."

"Right," Jopie agreed, "particularly if the idiot has studied ballet for more than eight years."

Mollified, in an almost civilized tone of voice, Nettie asked Petra to try once more, and then shrieked, "Enough! You haven't the vaguest idea what to do. Are you an imbecile?"

The room was suddenly silent as everyone stared at Nettie whose face was blotched with anger, contorted and distorted. Petra was shaking but wondered why no one defended her, to stop the insane, unjustified barrage.

Not even Jopie had interceded.

But pride saved her. Very quietly, now completely under control she replied, "It's really just as well. I've just recuperated from a terrible case of bronchitis and the exercise could aggravate it and cause a relapse."

In fact, she had never felt stronger, healthier or happier. And she had never had bronchitis in her life.

Several students gathered around, expressing immediate concern for her well-being, agreeing it would be best if she didn't risk aggravating the condition. But Jopie, silent and perceptive, looked at her, frowned, shook her head and made her understand she didn't accept the excuse for an instant.

Lying to Jopie, former nurse, present medical student, her tennis teacher to whom not a word about any illness had been uttered was futile. The chastising frown on her face was slowly replaced by an enormous grin.

"Petra, don't leave yet. Nettie is in charge of the performance but I am responsible for the entire production. I have decided we need you to sell tulips and cheese; in full costume, of course. You will stand behind the flower cart while we perform, and be a village woman observing the festivities. So, that is settled. "

Nettie sneered at her in disbelief but there was nothing she could do. Petra would not be allowed to dance but would participate anyway.

Jopie led Petra away from the others, put her arm around her and said, "Don't be upset. No one pays attention when she gets like this. Actually she is quite sensitive."

"Sensitive? I've never met her before and she deliberately humiliated me! You call that sensitive? I don't! What did I do to her? Did I say something that offended her? Why did she attack me?"

"You haven't done anything. Not directly. The truth is more subtle. And terrible."

Jopie sighed, "Nettie was five when the Germans invaded Holland. Her parents placed her with Christian friends, signed over all their assets to insure their child would be well-cared for and went underground. Soon Nettie forgot about them and during the occupation considered herself a member of the family, unaware she did not resemble her blond, blue-eyed 'brothers and sisters.' Sometimes she wondered why she was not permitted to attend church, to play outside with other children, attend holiday gatherings. In 1945 after the Allied liberation, she was suddenly allowed access everywhere, was in fact strongly encouraged to go to church. At first, still a child, she complied, but as she grew older and more cognizant she began to ask questions and demanded satisfactory answers. She wanted to know her real last name and insisted on using it; gave up Christianity although she didn't accept Judaism either; tried to find her parents through the Red Cross and learned they had been caught and sent to Sobibor where they were murdered in 1942. She chose to leave Holland immediately and was taken in by an American Jewish family in Boston. She is absolutely brilliant. And uncompromisingly bitter."

Jopie continued, unaware that her listener's eyes were full of tears. "All the Dutch students know her story. We try to be especially kind to her, let her get away with behavior we would not usually tolerate. Most of us feel she's suffered so much, we forgive her almost everything."

"But," Jopie said, "we never seem able to make her happy. She is always demanding, returns very little. I suppose she feels we owe her more than simple understanding and she's probably right. So, Petra, do not be too angry with her. You see, she cannot help herself."

She stared straight ahead, sad eyed and perplexed, "It still doesn't make sense. I thought she'd be pleased to have an additional dancer. It rounds out the group, four boys, four girls. Nettie the bride and Pieter van Hoorn her groom. Why should she resent you so, I wonder?"

Finally Petra spoke. "I don't know either, Jopie. Particularly since I am Jewish also."

Jopie gasped, "You are? I never thought about it when we met. The hair, the fair skin." Then she asked hesitantly, "When did you come to America?"

"Just before the war. A major decision to leave while we still could. My parents, brother, and I. The usual story for Jews, nothing we're not all born knowing. Or at least learn at an early age."

"Let me tell Nettie. It may make her feel better. Or worse, considering how she behaved towards you. She may ask you to perform anyhow. As an apology..."

"No, don't. I'll be busy enough and I really don't want to dance. Besides, my history doesn't change hers."

"Very well. Anyway, this one evening we'll make sure she shines in the light. It may be what she needs most and it costs us nothing."

As Petra left the gym Jopie called after her, "Costumes arrive Saturday morning at around 10 a.m. Be on time to pick yours up."

Chapter 10

Booth construction had been underway since before daylight on Saturday morning. The I. House looked more like a haven for woodworkers and painters than a ten-story dormitory. Every public area had been designated and assigned—the hallways, ballroom areas, conference rooms, study chambers on the first two floors.

Commands were being shouted in various languages and tones of voice. People waved at each other, cursed, laughed, worked. Men dragged huge pieces of plywood across the suddenly rugless lobby floor while bluejeaned women wearing a variety of university logoed sweatshirts carried boxes of decorations up and down the marble staircase.

The Netherlands had been allotted space directly inside the front entrance where all visitors would immediately see their display first.

Petra watched several Dutch engineering students concentrating on a mechanism that controlled the arms on an enormous, three dimensional papier mâché windmill, but so meticulously designed it resembled a real one with depth and substance. As she stood there admiring their efforts a small miracle took place. Someone pushed a button and the metal arms, the *wieken*, rotated slowly, majestically, exactly as planned.

To the right of the windmill two women were decorating a wheelbarrow with hundreds of crepe flowers in red, white, blue, while long strands of orange ribbon cascaded from its handlebars. Others were transforming a square table into a festively festooned "cart" with colorful paper wheels. Though only partially completed, the booth appeared professional; the Dutch students and every other group represented had their national honor to uphold. All of them did their best.

After digging in a large box of clothing, Jopie handed a bundle to Petra, pointed towards the women's wing and said, "Here, try these on in the bathroom. I'm sorry but we're short on aprons. Since you're not performing, you don't really need one."

Petra tried on the clothes. "They're fine, Jopie, but badly need pressing. All the folds are in the wrong places."

"Good. Here's the cap. Wash and starch it. Wear black pumps tonight because we're also short on *klompen*." Then she paused and asked, "Do you mind very much being second-placed this way?"

"If this was a fashion show I'd walk out. But I have memories of blistered feet from wearing those horrors. Use the *klompen* with my blessings. I'm going to be nice and comfortable in my I. Millers!"

"Thank God you're not being difficult. The public will be allowed in at 10 p.m. Try to be here half-an-hour earlier so we can fix any problems." Then Jopie reached into a smaller box, pulled out a triple strand of beads and handed them to the girl.

By 9 p.m. the washing, starching and ironing were completed and Petra was ready to put on the costume. It was the first time in many years she had worn a dress from Volendam. The brightly striped flannel skirt, soft and warm, felt familiar around her legs. Then on went the first flowered shirt and over it a black, braid-trimmed blouse with a low-cut square neck, all adhering to traditional materials and designs, the basic patterns unchanged for centuries. Around her throat she fastened the blood coral necklace with its huge, ornate clasp meant to be worn in the front as an additional ornament. She brushed her hair, regretting there had not been time to set it in the corkscrew curls, which were actually traditional. It hung incorrectly straight, but clean, below her shoulders.

Then very gently she picked up the all-important lace cap. "Please, let it stay up," she murmured. If the starch had not taken or the iron was not hot enough, the point would simply flop over to one side, looking ridiculous and spoiling the entire effect.

She looked in the mirror. The two side panels resembling small lace birds in flight flew around her face, showing off her long hair beneath their edges. The lace point jutted straight up in the air, just as it was supposed to do. Of course the brashly colored skirt begged for the pragmatic sanity of the black apron which belonged over it, but there was nothing to be done. Besides, as Jopie had said, she would not really be on display. She slid into the black pumps and hurried next door.

"Nettie isn't here yet," worried Jopie, obviously tired, and put another crepe flower on the cart. Then she looked at Petra again, gasped, snatched the remaining apron from the box, handed it to her and said quickly, "Here. Put this on. Hurry up!'"

"What about Nettie?"

"Never mind about her. I want you to wear it. Now do what I tell you."

She watched Petra struggling awkwardly with the long ties and finally snatched them out of her hands, with an expert's touch tied them herself and stood a few feet away her eyes gleaming with pleasure."Oh Petra, if you only realized how lovely you are!" she exclaimed. "Go, look in the mirror."

All Petra saw was her usual face and ordinary body, this time dressed in the rather unimaginative but picturesque costume of Volendam, the one most familiar to tourists but not the only and certainly not the most beautiful of the many regional attires in The Netherlands. No one special, no one particularly striking, and no one any Dutchman would consider glancing back at should he pass her on a street in Holland. The stereotypical blonde hair, fair skin, medium size, light-colored eyes. So what?

"I look just like every Dutch peasant woman," she told Jopie, feeling disappointed and unable to understand why her friend looked so awed.

"Yes, you do. Exactly! And when you walk into the Metropolitan Museum you'll see your face gazing down, time after time. Vermeer, Rembrandt, all of them. Go, look at their paintings. Your hair, your smile, your face, they've painted you a hundred times."

She added, "Ironic, isn't it? You, a Jewish girl. The personification of the classical Dutch woman. How do you suppose that could have happened?"

"Probably two reasons," answered Petra innocently. "The salt air and the northern sun eventually bleached us and turned us into mutations. It took only a few generations, and my family has been in Holland for hundreds of years."

"And the other reason?" A skeptical retort, followed by, "The real one?"

Petra grinned, "The bedroom, of course!"

Jopie scowled, muttering, "Sun-bleached mutations, indeed! Do you think I've never studied Mendel?"

Just then Nettie arrived. "Hurry up. I want my apron," she commanded.

"There aren't any more."

Nettie look startled, turned to Petra and began... "Then tell her to..." stopped suddenly, looked for an instant at the girl, picked up a flower garland, put it around her own neck and waited in uncharacteristic silence for the signal to begin the performance, paralyzed by her own hostility and the wall of bitterness that enclosed, isolated and protected her.

Chapter 11

Approximately thirty individual countries plus several closely related nations were scheduled to perform. The Latin Americans had banded together, the Indians and Ceylonese, students from the Middle East, as well as representatives from various African countries. Five skits were performed simultaneously every fifteen minutes, followed by a different set of five: Eventually each group would have performed three shows, allowing the audience enough opportunities to see them all at least once. During their own rest-times I. House participants rushed to see the others.

Tickets cost a dime, since most of the actual proceeds would come from the sale of arts and crafts or donated food. Minutes after the front doors were opened, the hall was packed almost solid with a huge, joyous crowd. Suddenly, with maracas shaking and boisterous shouts, a line of Latin Americans wearing carioca-colored clothing, snake-danced through the lobby.

"Come to the fiesta. Everyone! Enjoy our carnival in October. Upstairs in the ballroom, starting in five minutes!" they chanted, pushing through the people while wiggling their brightly costumed bodies.

Immediately behind them and taking advantage of the rapidly closing opening, approached the white robed, burnoosed figure of a tall Arab, who called out, "We invite you to the casbah, the Middle East at its most provocative and mysterious. Drink a cup of the best coffee in the world while you watch our beautiful belly dancers entice you with their unforgettable performances! Starting momentarily, upstairs, ladies and gentlemen." And he waved invitingly towards the marble staircase.

Jopie and Petra watched the jubilant faces around them and almost forgot it was time to present their own show. They hurried back to the booth.

To everyone's astonishment, Jopie, who much earlier had planned exactly what she would do next, stepped forward and announced, "You are watching a Dutch wedding celebration. The civil and religious ceremonies have already taken place. Now all her friends will dance for the bride!" Then she gestured quickly towards Petra standing beside the flower cart.

Nettie, surprised and angry, frowned, but the damage had already been done: The blonde last-minute interloper would not be allowed to dance but Jopie had placed her in the spotlight just the same!

Petra stood aside and watched the costumed students whirling in front of the windmill with its smoothly gyrating arms, and listened while they stamped their wooden shoes with so much enthusiasm the entire lobby floor trembled.

Stoically because there was no alternative anyway, Nettie took Pieter van Hoorn by the hand, danced around and around with him, clapping in time to the music, momentarily able to suppress the insistent nightmare hovering in her semi-consciousness. For an instant, the customary grimace, which always uglied her features, was replaced with radiance, and she became glowingly beautiful, exuberant. But when the music and the dancing stopped, there again appeared the familiar sour expression. She bowed to the applauding spectators, gave a stilted smile, held on to Pieter and disappeared with him into the crowd.

Jopie squinted after them and murmured, "Dear God. Let it happen. Please, please let it happen."

"Shhh," whispered Petra. "If we leave them alone, maybe it will."

"Hmm. You caught on to the Pieter connection quickly. Have you actually forgiven her for the way she behaved to you?"

"I have no choice. What happened to her in the war could have happened to me. But for sheer luck our stories would have been the same," Petra replied as her eyes darkened.

"But it didn't happen to you! Empathy is one thing, reality quite another. Anyway let's have happy thoughts the remainder of the evening. Hmm, guess who's heading this way? It's our handsome Indian."

Petra turned around and saw him grinning at Jopie, the dimples in his cheeks deep and taunting, like fellow conspirators, she thought to herself. Then he faced her and said, "Hello. How pretty you look!"

She thanked him while thinking, "That's either his over-used line or he's having problems with his eyesight. Next to the gorgeously gowned Indian women I feel like a frumpy farmer!"

She noticed his neat dark business suit and said, "I guess you're not participating in your show, are you?"

He laughed. "Oh, but I am! This costume is quite perfect for the role I am playing." He winked at her and explained, "I have been appointed exclusive gate-crasher watcher. No one may leave or enter the gymnasium without personal permission from me."

"Aha," she countered, "you're selling tickets!"

"Correct, my lady. A most important assignment, don't you agree? By the way, have you seen our skit?"

"Not yet."

He glanced at his watch, "It will begin in approximately three minutes. Come with me and I will sneak you in ahead of the line. People were already waiting for the next show when the other one was ending!"

Since the I. House was packed with overly generous paying guests, she doubted the Scholarship Fund would suffer irreparably due to one less dime. He took her elbow and maneuvered through the packed hallway, strolled confidently to the front of the line, led her to a place in the dimly lit gymnasium and disappeared to fulfill his ticketing duties.

A spotlight came on and there stood Chedda, silk robed and turbaned, his hands aloft in blessing, while a Ceylonese bride and groom kneeled before him. Parvati, dressed in a red sari trimmed with gold, her hair encircled in white flowers, appeared carrying a bowl from which the young couple drank. Sitar melodies and drum beats streamed from the rear of the room while a dancer using her hands, body, face and eyes made intricate symbolic gestures, which Petra could not interpret. After more prayers in Hindi or Sanskrit, the couple were considered married.

The lights were turned on and to her surprise, Dev was sitting next to her. In the darkness she had not been aware of him. "Enough of India," he exclaimed. "Let us go now and see what everyone else has thought up, or must you return to your booth?"

"Just one more performance in a half-hour." Again she gazed into his face and thought, "What does he want with me?"

Around them the silk-swirled women smiled provocatively, some breathtakingly beautiful. She felt clumsy and uncivilized near them, the flannel skirt and black apron as elegant as the milkmaids for whom they were intended. But he held his head high, immune to their coy or open invitations.

The bewilderment still coursed through her as she heard a familiar voice saying, "Ah Dev, it is you. See that you take proper care of my daughter!"

"Ah, don't worry, father," he teased immediately.

But the flippant retort apparently infuriated Baboo because he sputtered, "Look to it, Dev. Do watch over her. She is not one of your other girls."

The boy recoiled as if he had been physically attacked, recovered, and nodded to the older man.

Baboo, meanwhile, leaned over her and murmured, "Come to my booth. I am telling fortunes. There is a long line and I am already very tired but you will not have to wait." Raising a thin, elegant hand, he attempted to push a path into the crowd to go upstairs, barely succeeded in creating a small pathway and disappeared completely.

"Well, now let us explore together." The shocked expression on Dev's face had vanished.

They entered the nearest booth and walked into a fairy tale. Before and above them loomed the pure whiteness of a mosque, noble, perfect, with fragile minarets scraping against a midnight blue heaven, in which myriads of stars twinkled. Like the windmill, everything gave an illusion of depth, a trompe l'oeil replica which must have taken hundreds of hours to construct. At the entrance they were greeted by an Egyptian doctor, whom Dev had met once or twice.

"Welcome to the Arabian nights. Do you like our display?"

"It is perfection. How did you manage to do it?" Petra answered.

Obviously pleased, he chuckled, "Just a plaything for our ancient talent. Don't you know we are the greatest architects in the world? Although I do have to admit this morning the mosque was witness to some highly sacrilegious outbursts.

Something about sons of dogs and walls refusing to stay up." He laughed. "Of course I had never heard such Arabic before."

"But," he beamed with justified pride, "somehow problems were overcome and there it stands. I hope for a few more hours! Have either of you ever had Persian coffee? No? Good! I highly recommend it." He glanced at a counter inundated with people placing orders. "So, you both will be my guests. Meanwhile, please watch our entertainment."

A bright light shone down on a beautiful woman, lightly veiled, the sheerest fabrics covered her face and body, both laden with sparkling chains, and emphasized the diamond in her naked belly.

To Petra's discomfort and Dev's blatant delight, she wriggled, swayed, leaned backwards, allowed her long auburn hair to fall to the ground behind her, while her bare feet beat in time to the drummed music. Each gesture was a provocation, her breasts, eyes, hair and hands offering pleasures which the men present could only too easily imagine. The room had already been stifling hot, now it absolutely steamed.

Petra suddenly recognized the dancer. Thalia! Whom she had met at Baboo's dinner, sitting demurely next to Parvati, nervously awaiting the results of an exam in International Law, thick tortoise-shell glasses covering her eyes, wearing an unimaginative brown turtleneck blouse over a monochrome skirt, and so frightened she could not carry on a conversation!

The drumbeats stopped, Thalia bowed, placed her hands together in deference, and left the place momentarily in darkness.

"Interesting performance, don't you think?" choked Dev, feigning objectivity but not succeeding very well.

Their host returned with the coffee in tiny, delicate cups. "Perhaps you prefer it with sugar, but it is delicious this way too." He immediately refused to accept Dev's money. "You are in my house ."

Petra sipped, quickly disliked the grainy consistency of the beverage but battled simultaneously with a conundrum. One more swallow and she knew she would have to cough, but she didn't want to insult the generous Egyptian standing next to her.

Dev also seemed uncomfortable but set his jaw, determined to finish the drink. The doctor was not fooled. "Do not be ashamed to admit you find it unusual. It is an acquired taste. Truly, I am not offended." He promptly took the little cups away but Dev was frowning, embarrassed to have participated in such an overt, social faux pas. All he could do was thank their host and extend a promise to meet him for dinner soon. Spontaneously, the two men embraced.

As they left the mosque Petra wondered, "An Egyptian? Generous, polite! But everyone knows they're barbarians whose major interests begin and end with murdering Jews!"

While Dev muttered, "But this is not possible! How can I have a Muslim as a friend?"

He looked at her and read her face. "The I. House," he whispered.

For a moment they watched the shoving, exuberant mass in front of them until they were momentarily surrounded by the Latin American conga line, between maracas, bongo drums and kicking dancers.

Dev shouted, "Let's follow them, shall we?" grabbed her arm and hung on. In the crush of moving, singing people it would have been easy to lose each other. Although Dev had absolutely no intention of letting that happen. At least not tonight. Not yet.

For an instant as they were herded up the marble staircase, Petra wondered if Baboo had ever made it back to his booth or was still being shoved around somewhere in the middle of the I. House, hopeless, frustrated, brilliant and beloved. Then she and Dev ran after the musicians.

They were snake-danced into a large enclosure whose ceilings and walls were completely covered by tropical plants and fruits. Palm trees and high potted branches brushed against their faces as they entered, while orchids, plumeria, and birds-of-paradise mingled in a luxuriant abundance of colors and textures. Glowing sunlight had been simulated through clever use of hidden lights behind the stage.

A single guitarist, dressed in a serape, his face almost obliterated by a huge straw sombrero, began to play and sing a dismal, saccharine lament but soon was joined by other musicians and drowned out by exuberant flutes, violins, tambourines, and drums.

Now the jubilant dancers re-appeared, their bodies twisting sinuously to the throbbing tempo. They sang raucously, shouted wordless words as they moved, their abandonment contagious. Most of the onlookers unconsciously moved their shoulders and heads in rhythm with the performers.

Petra realized that Dev was glancing at her, as she, too, reacted to the music, the lace cap bobbing in tempo, her face radiating unconfined pleasure. He said nothing but obviously lacked any appreciation whatsoever for the sensual, hypnotizing melodies, as far removed from his ancient culture as the mysterious gestures made during the Indian wedding ceremony had been alien to hers. Indeed, he could barely hide his contempt at the blatant sexual exhilaration being thrust into his face, and she was silently amused as he watched the simulated orgy with haughty regal piety.

But when they looked directly at each other, he immediately ceased brooding and smiled. She blushed, and the reticent confusion haunted her again: What did he want? A momentary diversion?

Baboo had specifically warned him not to have any such ideas about her!

The shaking, vibrating bodies finally stopped dancing and again they wandered through the lobby with its crawling, undulating file of spectators.

"Now, on to Baboo. What does the mysterious future hold in store for me?" laughed Petra cynically.

"Don't joke about that!"

"About fortune telling?"

He scowled at her, "You must not condemn the beliefs of others simply because they are not yours! In India, at a baby's birth, the astrologer immediately casts its horoscope. Not for a week or a month, for the duration of the child's life."

"Don't try to convince me Baboo uses a horoscope as a guideline for his life. The man is a scientist! Did the stars tell his parents what he would become...or where he is right now? Or will be in a year? Nonsense!"

Dev appeared frustrated and a little angry, but overcame it and said softly, "After the horoscope is cast, it is locked away and will be consulted only much later in adulthood, to see whether specific events and the times they occurred took place as predicted."

"Well, what's the sense of having your future told after the fact?" she scoffed.

This time he was not upset. "Our priests realize the apprehension connected with facing an oncoming tragedy might be worse than the experience. The fear itself could have terrible consequences."

"Have you seen yours?"

"No, not yet. But my father showed me his and it correctly predicted he would almost be killed in an automobile accident and when it would occur. Many events that had already happened to him were also recorded. Go now to Baboo, see what he has to tell you."

He left her standing there.

Perhaps, she laughed to herself, his horoscope predicted a quickie in the hay with her. Well, if so, that was one prediction which would not come true! Ignoring the line in front of Baboo's booth she raised the curtain and was welcomed.

"Come here, daughter. Sit down." He motioned her to a chair opposite his and directed her to place her hand on the table between them. Gently he grasped it, noticing how small and childish it was and peered deeply into what she considered the unmysterious epidermis of her palm. To her it appeared grooved where it was supposed to be and un-grooved everywhere else.

"You will marry and have three children," he began, "and fall in love with a man from a land you have never seen."

Although she adored the frail genius, Petra was not impressed with his omniscience at this point. Fortune telling depended on generalities. These were definitely generalities.

"Your life will be very interesting, little one..." His voice was calm, steady, as if reciting a familiar mathematical equation. He had not cracked any eggs or peered into a crystal ball. In fact, there was no crystal ball and he would have considered wasting eggs for such a frivolous purpose obscene.

Baboo was Baboo, not a charlatan wearing a peaked cap or bejeweled turban, but rather dressed as always in a carefully cut, immaculately pressed business suit.

She had learned to trust and love this man who, as he had promised, allowed no one to hurt her. He actually had become a second father to her, available for counsel and comfort, gentle, intelligent.

Then he mumbled, "There is no more." The shift in his attitude startled her.

"Baboo, what did you see? Tell me, please?"

But he continued to edge her out of the booth. "Everything is just fine, really. It is all silly superstition anyway. Go now, child. You see, there are many others waiting."

She suddenly remembered the essence of Dev's words, the knowledge of a predicted event could be more terrible than the reality of the event itself.

In the I. House's crowded lobby she stood still and pondered. Baboo was brilliant, no illiterate farm boy from a village in the Asian hinterlands, a scientist who would find it anathema to accept abracadabra and hocus pocus. On the other hand, she reasoned cheerfully, at this moment he was undoubtedly again babbling nonsense to some other person. Well, she reasoned, whatever Baboo refused to divulge would be his burden and he was stuck with it.

She returned to her own booth for its final performance. Instead of the introspective mysteries of the East, she gloried in the robust simplicity of the Dutch peasant dances, as obvious and uncomplicated as the countryside itself.

Chapter 12

Too soon it ended, all the participants disappeared, and she was standing alone in front of the windmill with its huge arms now at a standstill, perusing the gaily decorated but completely empty cart and table, where every product had been sold.

As expected, the familiar loneliness threatened to overwhelm her and she wandered upstairs past the entrance to the Indian booth.

Wondering.

Dev wasn't there.

She assumed he was inside being entertained by a willing member of his infamous harem. Entirely his prerogative, of course.

Indifferently, without even realizing it, she was being pushed in every direction by the mass of people, having herself no set destination.

Lost.

The French had erected an indoor "outdoor" café complete with soulful-faced accordionist. Visitors wandered through the display, drinking imported wines and munching on slices of cheese, while the striped marquee stretched above them formed mattress patterns on their florid, sweaty faces. Dispassionately she bought a ticket, a glass of Bordeaux and watched a pair of enthralled-with-each-other Apache dancers meet, entwine from head to foot, and throw each other furiously across the floor all-in-the-name-of-love.

She recognized no one in the café and soon fled into the confused impersonality of the crowd. And there, separated by hundreds of shoving people, she looked up at the staircase and saw the white, white smile and the mischievous eyes. The happiness she felt even surprised her.

"Hello!" he shouted. "Where are you going now?

"I heard the Israelis are putting on an impromptu and it's supposed to be marvelous. But I don't know exactly where they are. They're not listed on the program."

"I know where it is. I have seen it but it is not so terrible if I see it a second time." He pushed his way to her and then bulldozed them both to the location.

Although initially denied a place on the schedule, a group of Israeli students had insisted on being included, to contribute to the fund-raising efforts. At the last minute on Halloween Eve itself, they were brusquely pointed to a dark, distant corner in the second-story hall, far away from everyone else. There had been time for just one ad hoc rehearsal, no money was available for costumes or sets, but they had managed to scissor and paste a show together.

Three men were seated on the floor playing flute, drums and accordion. A fourth sat off to the side, strumming on a guitar. The area was in semi-darkness but they had created a "campfire" with orange crepe paper and hidden flashlights. Four women dressed in simple cotton blouses and skirts, their hair long and loose, waited barefoot for the music to change.

The accordionist signaled, suddenly switched tempo and they jumped into the center of the area, raised their heads and arms and began to dance. From the sidelines four boys joined them and in no time the hall was vibrating with Israeli folk music, its Slavic-Oriental influences and rhythms hypnotizing the audience.

Meanwhile, performers from other booths, their shows finished, wares sold, heard the music and came upstairs to see what was happening. The Israelis who had formed a circle were now dancing the overly familiar hora, while their originally isolated corner was crammed with students still wearing their own colorful national costumes.

The musicians stopped playing, the dancers bowed and the performance ended. The audience erupted with clapping and raucous ululations.

No one left.

Rising and waving to the audience, the guitarist who was apparently the Israeli group's leader, thanked everyone for coming. Then as the applause continued and no one appeared to be leaving, he talked quickly in Hebrew to his friends and they performed yet another song. More enthusiastic applause. Still no one left.

In fact, more people appeared on the staircase and ran down the long hallway.

The guitarist, suddenly aware of what had happened, his face glowing, announced, "Now, we have danced and played for all of you. We are thrilled you have enjoyed our efforts so much. We understand you want us to continue!"

Loud cheers and clapping!

"But there will be a small difference. You must dance with us. The ballroom is no longer being used and here it has become very crowded . If no one objects, let us move there and we will show you how easy the steps are!"

Someone turned on the lights in the ballroom and instantly a huge circle formed. The Israelis demonstrated the hora, the guitarist rejoined his comrades and immediately the exuberant music rang out again.

.   Dev, delighted with a ready-made opportunity, took Petra's hand, the first time their naked fingers had joined, and led her to an opening in the ring. His left hand was grasped by a woman with a black lace mantilla crowning her head, while Petra's other hand was clutched by an Apache, his beret appropriately askew. The gorgeous Ceylonese bride, dressed still in her exquisite golden sari, a large solitaire diamond piercing her nostril, whirled past, held tightly by a tall, laughing African in colorful stripes who was bravely but futilely trying to master the steps.

Very far away, on the other side of the enormous room, Nettie radiant and flushed, was still being partnered by Pieter. Although they too were surrounded by others, they bent to each other, obviously experiencing only their own world. She totally ignored the girl on the extreme opposite side of the circle, wearing the apron initially meant for her, and gave herself up completely to the infectious music of Israel.

Beside her, Pieter dared to hope. He had no illusions about being able to heal her but he could help her endure and perhaps suffer a little less. Would it be enough? he wondered. Would she even allow it?

Meanwhile Chedda, making fun of his overly healthy waistline, was protesting to Salmi and Ellen that he didn't really think he could manage such vigorous exercise anymore but then joined in anyway. The Latins, still wearing their colorful costumes, were immediately attuned to the unfamiliar rhythm, adopted the music as their own and soon improvised original steps to it.

For another forty-five minutes the Israelis, unscheduled and originally denied participation, entertained and were entertained. On their faces dark lines of perspiration formed, but in their eyes burned an enormous satisfaction.

Tightly, Petra held Dev's strong, beautiful hand and whispered, "If only the rest of the world could share this, dance, sing, join together, maybe there would finally be a chance for everyone to live in peace."

He glanced down at her. "Look over there," he said and gestured towards the back of the room.

In a corner, not dancing but observing quietly, stood the Egyptian doctor who had taught them both so much already this evening. And he too, had a thoughtful, hopeful smile on his face.

The musicians, exhausted, finally stopped playing, but Petra was suddenly incapable of speaking to the boy next to her, still lightly holding on to her hand.

He was silent also. Then softly said, "It is after three. May I walk home with you?"

"Yes, please," she replied, overwhelmed with the evening's impressions, still incapable and unwilling to converse.

In fact, he was having a similar problem, wanting to remain near her but uncharacteristically tongue-tied. Outside the quiet cleanliness of the autumn night contrasted sharply with the noisy closeness of the festival in the I. House. Slowly they walked towards the building where her ugly, impersonal little habitat awaited.

"But are you really tired?" he finally asked when they reached the building entrance.

She answered simply, "No. What about you?"

"I feel the same. Shall we have some pizza and calm down a bit?"

She didn't know if she could digest pizza at this hour of the morning but wasn't ready to bid him "goodnight" either.

He led her farther into the clear night and to a little Italian restaurant on Broadway where many of the I. House residents frequently ate. The place was packed! But they were fortunate and slid into a booth being vacated just as they entered, then held hands on top of the table, not needing to say a word, completely aware of each other.

He gazed at her with amazement, while she stared awed by the gentleness registered on his face.

Earlier they had left the pandemonium of the festival and traded it for the deafening noise and waves of cigarette smoke in this location. They heard, smelled, sensed all the annoying influences, but none of them mattered—as if everything outside of themselves was occurring somewhere far in the distance.

A waiter came and they ordered automatically, not really hungry nor thirsty.

"Hey, Dev! How are you? May we join you?" called Chedda from the doorway, escorting a lovely American girl to their table.

The boy consented immediately. What else could he do? There was not one empty table in the entire restaurant and he could certainly not refuse his friend.

There followed chatter, endless, aimless, amusing, boring, continuing for an eternal, flavorless, shared meal, devoured by two ravenous participants, ignored or barely picked at by the other two.

At last Dev's head began to visibly droop, and with a veiled, exhausted smile he said, "It is time."

As he stood up, a still wide-awake, exuberant Chedda shouted, "So, young people, where are you going?"

"It is five o'clock in the morning! I am going home," replied his countryman.

Petra reached for her coat but Dev was already holding it, inadvertently touching her shoulders slightly as he helped her put it on. The contact as light as it was caused an involuntary shiver of complete pleasure to race though her body.

And his.

Which he had not expected!

Shaken, he went to the cashier, paid, opened the door for her, and together they emerged slowly into the brightness of upper Manhattan, alight even at this hour with neon signs and street lamps. The ugliness of the elevated tracks hung above them on 125th Street, from where they receded into the heart of the great city in one direction and the multimillionaire neighborhoods of lower Westchester in the other.

Petra shivered again and Dev put his arm through hers. "I am not really that tired. Just wanted to get away, " he admitted. "Let's walk a little more. I don't think I want to go home yet."

When an hour later they returned to the building where she lived, chased there at last not due to fatigue but rather the onset of freezing cold winds, he rode up in the elevator with her, memorized once more the look on her face, closed his eyes for an instant in ecstasy, squeezed her hand and ran down the stairs.

He walked to his own apartment on Riverside Drive, totally confused for the first time in his life.

Chapter 13

So...was it actually simply coincidence that in the ensuing week Dev was able to finish reading the necessary assigned cases for his law classes more than in time to appear in the crowded, stuffy Waffle Wing around dinner hour to debate problematic issues with some of his I. House resident classmates (always available for such group discussions), rather than opting to work them out by himself, weighing each facet with concentrated introspection, in the quiet river view room he rented several blocks away, which until then he had often declared he much preferred?

Breathe!

And was it also happenstance Petra suddenly politely refused to accompany Ellen to several more interesting dining establishments, citing the reasonable prices at the I. House and her truly meager budget, as well as the stultifying fatigue "Mr. Burken" induced with his endless demands for have-to-be-written-before-you-can-go-home-inane-news-releases-and-no-extra-pay-for-overtime, as perfect excuses for choosing Waffle Wing hamburgers rather than to indulge in much more expensive but authentic Spanish paella?

Breathe again!

Whatever the real reason, they could count on meeting each other every evening.

He, either sitting alone, writing, or surrounded by other law students who were loudly talking away irrelevancies. He listened but seldom joined the conversation, silent, expectant, pretending to be attentive to his friends. Never mentioning her name.

She, usually arriving later, not seeing who was already present, rather immediately taking a tray and deciding what to have for dinner, looking around innocently, ostensibly to search for an empty table, noticing him gesture in feigned surprise at seeing her there, inviting her to join him.

They became friends.

He found her sensitive, insightful, her fair coloring an exotic change from the women he had known, but hiding a mystery, which he sensed formed the core of her identity.

To her he was simply Dev, warm, intelligent and perceptive. And although the most physically beautiful person she had ever seen, also the least vain.

One evening as they were drinking coffee, a well-dressed man approached their table. "Uh, pardon me, young man," he said to Dev. "Are you Italian?"

"No."

"Doesn't really matter, son. Say, would you like to take a screen test? I think you have a great chance of making it in the movies."

"I'm sorry, but I am a student. Show business does not interest me."

"Could finance your education, my boy," he persisted; "with your looks, you could buy the whole school in just a short while."

"Thank you, but I don't want the money."

"I hope you appreciate what you're throwing away. Think about it," he wheedled.

Exasperated, Dev picked up his coffee cup, turned around and ignored any further conversation.

The insistent man put a card on the table. "In case you change your mind," he said and left.

After he was out of sight, Dev asked, "What do you think, Petra? Should I follow it up?"

"Decide for yourself. Many people would be thrilled with such an opportunity. But it's your life."

The famous mischievous grin appeared. "Ha, I can see myself now, cockatooing before a camera, worrying if my lipstick was the proper shade, screaming at the cameramen for filming the wrong side of my elbows." He paused for an instant and added, "My parents would kill me if they thought I would accept such prostitution!"

Petra shook her head. The man was right, of course, she thought. Dev is extraordinarily handsome, but his greatest beauty is his complete unawareness of himself.

Even if he accepted it as shrug-shouldered fact, whenever she glanced at him, every nerve in her body was attuned to him: Knowing he consisted of many more layers than a mere facade simply added to the attraction.

Chapter 14

Four weeks into the friendship, both of them were secretly nervous wrecks. He, because he desperately wanted to ask her for a date but knew it would be challenging wisdom. She, because she couldn't understand why he wouldn't.

One sleepless night, while yet another of an endless supply of sated enamored females dozed next to him, he asked himself the questions he had so far avoided. Why had he been both compelled and impelled to approach her that October Saturday afternoon?

Wide-awake, confused, he relived the instant he had first seen her, the whiteness of her face and the paleness of her hair, accented by the rosy glow on her skin from the tennis lesson. Why had he forced himself, robot-like, to purposely ignore her and instead approach her companion, ask for and receive an invitation to sit down at their table, and after all that preparation, to wait deliberately until just the proper moment to speak with her directly?

It had happened without any control from him whatsoever, as if he were being led on a leash. And he both liked and disliked the experience.

Worse! The same inadvertent behavior had guided him Halloween Eve at the festival. Usually a rational man, he had hidden behind a column in the lobby and watched as she smiled at potential customers, received and made change; then, most irrationally, he had appeared and apparently quite spontaneously asked her to be his guest and watch the Indian wedding, aware several women acquaintances would be furious! He had been angry at himself as well for being so unusually vulnerable (a male child used to being in control of and having his way with women since he was a teenager), and made an instant decision to ignore her for the rest of the evening.

Oh, and by the way, just in case there might be a misunderstanding.

Forever.

Instead, he found himself behind the same column, furtively observing her again, noticed the dejection on her face and read it correctly when she did not find him, felt strangely pained as she somberly tried to swallow the French wine, and consequently could not bear to watch her suffer an instant longer—ultimately surrendering—supposedly having gotten lost himself in the throng so he could "find" her again.

But!

Surrendering to himself was one thing. However, he had no intention of surrendering to her!

Ever!

Still, he considered, perhaps it would be wisest to ask her out for one Saturday evening dinner, take her to bed and end it there. Which was his usual modus operandi and would certainly work with her as well. Women, he had learned many years ago, were there for his personal enjoyment and, so far, all including his presently sleeping bedfellow appeared to have been grateful for his ephemeral attentions.

And so, most certainly, would she.

He was aware by now that every other Friday, directly after work, she returned to Washington to be with her family, but the coming weekend she would be here, in New York.

When he invited her to have dinner with him, he was not surprised she accepted. What did surprise him was his own delight they would be together. Alone. He recalled the shiver that had coursed through his body when he touched her at the restaurant and could almost imagine he felt it again.

Even without her presence.

On Saturday he was shaved, showered, dressed and ready to go more than an hour before their appointed rendezvous. Earlier, for the first time in his life, he had picked up and hung in the closet a month's worth of strewn-around clothing; borrowed and learned how to operate a vacuum cleaner; torn a Madras shirt into a dustcloth; converted an almost new towel to a mop; and swished bleach and scouring powder around the toilet with a just-purchased bristle brush until the bowl gleamed virginal porcelain. (At home the servants took care of such trivia, while here the landlord from whom he leased one room in a five-bedroom apartment did include a badly needed, insufficient, once-every-three-weeks cleaning service as part of the rent.)

All was now as ready as he could control for the evening (and night) ahead.

He tried to concentrate on reading *The New York Times* while enjoying two cups of strong tea. There was nothing that interested him in the paper, and the tea was beginning to taste too bitter. He got up, polar-beared around the room once more to ensure all was as neat as he could get it, watched the discarded beverage slither down the drain in the tiny sink, washed the cup, and was relieved to note it was now finally almost seven o'clock.

He locked the door and went out into the street where the weather had turned winter bitter.

October in New York was glorious: Indian summer, refreshing nights and balmy temperatures.

Early December was freezing cold with much worse to come. He buttoned his jacket, walked towards the I. House and didn't even notice the weather.

They dined at Tony's Italian Kitchen on 79th Street. He, exulting in snowy linguini with clam sauce while she ordered cannelloni. Then they sprawled laughing into a cab and rode to Greenwich Village for dessert, coffee and whatever else the night might bring.

Although he was a foreigner, Dev actually knew New York at night far better than she did, and it was automatic for him to take the initiative. Her teenaged knowledge of the great city and its diverse activities had usually stopped at late afternoon, unless she was accompanied by a parent. (Or later by college friends who could only afford a little cash for the cheapest beer halls, preferring to save most of their funds for Broadway shows, concerts and the opera.)

On the other hand, Dev, who had never known what money problems were, had experienced the Manhattan bachelor life for well over a year and was perhaps too intimately acquainted with its after-sunset diversions. He ordered the cabby to drop them at the Jumble Shop and took her inside.

As usual it was crowded and noisy, filled with oddballs, rich kids trying to act poor but unable to shed the aura of their own importance, poor kids not wanting to seem broke so their potential lovers wouldn't catch on and reject them, the blue-acid stench of cigarettes and cigars mingled with Joy and Woolworth's best.

And music—too loud and too trendy.

Unable to breathe they quickly finished dessert and drinks, and, gasping escaped into the freezing streets. Dev was more used to warm weather, but he wore a light suit, no coat and appeared immune to the cold. She was bundled into winter clothes, a turtleneck sweater and Campbell tartan pleated skirt, and over them a camel wrap-around coat with a belt but no buttons. As they wandered through the windy lanes, unsure of where they were actually headed, the belt broke free and the coat opened, allowing cold air to reach every part of her body. He looked at her and saw she was trembling.

Scowling, he noted, "That is much too impractical in this weather," and adjusted the errant belt and coat so they enclosed her again. Just to insure they would not reopen, he put his arm around her tightly and guided her close to the walls of the buildings, away from the cutting blasts which whirled through MacDougal Street.

But their huddled attempts at surcease did not succeed for very long. In ice-cold desperation they entered the nearest doorway and stumbled into a lovely cocktail lounge, with soft rugs on the floor, deep plush armchairs, coffee tables with hooded candle holders, and in the center a rosewood paneled fireplace emanating warmth and light.

Somewhere in the semi-darkness, a woman was singing folk songs and accompanying herself on the guitar. For the next few hours they remained there, talking, drinking wine, staying warm, not eager to return to the outdoored death.

Towards one o'clock they mutually decided to go home. Fairly quickly he was able to hail a taxi, gave the driver her address and when they arrived ordered him to wait, rode up in the elevator with her, waited until she was safely inside, then hurried downstairs and went home.

Alone!

To the room he had spent all afternoon cleaning in preparation for her arrival. He looked around it, sighed, then laughed cynically at his own stupidity and recently proven cowardice.

Not even a kiss.

On the cheek, for God's sake!

Not even that!

The woman three doors down the hall heard him come home, had been listening for his return, waited a few proper minutes, put on slippers and a bathrobe over her nightgown, walked determinedly to his room and knocked.

He didn't ask who might be visiting at this late hour, simply opened immediately, nodded a silent greeting, stood aside and let her in.

She kissed him quickly on the lips—a kiss he accepted but did not return—pushed him towards the bed, reached for the zipper on his slacks, pulled them down and knelt.

Again he sighed. But with relief.

Part Two
ANDANTE

Chapter 15

WASHINGTON D.C.

Petra, completely immersed in a dream, floated into her room, hugged herself, unwilling to remove the coat he had embraced to keep her warm (still imbued subtly with his scent). Dev's quiet confidence had given her a sense of security she had never experienced with another man. And there had been plenty of them. In fact, one passionate suitor was waiting patiently right now for her to return inevitably to his arms in the Washington, D.C. suburbs.

After tonight his wait could become interminable.

She felt as if she finally had come home, found the shelter she had searched for throughout her life. Dev hadn't even tried to kiss her, only held her hand, possessed her waist through the thick woolens. Yet she assumed he must be attracted to her. No, she KNEW he was!

But if he chose to proceed slowly, to wait, she would abide by that, allow him to lead at his chosen pace. For once she knew she could follow blindly without considering the consequences, trusting him implicitly.

Baboo need not chide his countryman for actual or implied fickleness.

And so she was completely unprepared for the total silence that followed their date.

Dev did not appear at the I. House the entire week, apparently having found more appetizing places to dine. The black, horrible phone (on which she was allowed to receive calls but not place any) remained stunningly ringless.

By the weekend, when she was due to make the family pilgrimage, she accepted the truth.

She boarded the train at Penn Station, prepared for a long, dirty, tiring trip followed by an even longer, boring weekend spent convincing Albert he needed to move on.

Albert!

The train roared on through the countryside, and her thoughts returned automatically to how their relationship had altered and what else she could do to extricate herself permanently from it.

It began two years ago with Ilse, a pretty but vapid-headed, future elementary school teacher, struggling to comprehend the mysterious thought processes of T.S. Eliot in an upper-level English Literature class they shared. For a few months they were friends, until Petra realized that although Ilse was carefully-groomed-attractive, beneath her brown, stiffly sprayed coiffe resided a colander instead of a brain, and the friendship ended due to sheer tedium. But not before Ilse had introduced her to Albert, her far more intelligent brother...birthing a friendship that would survive despite Petra's efforts to end it.

At twenty-eight he was more than eight years older, an Army veteran who had earned a degree in electrical engineering under the G.I. Bill, currently labored mightily for a government agency, was (like his sister) culturally ignorant and not eager for enlightenment, lived at home with her and their widowed mother, and maintained neither proudly nor ashamedly he was still a virgin.

And he was Jewish.

Sofie, Petra's mother, was ecstatic and asserted Albert, so kind, so handsome, so intelligent, needed to become a member of the family. Although prior to meeting him, Petra had been no wallflower, he was the first man she was heavily encouraged to consider seriously, a mate for the rest of her life. Initially, because she was extremely young and didn't want to defy her parents, she talked herself into being in love with him, suffered miserably because it appeared her feelings for him were unrequited (while he continued to ask her out and gloried in describing his adventures with the other women he was seeing simultaneously). She was bewildered and wounded, unable to comprehend why he was so sadistic but far too insecure to defy him or defend herself.

The first year they dated, he definitely had the upper hand, arrogant, confident she would love only him forever and callous enough to continuously manipulate her emotions. But during the second year, she met someone else and realized Albert was not a particularly great catch, in fact sexually was probably a disaster, an immature child unaware she was outgrowing him.

His unexpected rival, a brilliant Ph.D. candidate, secure, masculine, down-to-earth and absolutely honest, proposed to her within two months after they met.

And Steve, too, was Jewish. Being with him was exhilarating, and together they attended concerts, the ballet, parties and football games. His friends were intelligent, aware, and she constantly learned from their impromptu discussions, which could last until the early morning hours.

Albert had no friends, and his favorite way to spend a Saturday evening was to attend a movie (preferably a Western), followed by ice cream at a Hot Shoppe in Silver Spring.

Now with a basis for comparison she found Albert undefinably but also undeniably lacking.

However, she wanted to please her parents, and for a traumatic month, actually observed both of them dueling on the phone for equal dating time, heard each declare unending love and offer marriage (and to her dismay really cared for them both), should have savored being the female fervently desired by two eligible males, was assured she was the hub of their lives (a situation that should have been to her advantage but actually caused her even more confusion and anxiety).

Predictably, Sofie became a menopausal maniac, who constantly referred to her daughter as a whore, threatened immediate disownment, hounded and screamed at her. With whom, Petra wondered, did she whore? To date, Albert's amateur gropings at her outer clothing had been her most intimate sexual experiences. Steve hadn't even progressed that far!

In keeping with the impossible moral code of the Fifties, she was expected to be emotionally and physically mature, but had to adhere to the unscripted ordinances governing a "nice girl's" behavior. And God help any woman who somehow got a "bad reputation!"

Deserved or not.

After putting up with the two ring circus for eight months, submitting to some deep introspection and ultimately comprehending even all by herself, Sofie outnumbered him, Steve had enough and left for California to complete the necessary research for his dissertation. And to hopefully find a mother-in-law who would appreciate him more!

Sofie congratulated herself for having salvaged her daughter's almost-in-shambles future and for kicking the overly eager and smitten rival far away to the Pacific Coast, a man too strong for her to manipulate, as she had feared all along.

Ironically, she had not even been able to use the difference in religion to break up that misalliance, resorting instead to describing him as low-class, culturally confined, the Eastern European offspring of pogroms, programs and peasants (although she admitted only nominally that Albert exactly fitted the description as well).

While their family were refugees, well educated and established for centuries in their tiny, peaceful country, contributing attorneys, manufacturing magnates, doctors and musicians, respected faculty members at universities in Leiden, Delft, Amsterdam, and so on and on.

Petra and her brother not only owed to Sofie their initial births but their subsequent lives as well, she constantly reminded them.

She was right, of course. They would have perished along with the more than one hundred thousand other Dutch Jews if she hadn't insisted, raged unceasingly against her usually compliant husband Sam (initially unwilling to leave a lucrative position with years of seniority and a life of ease), and in concert with her father Pierre (who while on a trip in Germany observed both the actions and non-reactions of government authorities and local citizenry as the persecution of the Jews escalated—and hurried home to Holland to warn Sofie and Sam of the danger) ultimately threatened to take her two children alone to a strange country (rather than remain in the luxurious environment she only had known) since they had (correctly, it turned out) perceived the direction Adolf Hitler and his legally elected Nazi Party next door would follow.

Take another breath!

Opa Pierre (after whom Petra was named) remained in Holland trapped by an extended family unwilling to believe his repeated warnings and was murdered (as were they) in Sobibor. In time the crucial role he had played in their escape decreased and Sofie's own increased, as the story was told and retold. Through it, she was able to repeatedly convince the four surviving members of her family that she always made the best decisions concerning their presents and futures, as their pasts far too sorrowfully and presciently confirmed.

Her son joined the navy and escaped the chains. But she swore no one would alter the plans she had made for her compliant daughter. One day she would attend Petra and Albert's nuptials, superintended by her personally, of course.

The bride would wear a simple silk pastel dress (since Sofie considered wedding gowns ostentatious wastes of money), the groom be appropriately handsome in a navy blue suit. They would not require the services of a rabbi (they didn't even belong to a shul). Just a civil ceremony, followed by a reception for a few friends.

Classic, elegant, unobtrusive. Exactly as her own wedding had been many years ago.

The young marrieds would be happy (but even more important would remain close by and be easily malleable).

She didn't realize she had an even more controlling mirror-image in Albert's mother! But whereas Sofie wanted desperately to see Petra married to Albert, this leonine matris familias ferociously feigned to keep her son from doing anything of the sort.

Gertie Shapiro, widowed ten years earlier, squat, red-haired, cigarette voiced and, like Sofie, used to being obeyed instantly (and keening pathetically if she didn't get her way), consistently made all major and minor decisions for her two children.

She tried several techniques and pragmatically discovered the most efficient one (to which they never became inured and which invariably wounded them instantly into obedience) was to lament softly, pitifully, at length, and to compare the despicable behavior of her ungrateful offspring with the saintliness of the wonderful, sweet, loving man who had fathered them. How could they, by not concurring in and complying with the few requests made by the spouse whom he had so completely adored, whose advice he trusted totally, sully his blessed memory this way? How angry he would have been, how concerned about their loving mother's feelings, her unselfish tears, her ultimate welfare and the terrible treatment she endured at the (sob) hands of their own children! How he would have berated them and come to his never-wrong beloved's defense!

"Milton, oh Milton. Look down and help me!" she would cry in final anguish, as Ilse and Albert inevitably ran to embrace her and conceded they were (as always) contrite and wrong.

Of course while the poor man was alive she had used the same tactics but dissimilar semantics to control him, until exhausted with the constant exhortations of— "Milton! Just look at them! Your own children whom I bore for you with such grave danger to my own life! Twenty grueling hours to give you your son, even longer for beautiful, darling Ilse. Milton! Will you listen to me? For you, to make you happy, I went through all that suffering. So how can you treat me like this? The mother of those wonderful children. Your loving wife, uncomplaining mother, passionate lover? Milton! Who never asks for anything unreasonable! Just a house, Milton, in the suburbs. And my portrait painted! The car is already two years old! Milton? MILTON!" –the truly good man's heart gave out and he achieved the one thing he craved most...distance away from his diabolical oppressor, even if it meant death!

And now she used the entirely fictitious memory of their perfect marriage as the primary weapon against her gullible offspring.

Same tactics, different targets, equally effective.

While still in college Ilse once attempted the clichéd escape, affaired passionately, and even temporarily contemplated eloping to Tampa with a college saxophone student summering as a Good Humor ice cream truck driver, who wooed his blatantly unhappy customer by steadfastly ringing the bell, thus summoning her from inside the house to his side, offering her free popsicles and one night inevitably inviting her to ting-a-ling his bell in return.

The ensuing *Te Deum* temporarily silenced the unending requiem mass in her skull and, although it did not result in the composition of a masterwork of symphonic proportions by the itinerant musician, it did lead to several explosive crescendoes achieved during a week-long August concert series and a heartfelt "gosh darn," which escaped lyrically from deep within his innards as he untangled himself from her carillon-playing ministrations.

Several weeks later Ilse appeared greenfaced at breakfast. Correction: appeared greenfaced but did NOT appear at breakfast and Gertie sternly suggested two alternative solutions. One entailed the use of a coat hanger, the other hinted at Albert's military-acquired knowledge of firearms.

They took the hint and also took off.

En route to Florida she raced to a service station bathroom, experienced a few slight cramps and emerged spontaneously fruitless and free, joyfully dumped the ice cream salesman and returned to her sobbing mother's nurturing arms, repentant and swearing to obey forever. Which she did.

It now became Albert's primary duty to look after his sister, who had proven she could not do it herself. Soon after she introduced him to Petra, she met another potential suitor, an accountant dazzled with her dark-eyed stupidity, and Gertie stepped in, ordered her daughter to play the mandated virgin—no more hanky-panky until the hankies and pankies came off on the wedding night.

At first the older woman was not threatened by Petra, recognizing with satisfaction the safety factor inherent in double dating. The accountant proposed in late September, Ilse showed off a ring in October and the wedding was set for January. Until then Albert would act as benevolent chaperone, guarantee that the two lovers were not left alone together, insure his sister's "chastity."

Gertie was pleased. The bride standing under the *chupah* would be pure until proven otherwise.

As for Albert? He had years left before embracing connubiality. In the meantime she needed him.

A lot.

But to her dismay she realized he actually liked Petra. Surmised as much when her usually pliable, submissive son suddenly wanted to go out Friday and Saturday evenings alone with her.

Not on a double date with the engaged couple!

Leaving her, his poor, widowed mother at home to mourn, unheard, the death of her adored (and undoubtedly disapproving) husband. But she was determined to fight this fight, and win it gloriously!

Gertie found excuses to keep him close. (Albert, Albert dear, would you listen to me? The water pipes must be painted this weekend. If you don't do it immediately they will rust and break. Just look at how corroded they are!) Or as he was preparing to leave the house, "First, darling, do make sure you throw your dirty laundry in the machine and fold the stuff in the dryer. My back is hurting so badly! And could you stop by the pharmacy to pick up some toothpaste? I forgot to get it this morning," thereby insuring he would arrive late at Petra's house.

Petra felt the woman's resentment, noticed the hypocritical smiles, didn't understand what she had done to offend her and naively assumed Gertie would eventually like her.

How ridiculous!

Once she realized Petra was a serious threat, who might, in fact, steal the-desperately-needed- by-his-mother-only-psychological support of adorable Albert, the older woman, mouth smiling, but eyes glittering with jealousy, attacked.

"Tell me the truth, dear. How old were you when you first started bleaching your hair? How often do you do it?"

"Are you on a diet? Or ill? You look a little puny and your skin looks so pale. Don't you feel well?"

"You know, blondes should never wear red. It makes them look like streetwalkers."

Petra, continually being convinced by Sofie that she was in love with Albert, found herself reviled by the one person she really didn't want to anger, confused and unable to deflect even one venomous remark, but hoping and imagining Albert would come to her defense.

He didn't. Rather, the situation amused him. Imagine two women fighting over him, a luxury the weak little man had never imagined! Even if one of them was his own mother.

Gertie knew perfectly well the power she presently had over the girl, decided to take advantage of it and cajoled her into giving a wedding shower for Ilse.

Petra paid for everything, because after the invitations went out, Gertie informed her that was the responsibility of the hostess. Refreshments and decorations weren't very expensive. Then she withdrew some funds from her savings account and went to the best store in Washington to purchase Ilse's present. She chose a crystal vase, handmade and perfect. When she pinged against it with a finger, it belled loudly and clearly and, when held up, sunlight broke into rainbows from its heart. It cost far more than she had ever spent on a wedding gift.

The few friends who accepted the invitation gave Ilse place mats, kitchen tools, black panties, pot holders, a straw bread basket. All the gifts were gushed over and admired.

But when Ilse opened the box containing the vase, Gertie loudly exclaimed, "Oh, how about that! Cut glass! We have boxes of it packed away in the basement! Lots of it. Just junk we never use."

Petra, devastated, finally recognized the enemy.

When she told her mother what had happened, expecting some kind of angry reaction, Sofie noted calmly of course, Gertie was an uncouth, vulgar, jealous peasant but insisted Albert was not like her and Petra should not judge him by her actions.

She wondered how her mother could condone such behavior and not be concerned that her daughter might be subjected to much more mother-in-law-initiated abuse should she marry him.

And had, of course, no idea of her mother's own unresolved feelings toward Albert.

Chapter 16

Several Saturday evenings later, as they were in their customary (after-the-usual-Western-movie-followed-by-ice-cream) parking spot to indulge in some (what he considered) heavy necking, he informed her that she would not find him as passionate as usual.

"I had sex with a woman last night."

"Oh."

"She doesn't mean anything to me. I just wanted to find out what it was like."

"Oh," again.

"What do you think?"

"About?"

"I'm not a virgin anymore."

"Congratulations."

"Don't you care?"

"No."

If he thought he was less passionate that night, she never noticed a bit of difference.

Chapter 17

Steve's appearance and disappearance affected her strangely. She really missed him: the fun, the discussions, his honesty and integrity.

Unconsciously, the weeks of confusion when she didn't understand how she could love two men simultaneously had strengthened her.

Steve was dependable, mature, unafraid of his own introspection, and she respected him far more. But love? Him or Albert?

Love was complex, much too abstract for her to absorb as a preliminary judgment for settling her entire (long or short) future. She knew (as Steve sensed also) she was years away from making such an important decision.

And she was overly aware she owed a huge debt to the woman who had given her life and guaranteed its continuance with enormous sacrifices.

Who, had never washed a dish or cooked a meal before coming to the United States.

Who though volatile and violent, demanded and was entitled to a great deal of consideration.

During those months, a terrified Sofie phoned Albert at his office to warn him he had serious competition. His exclusive presence had been preempted.

"Move your ass, Albert. Or you'll lose her!"

He, unexpectedly forced to commit himself, finally declared he loved Petra, only her, was no longer interested in any other woman, begged her to stop seeing other men.

Even despite her frequent lamentations, defied his mother to spend extra time with her.

Gertie was furious; Sofie, triumphant.

Petra thought she probably loved him, wanted to please her parents, but the situation had changed. For the first time she felt empowered and dared to test her strength.

She was no longer willing to endure Albert's childish games, games in which she had always been the victim, too frightened of losing him to protest.

His favorite, played to perfection each and every time during the pre-Steve months, was to arrive at least thirty minutes late for their dates, assuming (correctly) she would be nervous, anxious, afraid he might stand her up and be touchingly (although he was not touched) grateful when he finally arrived.

The excuses he offered were transparent.

Stronger now, aware, she determined to seize the reins and never relinquish them again!

"I'll pick you up at seven Saturday and we'll have dinner at Napoleon's," he informed her on the telephone.

"Are you planning to be on time?" she asked innocently.

"Why?"

"Because if you aren't you'll find me in blue jeans."

"Sure," he said laughing, throwing the threat back at her, "sure I will."

On Saturday by seven o'clock she was dressed, made-up ready to leave.

And obviously as usual, no Albert.

Seven fifteen.

Still no Albert.

Five more minutes.

She went to her room, took off the silk dress, nylons and high heels, changed into a pair of paint-spattered dungarees, a flannel plaid shirt, thick socks and scuffed loafers, washed the makeup from her face and lathered it with cold cream, put the Goldberg Variations on the record player and lay down on her bed.

At 7:45 the bell rang.

"He's here," hurried her mother, still thrilled about Steve's demise. "Quickly, get dressed."

But Petra replied, "I am dressed."

"What? Don't let him see you in those old clothes! You look like a tramp. Now hurry up and change. I'll keep him busy meanwhile."

"Oh," she replied nonchalantly, "just send him to my room."

"Petra. You cannot do this!"

For once she defied her mother also. "Indeed, I can!" she answered.

A few minutes later he knocked on the bedroom door, stared at her and said, "I'd better change our reservations to a little later."

And, deeply embarrassed, unused to public humiliation (although he had until then cavalierly and frequently humiliated her in front of her parents) humbly asked Sam if he could please use the phone.

In absolutely no rush, she took another extraordinarily leisurely bubble bath, applied new make-up with extreme care, dressed very slowly so as not to wrinkle the delicate silk dress or risk getting a run in the nylon stockings, and emerged an hour later, relaxed, elegant and prepared to enjoy a gourmet French dinner.

Meanwhile Albert, "entertained" with anecdotal inanities by Sofie (and observed by the wordless but obviously amused Sam, who silently blessed his rebellious daughter and fought to keep from exulting aloud!) had been forced to update the reservation times four.

    He was never late again.

Chapter 18

On their next date he made a fatal mistake, one she could not forget or forgive.

With a great deal of hubris he informed her (confident of her emotions and his-fast-disappearing-power) that prior to each date and (in fact) for the entire previous year, he had always determined just "how far" he would advance sexually with her (a pragmatist never losing control of the situation), shocking her immensely (since she was still attempting to please her family and continue a relationship which might eventually lead to the much-hoped for engagement) but instantly and forever squelching any naive perceptions she might have had about his romantic spontaneity.

It killed hers, too, of course.

She resented being made to feel she was his Trilby, to be machinated at his pleasure. With that sneering statement of his omnipotence he lost her.

Permanently.

But didn't know it. Yet.

He noticed she seemed more independent, less pliable, criticized him without being at all tactful. Wondered why she shied away from his touch, kissed him dispassionately if at all or pushed him away when he tried to approach her.

He didn't realize his slightest touch was beginning to disgust her.

He had a habit of stroking her hand, back and forth, back and forth, until the area became irritated from the constant friction. She was even more irritated herself, understanding for the first time what the cliché "made your skin crawl" actually meant and finally demanding that he stop. A few minutes later he tried again. Fuming, she took her hand and placed it in her lap. Then he began the same technique on her arm, although she tried to edge away.

The amorous feelings she had once felt for him changed rapidly and she understood they had been planted, nurtured, and pruned by her mother and were actually not seeded in her own emotional earth.

Albert, secure in his accustomed spot in the family, no longer concerned with the competition, welcomed the new leave-me-alone challenge, pompously aware she would welcome him back eventually. Meanwhile, finding he was required to be more attentive, behave as the suffering suitor, surprised the hare had somehow escaped the snare (and the marital cooking pot!), the formerly disinterested hunter suddenly discovered he needed the hunt to survive!

He phoned more often just to hear her voice, listened for the first time to what she was saying, learned to ignore his mother's constant whining weekend demands, increasingly eager to be with Petra during his limited spare time.

The inevitable had happened.

He fell desperately, deliriously, in love with her. Suddenly noticed her skin was translucent and absolutely flawless, her body with its minuscule waistline and gentle breasts the epitome of womanliness, the haughty line of her head when she refused him even the slightest endearments, her eyes huge and green with anger, challenged and enchanted him. Where had this fascinating woman been hiding, he asked himself? Was this the same frightened little girl whom he had met a year earlier, pliant, insecure, unable to challenge him in the least?

At work he found himself thinking about her...and inadvertently felt his penis swell and thrust.

Simultaneously her general attitude towards Albert became that of an older, annoyed sister, frequently irritated, critical of his actions. Impatient and insensitive.

Familiar behavior. Exactly like his mother!

He began proposing even before Steve was gone. To his surprise she refused him, and consistently refused, each of the numerous times he continued to suggest it.

"Take your time and think it over," he replied.

She liked him as a friend, she insisted. Nothing more!

He didn't believe her for an instant, wouldn't accept she no longer responded to the old, manipulated techniques, which had worked so well. And now he acknowledged to himself he was in love with her. Desperately, insanely, patiently, submissively, but never hopelessly. He swore even if it took decades he would win back her trust and her love.

He had absolutely no doubts of his success.

When Petra announced she was moving to New York...a tactic he instantly recognized with some amusement as a naive device to force him to admit his love and to mollify her, easily resolved with yet another (not to be implemented until next year) proposal, (immediately refused to his astonishment), he was horrified, slowly perceiving she actually was leaving, and called Sofie in a panic (who secretly gave him her address and promised to keep him informed of any news). She also advised him to telephone every weekend that Petra was in Washington.

He did. And called Sofie days in advance to guarantee the contact would never be broken.

He also made several changes in his own life.

True, he still lived with Gertie (so alone and lonely since her beloved Ilse was married and how would the suffering and martyred mother survive without her?), but he had also applied to and been accepted by the Georgetown University School of Law.

In a little over a year he would be an extraordinary catch, a man with unique qualifications and the undeniable financial benefits which would accrue with them. Since he was presently overwhelmed with maintaining his regular job and attending law school at night, he was really too tired and harassed for strenuous socializing, and (after he got over the shock) noted with irony her move out of town and romantic reticence fit perfectly into his present plans. And he knew for a certainty after he passed the bar exam, she would marry him.

The old feelings were not dead, only dormant, waiting to be resuscitated.

More frequently now as he attended lectures, read up on cases in the law library, his mind was suddenly diverted as he remembered the kisses and caresses they had shared, and dared not move from his seat until the inevitable erection which followed had subsided.

Sofie, cognizant of every refused proposal, was far less patient and temperate towards Petra, turning the Washington weekends into nightmares, screaming, screeching, cursing at her stubborn daughter, accenting some harangues dramatically by smashing a few unwanted dinner plates (a good excuse to buy new ones) and constantly denouncing her as a filthy slut, then followed the volcanic accusations with hours or even days of icebergian silences.

Sam, gentle, overwhelmed, helpless, shook his head and mourned for his child's suffering but did nothing to alleviate it.

Now as the train pulled into Union Station, Petra wondered how traumatic the next few days would be and wished they were already behind her.

Chapter 19

The minute Petra arrived, Sofie noticed the difference, the glow, the distracted stare, the softness surrounding each gesture. She had behaved exactly so when first she met Albert—and now, hallelujah!—the magic was back! In fact she had not even realized her daughter's tranced state was gone until its present, very obvious return.

"He's phoned twice already," she gushed.

But instead of rushing to return his calls Petra murmured, "I just want to rest a little while, Mom." An hour later he rang, not willing to wait until she got around to it, heard and ignored the hesitation in her voice but invited her to a movie the next evening anyway.

She declined.

Not discouraged, he invited her for brunch at the Wardman Park Hotel on Sunday and she declined again.

"I understand," he said "When are you leaving? I'd like to take you to the station."

She accepted that offer, since little or no physical contact would be necessary and the encounter would last at most thirty minutes.

Her mother watched in silent frustration as Petra pawed through her clothes closet, choosing outfits she needed for New York but refusing to discuss Albert (or why she was rejecting his invitations).

Early Sunday afternoon Sofie came to her room cradling a white strapless voile gown embossed with black velvet ivy leaves and tiny embroidered flowers.

Without telling Petra, she had purchased the material and worked on it for weeks, but now could no longer continue without a fitting.

Petra gasped when she saw it, so simple and beautiful, embraced and thanked her mother, aware again despite the often unreasonable, untethered temper tantrums, in her way Sofie loved her child. But it was a love secondary to a more urgent, primary need for total control. A love which changed from moment to moment leaving everyone (including Sofie herself) completely confused.

She made some adjustments to the dress, admired how lovely it looked and promised to have it ready the next time Petra came home.

A little later, Albert arrived (promptly) to take her to Union Station.

"Will you be here within the month?" he asked, not particularly concerned about her reply (knowing Sofie would tell him anyway).

"Probably. This wasn't such a bad weekend but sometimes my mother doesn't make it easy."

"I know. But my law school fraternity is giving a formal at the Shoreham. Do you think you could be here for it?"

"My feelings haven't changed. I don't love you, Albert."

"But you aren't engaged? To anyone in New York? Or seeing someone special?"

The one apparently disastrous date with Dev didn't qualify for either definition.

Albert took her left hand, glanced at it and said, "I don't see a ring. As far as I'm concerned you're still available. So, will you come to the dance with me?"

She sighed. "All right. But no pressure, please."

He promised, picked up her suitcase and helped her board the train, then waving and smiling watched it disappear.

The verdant hills of Maryland were still visible in the darkening afternoon, replaced by Philadelphia's distinctive suburbs and then through the moving windows gleamed the lights of upper Manhattan. At last total darkness as the train entered the tunnel beneath Penn Station.

It was just after five o'clock.

She grabbed her weekend case and headed towards the subway, extremely relieved to have left Washington but equally ambivalent about returning to New York and what might face her at the I. House.

Chapter 20

Still confused by Dev's silence but assuming he must have a good reason, Petra hurried to ask the landlady if there had been a phone message for her but there was none and the phone remained darkly mute throughout the next few weeks. Dev did not appear at the I. House, or if he did she did not see him.

Baboo noticed her immediately one Friday evening as she glanced around the cafeteria, and motioned towards her to join him and Alan at their table, which had been pushed against two others. She was relieved to see him, brought her tray, unloaded it and tried to choke down a hamburger.

Unable to resist she asked timidly, "Is Dev all right? I haven't seen him for a long time."

"Oh, that one," remarked the always cheerful Alan who had overheard. "He has a million women. Do not waste time thinking of him. No one can hold him for very long."

It occurred vaguely to her that he seemed happier than was necessary when he delivered this declaration and did not seem aware she said nothing in return, remained stone silent. Not that his comments surprised or hurt her. In fact they were valid. She had seen the women staring, heard the remarks about him, and modest as Dev appeared to be, he was neither deaf nor blind.

A small thrill of pain raced through her as several of his best friends arrived. Without him.

Now a semi-serious discussion began between two heavily made-up Japanese students, an American mathematics professor at Columbia University and several other people. Baboo, Alan and Petra listened but had not joined in.

"I am convinced society is at its most decadent level in history," Jerry Roth the professor postulated. "The sheer magnitude of atrocities committed against the Jews by the Germans would have shocked the barbarian hordes! Modern man is unchallenged when it comes to sheer calculated brutality. Intellectually committed mass murder, cloaked under the guise of religious or philosophical ideology (actually an excuse for politically institutionalized robbery) is, I know, not at all unique. It has been so throughout history. The difference is the efficiency, the scientific objectivity to enact it to such a degree without the least qualms of conscience! Six million innocent victims, among whom one million children!"

"You cannot blame all the German people," interpolated Baboo, "Germany has produced geniuses like Goethe, Schiller, Schopenhauer, Beethoven, Brahms."

"And Heine, Einstein, and Mendelssohn," Petra added quickly. Jerry, startled, looked at her and nodded. They instantly understood each other.

"Yes," he repeated softly, "and Heine, Einstein and Mendelssohn."

"I saw a documentary once about some camps," one of the Japanese women offered, "but I do not believe they actually existed. I have met many people from Germany and they were very kind. I think this must be propaganda." She smiled vapidly, awaiting confirmation of her theory. "In fact, of all the countries I have visited in Europe, ah, that one is by far my favorite. I felt quite at home there."

Petra looked at the well-intentioned face, the eyes carefully outlined, lipstick applied perfectly, smooth black hair fashionably groomed, heard the girlish giggle of embarrassment when no one spoke, felt the muscles around her stomach tighten, recognized the familiar symptoms of her own withdrawal.

Just then Dev appeared.

Alone.

If he had plans for the evening he wasn't dressed for them. His white sport shirt looked clean enough and the grey slacks were only slightly rumpled but he was apparently not interested in serving as the living embodiment of the Brooks Brothers model.

She felt herself shudder as he passed their table, waved self-consciously at everyone and walked on. Baboo peered suddenly at Petra and made an instantaneous decision "Ha, Dev. Come here and join us too!" It was not a request but a quiet, not to be denied, command.

The boy hesitated for a moment, not daring to humiliate his countryman, and took a seat. At that moment one of the Japanese women emitted a soft moan and gazed at him in open adoration.

Petra knew Alan was right. There was no sense in attempting to harness an animal as magnetic and beautiful as this one. She took a deep breath and with regret, aware he had already made the decision for both of them, let thoughts of him go.

"I read some articles about one of the camps in a magazine. The doctors were supposedly doing medical research," a young man with a pronounced Southern accent drawled "If those experiments actually were carried out, they had nothing to do with bettering the human condition and those men weren't scientists. They were sadistic murderers. Do you know what they did with pregnant women?" and he proceeded to enlighten everyone, oblivious to the effect he was having or indeed completely unaware of whom he was addressing, he was blatantly babbling on, the garrulous center of horrified attention.

Jerry stared at Petra, stunned like her into silence.

She wanted to tell the well-meaning hick with his ridiculous twangy voice to shut up but was paralyzed, and the detailed, clinical monologue continued. Endlessly, it appeared.

She became panicky, felt tears blurring her sight, turned away to hide them and found herself staring terrified into the gentle face of the boy. He frowned, then said loudly, putting an end to the lecture, "They are showing a film in the auditorium. Let us all go there."

Blinded, Petra stumbled towards the staircase, sobs gathering in her throat.

Dev followed, said nothing, thinking of Karachi...and memories always close to his consciousness, the evacuation as a small child from the magnificent home which had been his birthplace, for a reason he was far too young to understand. Remembering with black humor and horror, the males all around him hurriedly pulling down their trousers to corroborate to friend or enemy the physical manifestations of their religious beliefs. Depending on who was holding the rifle, information which would determine life or death. A little child, with the face of an angel (although he did not know it then) being exposed to such insanity!

He rushed over to the staircase balustrade where Petra stood facing the wall, took her chin in his hand and put her head on his shoulder, completely shielding her from anyone else's view. She rested there for an instant, recovered her poise, then he took her elbow and led her into the darkened auditorium.

The movie was terrible but Dev kept his arm around the shaken girl and, once, leaned down enough to kiss her forehead very quickly.

He did it without thinking.

So that when the magnificent crystal chandelier above them was again alight, she was not prepared for the open expression on his face, tenderness, wonder, vulnerability.

She was overwhelmed and dared not look at him again. Seeing her reaction and immediately surmising what she had divined, he cloaked his eyes, turned away in embarrassment and soon regained the confident facade he usually wore, the cocky pride in his bearing, head held proudly high as befitted a man of his station.

The mischievous grin.

Back in control.

He would not reveal himself that way again, he swore. Let her think what she would, she had witnessed an aberration and it would not be repeated.

"Well, then, and where did you disappear to?" laughed Alan as they walked back into the Waffle Wing. "Want to go for a ride in my new car? It seems like a perfect evening to break it in."

Petra smiled shyly at Dev, hoping he would agree and joyfully followed him to the shiny green monster parked at the curb. He pushed the front seat forward to let her get in the back first but Alan interceded immediately. "No, she sits in front with me. You can keep Parvati company," and he grasped Petra's arm while pushing the saried doctor towards Dev.

"I am sorry, Alan. Not this time. She is with me."

The finality in Dev's voice apparently convinced the driver because he acceded, grumbling, "Oh, all right then," perfunctorily settled Parvati next to himself, turned the key in the ignition and shouted, "Now, Connecticut, here we come. You should see this baby move!"

"Faster than the water buffalo in New Delhi or don't you have those in such a sophisticated city?" teased Parvati smiling her sweet but ghastly smile.

Petra heard Alan make a retort, which had them both laughing, but was completely unable to converse herself, could only gaze at the gentle man seated next to her, watching her, closing his eyes from time to time as if in half-sleep.

She shut her own, drunk from what she read in his face.

Once, softly, he could not restrain himself and kissed her hair, nothing more and, so fleetingly, perhaps it had not happened at all.

In the front seat conversation, had stopped.

Petra leaned forward, glanced at the speedometer and gasped, "Alan, please, stop it! Slow down!"

In the mirror she suddenly saw the furious face of the driver. When he noticed her watching him he grinned back wildly and accelerated even more.

"Please, Alan!" she repeated helplessly as they flew past the Hartford exit, continuing to speed down the highway. "Where are we going?" she pleaded, trying to keep her voice from cracking.

"To Boston, baby. To Boston!" he replied with the insane grimace still painted on his face.

"Slow down, you silly thing. We'll all end up in a hospital!"

"So what!" he retorted instantly.

Now she understood and froze as his foot pressed the gas pedal down even harder.

"Dev, for God's sake! Make him stop!"

"Why? This is certainly a unique way to spend an evening, don't you think?" he replied, laughing and unaware of the danger, then looked at the speedometer and his face contorted with horror. "Jesus!" he whispered to Petra, "He's crazy!"

Parvati in front, had said nothing for some time, too paralyzed with fear to even react.

But Petra would not consent to her own death."Alan! Cut this nonsense out right now!" she commanded, controlling the terror in her voice. Then hoping to divert attention from his evident desire to kill them all, mentioned how much she admired his cooking skills, praised the diversity of the recipes and asked if he would be willing to share a few of his secrets with her, emphasized how grateful she was to have been invited to partake of the Indian meal, and hoped they would be friends for many years, watched intently as his hands slowly relaxed on the steering wheel, the foot eased minutely from the floor, the insane expression disappeared from his face.

Taking a deep breath, he took the next exit and turned the car around and headed back to New York.

Dev, deathly pale, helped Petra from the car and mused later, " Did we instigate this bizarre reaction? Enough to make him consider committing suicide and murder simply because you sat with me? Isn't Maria enough for him?"

"I think he considers me a child to be protected. Tonight he sees us together, doesn't know what to do and over-reacts."

"Perhaps, but he was also bothered by something else, not just considering your safety. I think he was jealous. Just plain green jealous." He escorted Petra home, hugged her quickly and left.

Ten minutes later he was lying naked on his own bed, awaiting the ministrations of the woman who lived down the hall. When she arrived, opened the unlocked door and entered, he nodded at her to begin.

Chapter 21

The next day he submitted and invited Petra to have dinner with him.

They went to a French restaurant downtown, wandered over Fifth Avenue, gazing in the store windows, merged with the tourists crowded above the ice skating rink in Rockefeller Center, agreed the statue of Prometheus was probably the ugliest, gaudiest most garish sculpture in the whole world (but the area wouldn't be the same without it), peeked in at St. Patrick's Cathedral, and finally took a taxi back uptown.

He paid and, as it drove away, took her hand, crossed Riverside Drive in front of the I. House, led her silently into the shadowed columns of Grant's Tomb, then savoring each unfulfilled second, kissed her slowly without passion, his mouth at first just brushing her lips, wandering gently over her mouth.

Then he opened his eyes for an instant, saw hers were shut and surrendered.

Finally! The kiss she had anticipated weeks ago, he had not allowed himself to even consider and both of them mutually, desperately wanted.

When they separated for an instant she whispered, "Why did you wait so long?" smelling the cleanness of his face at last so close to hers.

"Because I know myself. I knew if I held you in my arms like this, just once, I would never have the strength to let you go again. We Indians are under so many restrictions here." He gazed at her with pride and wonder in his eyes, no longer trying to hide his emotions.

"What kind of restrictions, Dev?" she asked.

But he refused to say more, just lifted her chin, kissed her again, said good night, and watched as the elevator rose and took her away.

The Jamaican elevator operator, insolent as usual, noted, "So, you like de Indian men, eh? Me, I am Indian too. West Indian. You like me?" She didn't respond and he leered, then laughed aloud, as she nervously put the key in the lock and quickly closed the door behind her.

The man had always made her uneasy, now she was beginning to fear him.

Dev walked home angry, happy, confused, cognizant, tasting her mouth on his own, feeling her warmth in his embrace as though he were still holding her.

As usual the woman heard him walking past her room and soon followed him. This time before opening the door he reconsidered, shrugged, did it anyway, and half-hoped she would be able to annihilate the exultation he still felt.

She cured his frustration but the exultation did not disappear. He was afraid to fall asleep in case it might.

Chapter 22

Sunday again, bell-tolling, late breakfasts, bright daylight, "*The Times Book Review.*"

Still reliving the first, longed-for kiss, Petra completely forgot the one rigid, never-to-be-broken commandment, and like one of Bluebeard's foolish wives, impulsively opened the forbidden door into the bathroom to take a shower, thus revealing in all his brown baldness and hairless chestedness, a poodle-naked little man splashing and reveling happily in the bathtub. He sputtered something unintelligible while she, stifling hysterical laughter, streaked down the dark hallway and into her room.

"Oops," she thought, "retribution will surely come!"

Ellen was weekending somewhere with Salmi and Petra was concentrating on the review of a recently opened art gallery when the expected summons came from Missus who invited her to meet with them in the living room. Mister, no longer *au naturel*, was attempting to be offhanded while trying to solve the crossword puzzle.

"Who is a famous Richard of opera?" he asked innocently.

Petra answered immediately, "Strauss, Wagner, Tauber, Tucker, Crooks. Which one are you looking for?" He didn't reply but his pencil moved energetically over the paper, although he never looked up or thanked her for helping him.

Missus, ever the prototype of the good German *hausfrau*, was industrially darning his socks and smiled endearingly at the girl.

"You must have forgotten it was Sunday today," she began benignly. "My husband mentioned you surprised him while he was bathing."

"I'm very sorry. I guess I was dreaming. I'll try not to make the same mistake in the future."

"Of course, my dear. I am quite certain you did not do it on purpose. Would you like some tea?" she asked unexpectedly, pointing to the Bavarian cups and saucers on the coffee table.

The girl accepted, poured for herself, while Missus put her sewing aside and went over to the old-fashioned arched wooden radio, waited for it to warm up and began twisting dials.

She stopped at WQXR.

Petra instantly recognized the Bruch setting for "Kol Nidre" with its beautiful, dolorous cello solo.

"Why, that reminds me of my childhood," remarked Mister suddenly.

Petra looked at him in confusion.

"Oh," said Missus still clothed in her cat-sweet-smile. "You didn't know? My husband is also Jewish."

Although in fact, just this morning she had actually seen him naked, Petra had not observed him long enough to either search for or notice the physical confirmation of his Judaism and accepted his wife's comment as Biblical truth.

But she was surprised.

"Personally, I find the Hebrew services very interesting, although my husband never attends anymore. But now and then we catch one on the radio on a Friday evening."

Petra didn't know if a comment was expected but simply couldn't think of one. Their religion or lack of it was not her business and didn't interest her. While her own beliefs were far too personal to discuss with them.

However, Missus wasn't going to drop the topic and blurted out, "I like religious music, but I hate it when those cantors begin to cry. It's so embarrassing, don't you agree?" Her needle jagged deeply into the argyle heel of the sock she was mending, the lamplight covered her head with benevolence: She was a painting/tableau of European domestic tranquility.

Petra retorted, "After two thousand years of persecution I think the Jews have a right to lament!"

The needle caught the light, flashed and lit up her kindly face. "But my dear, I have nothing against Jews," she replied mildly. Then looked fondly at Mister and said, "I have lived with one for many years, haven't I?"

"Yes, we came to the United States in 1936 shortly after we married, but returned to Berlin on vacation in 1937. My relatives still lived there, you see. It was quite awful. Mister had to wear a yellow star."

She paused, looked off in the distance, remembering the nightmare.

"And my poor parents and brother having to be exposed to such a thing. All the neighbors knew my husband was a Jew and gossiped about it. You see, the family was very prominent and their lives were made most uncomfortable until we left. A very horrible experience for Mama and Papa. I felt so badly for them!"

Petra, furious, expected Mister to protest or at least make some comment but he did not even glance up from his paper.

"What about your husband's feelings? Did you have any compassion for him?"

This time the astonishment was etched clearly on her puffy features. "Why should I feel sorry for him? What did he care? Besides, as you can see, I remained with him, didn't I? Even though he is Jewish!"

Petra excused herself before she lost her temper. She would start searching for a new place to live as soon as the budget permitted!

The fury continued to boil when she stormed into the I. House.

Downstairs, a group of South American students was having an impromptu jam session, drumming out sensuous rhythms, intermingling them with spontaneous dances. Who knew what Sephardic ancestor had given her the love for Latin music but it translated automatically into her feet, as if she, just as the amateur musicians, had been born to it. Here, as performed by native dancers, the steps were authentic, untainted by commercialism, strongly suggestive, primitive.

Bossa novas freed from jukebox interpretations, cha cha chas that barely resembled the conservative version danced in the Catskill resorts, merengues brought directly from the villages of the Dominican Republic. All were pure folklore. Wild movements, performed without inhibition.

Petra's wide black skirt with its pink and white petticoats underneath swirled around her knees, her hair fell loose from the pins which had held it, and she felt sweat pouring over her face.

Well, sweat was better than tears!

The stifled anger was being danced out. Damn her! Damn the bloody stinking German! Damn her and her whole rotten country! And as the music throbbed ever more passionately, her entire body responded, swaying, shimmying, whatever could move moved, an exhibition so erotic and spontaneous that within moments a circle formed around her and her partner.

Into this turbulent, tropical maelstrom, in a Manhattan-based international student facility, wandered the thousands of years of dignity and self-control personified and manifested by the young Indian who last night had for the first time kissed her. He watched from the outside of the circle, disgust on his face, waited until the music finally broke and grabbed her arm.

"What kind of performance was that supposed to be?" he growled.

She took out a handkerchief and wiped her face, still feeling the thumping of her heart and the thudding of the blood in her veins. "I was just dancing for heaven's sake. What is the matter? You cannot do these steps correctly and munch on a cucumber sandwich at the same time!" she fumed, anger at his provinciality twinned with the fury she still felt towards the landlady.

His voice was steel and fire. "You should have heard the men around me commenting on your gyrations. They are under the impression you are taunting them. You must be an easy lay."

She raised an eyebrow and hissed back, "Their problem. Not mine."

Just then the music began again, thankfully a languorous bolero. "Come, I will show them you are not alone." The anger simmered but was now under control.

He took her in his arms and immediately she felt at peace, glorying in the pressure of his hands as he led her slowly through the steps. His face was calm, and soon he leaned down and buried his cheek deep in her hair, a silken golden adornment he now felt he owned and never again wanted to relinquish.

The rhythm of the music changed suddenly—wild, abandoned, passionate—and the formal, civilized steps he had been taught in his English boarding school did not fit it. He sensed her desire to break free, how consciously or not, her body rebelled against his awkward attempts, recognized his inadequacies and her not-well-veiled dissatisfaction immediately.

"Well. You would much prefer to dance with someone else!" he stated, stalked across the room and instantly had a gushingly delighted brunette in his arms.

She watched them for a second, wounded far more deeply than she had anticipated, but soon she was asked to dance with someone else, and yet another circle of admirers formed around her, while she was haughtily aware he had stopped to watch also and ignored the obvious revulsion on his face.

At the end of the evening he did escort her home. Knowing she feared the elevator operator's unwanted interest, he went to the front door with her, waited until the elevator had again descended and then primly noted, "I am sorry but I must research several important cases next week and will not be able to get away. Perhaps we can have coffee at the I. House one day after I have finished."

She accepted the lie and had her own excuse ready. "That works out perfectly. I have to be in Washington this weekend anyway to attend a ball. So I won't even be here. Thank you for taking me home and good luck with your research."

He ran down the stairs without touching her or any additional comments from either of them.

Chapter 23

On Saturday evening Dev knew he could safely go to the I. House, but found himself searching for her anyway. He strolled into the music room, absorbed her absence, listened for a few distracted minutes to the Beethoven "Choral Fantasy," wandered into the library and fidgeted with a magazine without comprehending the intent of either the photographs or limited copy beneath them, and finally decided to get a cup of tea, feeling suddenly unusually chilly.

It was too early for his friends to have arrived and the cafeteria was almost deserted. He did see Pieter van Hoorn echoing his own disconsolation, gazing intently at nothing and slowly churning a soup spoon around and around in a thick mug while his clam chowder lukewarmed.

They had never met but Dev introduced himself as a friend of Petra's and asked if he could sit down, then asked innocently, "Where is your Dutch lady?"

"Nettie, you mean? She is in Boston visiting her American family. She'll be gone a week more." He smiled forlornly, "I am miserable without her, as if my entire world has been cut in half."

'Pardon me, but she does not seem an easy person from what I have heard."

"People don't know her. They judge her for her candor, the inability to be tactful, a pseudo-skill she considers foolish and hypocritical, doesn't realize not using it costs her friends. But she tells me all the time she has no use for friends anyway. The only person she trusts is Jopie and sometimes she won't trust her, either."

How garrulous he is, thought Dev, as if the young Dutchman needed to share even with strangers his deepest feelings, his reservations, a packed full casket of dry ice overflowing and venting without restrictions. He couldn't imagine talking about his problems so openly with someone he hardly knew.

"How long have you known her?" he asked, pretending interest in Nettie while starved for information about Petra, and finding a small amount of comfort from the proximity of another Netherlander, someone who had lived where she had lived.

"Oh, about a year. She fascinates me but cannot understand someone can actually love her."

"You've told her?"

"Often. She shrugs and laughs at me, then insists a Gentile could never truly love a Jew. She has good reasons, of course."

"The war?"

"And its aftermath. No family left. Learning her parents are not her parents, her brothers and sisters are not related to her, she is Catholic but not Catholic, actually belongs to a culture she knows nothing about. Her name is not even her name! A child goes to sleep one night perceiving herself one way, awakens the next and discovers absolutely everything she assumed about her life and surroundings is a lie. She learns what really occurred, tries to incorporate some aspects of the recent past into the present, but cannot. So she rejects it all, the phony name, the converted religion, the family that cared for her but never loved her, and begins entirely over. She is adopted by an American Jewish couple who try their best to help her readjust but are spectators of rather than participants in what she is experiencing."

Pieter stopped talking, stared with sudden disgust at the milky-tan skin which had formed on the top of his cooled soup, picked at it with his spoon, removed it and put it on a napkin, but did not eat.

"And then, just when she has found a little stability by studying, proving what a brilliant medical researcher she is, along comes her past. That's me! Dutch...when she wants to escape from any memories of Holland."

"And a Gentile," added Dev.

"The Dutch part we've resolved, I think. After all, she was born and raised there, still knows the language, even secretly (she told me) looks forward to Sinterklaas Day. But she is afraid to feel, to let herself believe in others, to be ridiculously, wonderfully young and free. I want to see her smile, let her be totally silly, show her the wondrous joys of life rather than letting her dwell only on its sadness. And, I cannot imagine my future without her. It's unthinkable."

Pieter took a deep breath. "I am seriously considering converting to Judaism. All religions are the same to me anyway. They are equally good and bad and although each one asserts it is the only truth, that in itself is a lie."

"You want to marry her, then?"

"I think she'd disappear in seconds if I proposed. But yes, someday I would like to marry her."

Dev tried to control his voice, to make the question he had to ask appear clinically objective. "Did Petra have family who perished in the war?"

"I don't know. The resistance movement had its share of victims. Most of the Dutch people suffered heavily but survived. However, the Jewish population was virtually eradicated."

"She is Jewish."

"Oh. Then yes. Probably," was all the startled Dutchman could say.

Dev wondered if Petra might have a similar background, remembering her reaction to the ad hoc history lecture by the Southern expert on concentration camps. Seconds later he relived the disgustingly provocative manner in which she had danced, flaunting her body, inviting improper commentary. Taunting him!

The war? One more legitimate reason to avoid her. Personally he needed no additional reminders to resurface about war at this time in his life. He had enough of his own. Partition! Memories he had spent years trying to forget! The women screaming, the babies crying, the men running, running, just as his own family had run. Away from his birthplace in Karachi to Bombay, a city most of his Hindu family had never visited but where practicing their religion meant safety and life.

He raised an eyebrow. Their individual experiences had occurred thousands of miles apart. Still, the practice of both their respective beliefs had resulted in somewhat similar mass persecution and its subsequent emotional consequences. And now they had met in New York at the International House where such conflicts might be addressed between enemies. How strange! How ironic!

"How poetic!" he scoffed cynically.

But dissecting and analyzing the profundity of such concepts were absolutely not his priorities right now, he postulated silently, staring at the distraught young man across the table.

He had to earn his law degree and earn it with highest honors! He had assured his parents and would do his absolute best. Everything else was irrelevant.

However, he had promised to phone Petra after she returned from Washington, intended fully to keep his word as a gentleman and, with that gesture, complete any leftovers undone. So why was he still sitting with Pieter?

He looked around and noticed Salmi, Ellen and the Appendage Kerim huddling in a booth, laughing, talking. She saw him and waved, Salmi merely scowled his normal scowl in curt acknowledgment, holding a cigarette almost girlishly in one hand. Kerim, staring stupidly resembled a bewildered child.

Just then his best friend Ram, accompanied by a radiantly beaming Baboo, and followed by Alan and Maria, walked in together. They spotted Dev, were introduced to Pieter and sat down.

"She's coming! In a few weeks!" laughed Baboo. "Gita! She'll be here by the beginning of the year! Come, everyone. I want to celebrate! I am so happy! Let us find an appropriate milieu at once!"

Ever gracious and sensitive, Baboo said, "Please, Pieter, you must join us too for the remainder of the evening. As my guest. No, I absolutely insist! We will find a place on Broadway with atmosphere and music. Most of us will not drink liquor but find fresh squeezed orange juice more than sufficient."

Pieter, delighted to be torn out of his Nettie-induced-depression countered, "Thank you so much, Baboo, I am a proud Dutchman, able to pay for my own drinks, and will gladly toast you and your bride with some good Heineken's beer. Orange juice invariably gives me indigestion!"

Chapter 24

Washington was clear and mild, perfect weather for wearing a strapless evening gown and a light wrap without worrying about either feeling or catching cold. Sofie had finished the dress just in time and proudly approved as Petra put it on. The fit was perfect, her daughter looked lovely in the simple black and white creation.

As usual nowadays, Albert arrived precisely on time, tuxedoed and so handsome Sofie had to remember not to flirt with him: Her young daughter should remain the focus of his attention and not she.

They were a beautiful couple, Sofie thought, as she and Sam watched them depart.

From the beginning Petra was the only woman Albert even considered inviting to the dance, although she had immediately reminded him they were merely friends. Good idea, he agreed; he could concentrate on the future in the future; right now the law was more important. And, he thought, how fortuitous: She wouldn't be pestering him with questions as to when they would be married and the inane but unavoidable trauma involved with pre-and post-engagements. Instead, they could wait until after he passed the bar next year. Her reticence he considered exceptionally well timed.

As for her assertion she no longer loved him? What nonsense! Of course she did! He could still manipulate her emotions whenever he chose, of that he was completely certain. Petra's feelings for him would endure unconsciously, nestled secure and dozing deep within her heart to be awakened at his pleasure.

He brought her a purple orchid, the one flower she absolutely detested not only because it was common and unimaginative, but because it resembled a large colored insect enveloped and trapped in silver ribbons. She half expected the thing to crawl out from under its festive array and attack her bare shoulders or vulnerable, strapless-gowned breasts and torso.

"Thank you," she said primly, pinning it on her waist where she hoped it would not be visible, then crumple quickly and die.

He was pleased she liked his choice, which Ilse, who knew all about corsages, had suggested.

To Petra the evening was endless. She pretended to be interested in what Albert was saying, but failed. Her skin revolted every time he put his arms around her to dance, tried to pull her closer and lay his cheek against her face.

"No," she admonished him, "you promised!"

"Oh well, I hoped you'd change your mind just a little," he answered.

It wasn't his fault the evening was an enormous trial, and the Washington that she had always hated had become even more hateful. Her thoughts were on New York.

And, despite the ridiculous quarrel, on Dev.

Where is he this evening? she wondered. With whom is he spending it?

***

Late Sunday afternoon, Dev kept his promise but only to announce he would not see her at the I. House for the weekly South American impromptu. "Too much work. Still haven't finished my research and I have to present it very soon. Perhaps another day. I hope you enjoyed your party in Washington?"

She was prepared for the rejection but unreasonably wounded just the same. And countered immediately with a fabricated exaggeration of her own. "The dance was absolutely marvelous! Someday if you ever go to Washington you must make a point of visiting the Shoreham Hotel. Particularly at night when the fountains and gardens are lit up, just like a fairyland. And so romantic!" she gushed into the black unromantic telephone receiver against her ear, paused for an instant and continued. "But I am glad you cannot make it this evening. I can't, either. Somehow I managed to wrench my ankle and my date had to carry me everywhere. Fortunately he is tall and strong" –Albert tall and strong?—"It's still a bit sore so dancing tonight is not a good idea."

Her words, carefully predetermined, were meant to cause Dev the most discomfort, and she spitefully imagined his annoyance when he assumed another man would not only have had his arms around her, but been in far more intimate contact with her body, his arms under her knees, her torso clinging intimately to his...

And she was right.

He fumed silently, helplessly, imagined the beautifully gowned women, the tall, strong men in tuxedos suave and handsome, while everyone stared as she emerged from the illuminated gardens, borne like a queen in the arms of someone else! Enough! He was done with her!

Politely, carefully, they said "goodbye" to each other and hung up.

Both independently agreed breaking up now was better than waiting until the situation became more complicated. They had left an infant-relationship with equal dignity and on fairly civilized terms.

Towards evening she slipped into her ballet shoes, three lacy petticoats, pulled on a long black skirt, a jersey top, prepared for an evening of exhilarating

South Americanism without the absurd inferences and unwanted interferences of her Indian acquaintance (with his medieval notions about modern women).

Joyfully she ran into the room where maracas and drums were already throbbing and was dancing immediately.

As she walked towards the dance floor with her partner, she noticed Dev standing in the doorway. He nodded at her, inquired about the injured foot and mumbled something about taking a break from the library. He watched with silent fury as Petra and a stranger tangoed, and the man dipped her towards the ground while her hair cascaded down, then spun her quickly causing her underwear to swirl indecently around her knees, held her tightly with one of her legs wound around him, and thought they might as well be having public intercourse.

Although he was disgusted he couldn't stop looking at them either.

The music changed and again she was asked to dance, knew exactly what he was thinking and in the middle of a mambo spin, left her partner in the lurch (my ankle hurts!) and stalked over to Dev, determined to at least be honest.

"Look, don't take this personally but I really want to dance. Most of the steps bore or offend you, while I feel happier with a more advanced partner. So, let's give each other freedom to do as we choose. No hard feelings. As long as we both lied about not coming tonight and got caught at it, we might as well enjoy ourselves but remain friends."

Her entire speech was blurted out without any thought, any pause for breath and without her daring to look at his face. When she was done she raised her eyes. And then he suddenly began to laugh, deeply, at length, a rollicking reaction to an enormous joke.

When he finally stopped, he put his hands on her shoulders and exclaimed, "Thank heaven! I have been so embarrassed and upset. I didn't know how to tell you and all week I have been trying to think of a way. We must not be so serious, Petra. You delightful girl! My adolescent excuses were not even necessary. You said exactly what I feel!"

She laughed with him, relieved neither of them was angry anymore.

Dev bowed formally, took her hand and said with extravagant formality, "Very good, my lady. We will pursue our individual pleasures. However, if I have not met the maiden of my dreams and you are not invited to perch on the back of a white horse belonging to a more enticing escort, I shall be most pleased to accompany you to your castle at evening's close. But, please don't make it too late. I really do have a case to present later this week, although I am fully prepared for it."

"Well," she replied, "my ankle is feeling much better but it probably shouldn't be exposed to too much additional exercise so quickly."

They stayed another half-hour before he took her home and in the hallway kissed her.

Once.

Just enough to leave them both starving-hungry for much more.

Chapter 25

Christmas was approaching.

The giddy insanity, New York's annual gift to its heterogenous population from just before Thanksgiving Day to the first weeks of the new year, was at its highest peak. Rockefeller Center, magnificent with its enormous decorated tree, presided over an army of wire-winged angels hovering between myriads of white and scarlet poinsettia plants.

The traditional gilded organ appeared again above Saks Fifth Avenue's facade, carols and hymns mingled with the staccato blasts of car horns and the grinding noise of busses as they braked and stopped. Further down the enchanted world which was Fifth Avenue, the usually stern and sterile lobbies of several banks had been converted into storefront North Poles with Santa Clauses and red-velvet, flare-skirted helpers (hired from the local modeling agencies) distributing candy-filled stockings to the children. One had installed a miniature ice skating rink complete with live performers who spun and twirled while gifting awed snow-suited gapers with giant red plastic canes containing small favors and silver-wrapped chocolates.

Huge electric Christmas trees, with branches extendending from roof-to-sidewalk, hung in front of storefronts and were visible the entire length of the crowded streets.

New Yorkers became one joyous mass, regardless of religion or background. Who cared whether a Messiah actually was born on December 25th? If true, then just an additional reason for people to smile at each other, shrug off for once without anger the unexpected pain of a stepped-on toe, exchange jokes with total strangers as they waited together in endless lines at the over-crowded stores.

Just once a year, when the weather was at its worst between blizzards and freezing rain, the populace found a reason to celebrate. Soon enough the dark nights would enshroud them again with nothing else to break the maddeningly severe winters.

Christmas, Diwali, Chanukah,— or whatever else its name might be, was the excusable psychological outlet which New Yorkers demanded to survive until springtime and the light returned, the ephemeral resurgence of gaiety and color, grasped at hungrily by the wind-wearied people.

Of course purists ranted about the commercialization of Christmas, oblivious to the exuberant millions of New Yorkers united in feasting, giving, suddenly impervious to each other's religious and racial backgrounds. A remarkable lesson in harmony and tolerance...and a phenomenon itself worthy of far more acknowledgment than myopic haggling over Biblical fact or fiction.

The universities were closing for a few days and Dev had been invited months ago to spend them with a classmate in Chicago. Petra had to work late on Christmas Eve (Burken wasn't due at a party until after eight), but they managed to have a nine o'clock dinner together, wandered through the icy streets to admire the beautifully decorated store windows, agreed to sneak into midnight mass at St. Patrick's, assuming no one would challenge them as to whether they were actually Catholic, and gloried with the rest of the congregation in the splendor of the magnificently adorned church and its joyous celebrators transcending every divisive religious boundary.

"Are you going home to Washington?" he asked much later as they stood in front of her door.

"Yes. I promised."

"Will you be back for New Year's Eve, then?"

"Will you?"

"Only if you consent to come with me to the ball at the I. House."

She reached up and kissed him. "Try and stop me from going with you!" She smiled, effectively hiding the anxiety she had been feeling while waiting for the invitation.

Early Christmas morning he flew to Chicago while she prepared a suitcase, filled it with presents and taxied to Penn Station.

Each one would have preferred to remain in New York.

Chapter 26

Dev was in trouble before he left the airport. His friend was waiting at the gate and had brought his sister along. She took one look and appropriated him, threading her arm through his and leaning her breasts against it, leading him quickly to the car. He started to take a seat next to Bob who was driving but she laughed and pulled him into the back. For an instant he chuckled, remembering a similar situation not too long ago in New York.

Petra, he thought, and his heart lurched.

"Bob's told us all so much about you. I hope you don't mind being pushed around like this but you're really another member of the family." He nodded silently.

She was pretty, vivacious, probably a year or so younger than her brother and a senior at Northwestern.

"Majoring in Asian History," she told him, "so I'm blaming you if I flunk my exams. I intend to quiz you on every aspect of life in India to insure I won't. In fact, I hope to make the professor feel under-prepared."

"And we begin this evening after dinner, with a special showing of 'The River,' directed by Renoir. No, not that one! His son," she added quickly, seeing the confusion on his face.

From the outset, Barbara was present wherever he and Bob went, a gracious, solicitous hostess who helped Dev explore Chicago. However, close to the agreed last day of the visit he was feeling uncomfortably obligated to her and also guilty towards the rest of the family. He was grateful for their hospitality but longed for New York. Among these loving, open people he felt inexplicably lonesome and recognized ever more clearly, miserably that his discomfort was not at all their fault.

He was packing for the early morning departure when Bob interrupted him.

"Do you really have to leave tomorrow? There's a New Year's Eve gala at the country club."

Dev mentioned he had already made plans.

"Break them. My sister will be crushed if you don't come. You've made more than a casual impression on her." He chuckled, "But I knew you would."

"I cannot. First, it would be ungentlemanly. Second, I cannot possibly reach the lady concerned."

By early noon the next day, Dev was back in his own room. He knew Petra would be at the ad agency and dialed the number.

"Miss Fresco" came the soft voice he had missed.

"Hello, doll. I am back."

"I am so glad," she replied, embracing the impersonal receiver with both hands, her eyes closed.

***

The time apart had been a trial for her as well. For the sake of family peace she pretended to enjoy herself, admired the presents, attended the *de rigeur* Washington cocktail parties, relearned the necessary calloused formula, "How nice to meet you. Where do you come from? Oh, yes, that is a truly lovely place" (if she'd actually been there) or "Everyone tells me it's absolutely gorgeous. I am looking forward to seeing it myself some day" (if it was unvisited territory), usually accompanied with an unsubtle glance around the room in search of more interesting or lucrative company and the standard, "We must get together for dinner or lunch soon. Here is my card," always followed with "Oh, thank you for yours, too! So glad to have met you."

At party's end everyone temporarily possessed a dozen or more new business cards made of various shades and grades of heavy paper and with more or less expensive embossing. No matter, by morning they would all land in the rubbish.

She did try to be civil but no amount of champagne and formulared conversation extinguished the stunning emptiness which enveloped her. Escorts and college friends remarked she seemed subtly changed. She found them dull and provincial.

Searching for an excuse to leave earlier, she insisted there was much work waiting in New York—at least five press releases to write and distribute before year's end—and finally alone and at peace, boarded the train aware Dev would certainly not have returned from Chicago.

And now she heard his voice.

"Did you have a good time with your family?" he asked, hoping she had been as bereft as he.

"It's over. So it doesn't matter anymore. What about you? Did Bob take good care of you?"

"Perhaps just a bit too well." Not elaborating, he continued, "I'll call for you at seven o'clock. We will have dinner and then go to the ball. Is that too early?"

"No. Burken's gone home for the day. He's been partying all week with the other account executives. None of them has been sober enough to concentrate on anything except their next drink. Between the liquor stench and the cigars, the agency smells like a brothel. I still have some things to finish but I could probably leave right now and they wouldn't even miss me," she answered, not caring what plans he had in mind for the evening, just thankful they would be together again.

So was he.

***

She carefully put on the delicate pink gown brought back from Washington, still financially unable to partake of New York's ample supply of fashion.

Without knocking, Ellen, tall, haughty, walked into her room wearing a simple crepe sheath of pale blue, which accentuated her eyes and the whiteness of her hair. She held a bottle of sparkling burgundy and two glasses, gave one to Petra, poured and raised her own and said in a voice huskied by cigarettes, "To the past year. It's been different! And the two of us and our ardent admirers for the coming one."

Before the next sip, the doorbell rang, and their escorts arrived looking somewhat uncomfortable at their simultaneous arrival.

For once, Missus allowed males into the virginal sanctum, assuming (correctly) that although voluminous, seductive nightdresses might well lead to sexual behavior (perhaps wanted by the roomers but absolutely not by their landlady!), the two women presently harnessed into whalebone-enhanced strapless bras and girdles were as unassailable as if they were keyed into medieval chastity belts (which, in fact with minor modifications, they were!).

The men were offered drinks, relaxed and found themselves *ad hoc* double-dating for dinner.

Salmi suggested a Greek restaurant on Broadway, and after they ordered, Ellen whispered to Petra, "Over there, near the window with the woman in the yellow dress. Another of the emperor's grandsons. A rich one. He probably has hundreds of brothers and sisters. Or maybe not."

When the quartet arrived at the I. House, they separated instantly. Baboo was standing in the lobby. "She's here, children. Gita has come. Please, at once, you must make her acquaintance."

He disappeared towards a corner of the huge hall and returned, leading a young, intelligent-looking Indian girl, wearing round silver-rimmed glasses behind which brown eyes glowed softly. She was dressed in a white and gold sari. As they approached, she smiled shyly, displaying perfect, lovely teeth, and although timid, was silently noting everything around her.

"Here, Gita. This is Petra my daughter and Dev my son. Children, kiss your mother!" His enthusiastic inclusion of Dev as part of the "family" could only mean the brilliant Indian engineer had surmised and drawn unchallengeable scientific conclusions.

Dev immediately bent down to obey his new "father," but Gita, evidently uninformed regarding her sudden elevation to motherhood, winced in confusion and seemed not at all pleased with her handsome son's failed attempt to show affection.

After Baboo, teasing but merciful, explained he had "adopted" Petra and Dev, she instantly held out her hands to both of them.

"We will be married next week in the Consulate," she said. "Please make every effort to attend the ceremony. After all, it is to the benefit of all concerned when children attend their parents' nuptial rites," she admonished them solemnly, while the gentle eyes behind the severe glasses gleamed with silent mirth.

Both she and her fiancé had chosen wisely. They were perfectly matched. The newly met and reunited family entered the ballroom together.

It was decorated with balloons, while gold cloth-covered tables and chairs circled the perimeter of the dance floor. Pink, silver, blue and white streamers cascaded from the crystal chandeliers, and banners with naked babies painted on them exhorted, "Happy New Year! Happy 1955!" On the stage a full orchestra was playing dance music. No one seemed aware of a dangerous Cold War underway, intent on forgetting reality for tonight. One evening of Lethean oblivion. Who knew what the approaching year would hold?

Several couples were already dancing, and Dev led Petra wordlessly among them. Twice, a hand tapped on his shoulders. Twice, she apologized and refused, not wanting to move from his arms for an instant. After a while the wandering males caught on, left them alone and searched for more appreciative partners.

Towards midnight, Alan unexpectedly appeared and when he interrupted them she was confused.

"It's all right," Dev whispered. "We have no choice. It's only for a few minutes and I will stand aside and wait for you." He released her and she watched him, feeling miserable and awkward in Alan's unfamiliar embrace, his arms firm and confident. Over her unwanted partner's shoulder, she searched constantly for Dev.

Alan purposely led her so that she faced the opposite direction and then said, "Don't worry about Dev. He will find himself another girl in no time. Just forget about him."

When she turned her head, she saw Dev had not moved, his eyes riveted on them, never wavering as he helplessly watched Alan lead her to a remote corner.

What is he planning? Dev wondered.

Suddenly the music stopped in mid-beat and the master of ceremonies announced, "Ladies and gentlemen. It is now twelve o'clock sharp. May I be the first to wish you all a Happy New Year!"

More balloons descended from the ceiling, confetti snowed in every direction and, as the lights began to dim, Petra saw Alan bending down to kiss her. Furious, she pushed him away and ran to Dev, waiting quietly, alone. With radiance illuminating his magnificent face, he held his arms open and she fell into them.

Gently he leaned down and kissed her, whispering, "Happy New Year, doll. My sweet, sweet, doll," and as softly she kissed him back, unable to speak at all.

Instantly Alan was there again, pulling them apart, insisting on being kissed by her as well. She moved her lips perfunctorily over his cheek, and he walked away scowling, eventually finding Parvati who was watching the festivities from the doorway.

But Dev and Petra were tired of the noise and feasting. He glanced at her with the half-veiled signal she had learned to interpret so well, they gathered their belongings and went next door, and he waited while she changed into a sweater, skirt and loafers.

They strolled along Riverside Park, quiet and deserted in the new year's first morning, and he led her again to the monument and held her safely for a few moments in his arms. Now and then a celebratory horn sounded in the distance, or they noticed another couple still in formal dress emerging from the I. House.

Chapter 27

Though there were few arrangements, they encountered each other frequently in the next weeks. An unsaid natural evolution of the relationship flowed automatically: dinners and impromptu meetings at the I. House, walks through Riverside Park at dusk, listening to Brahms Concertos in the music room while Dev tried to delve through a case and Petra unexpectedly found herself composing poetry.

Dev began to lose his appetite, looked pallid, thin-faced, the soft, dark eyes appeared haunted. Sometimes he seemed on the verge of saying something, then checked himself, shook his head and frowned, made suddenly mute by what?

When she asked if he was ill he denied it, but became gaunter and even more nervous as January melted into the middle of February. By early March he answered primarily in monosyllables and watched her, his eyes both gentle and anxious.

And continued to lose weight.

She didn't know how to help him and became increasingly concerned.

"I'm fine," he assured her, "really. First class. Just have a lot of cases to work through and I am tired. It's all right, doll. Now, eat your dinner before it gets cold. By the way, you are getting thin yourself," he noted hoping to deflect attention away from himself.

On a Saturday evening, between the inevitable twice monthly weekend visits to Washington, when neither had been able to finish even half of the food in front of them, he asked cautiously if she would go with him...

"...to my room. To learn some dance steps," he teased.

"Yes," she responded simply. The embraces in the darkness of the park, behind the columns of the monument, or in the overly lit hallway of her building, were no longer enough.

For either of them.

So finally he took her with him, to the immaculately clean room he had readied repeatedly for many weeks and gallantly turned on the radio. But neither of them heard any music. Or cared about it. Dance lessons? He put his arms around her. The lessons never happened. He held her tenderly, as if she would break but couldn't move his mouth away from hers. She closed her eyes, feeling for the first time in her life, secure, safe, sheltered forever, knowing this man would never betray her.

He placed her on the bed but did not attempt to disrobe her, just lay down himself and gazed at her. Suddenly, the anxious, frightened expression appeared again and he turned his face away.

"What is it, Dev? What is bothering you?" she implored, horrified by his obvious suffering.

He drew her close, buried his face in her neck so she would not see his face and whispered, "I cannot fight any longer," then pushed her away and said, "Look at me."

Bewildered, she obeyed.

The anguish written on that glorious face was excruciating...and then he mumbled words torn from the depth of his innards, as if each was its own innate instrument of torture, dragged unwillingly into his throat from some deep recess within his body, changing his voice into an unfamiliar echo of itself.

"You have won! I–have–no–strength–left–anymore."

With tears in his eyes, he collapsed against her shoulder. She trembled, not knowing what was coming next.

Then taking a deep breath he lifted her chin, looked into her face and gasped, "I"—another deep breath—"love"—gulp of air—"you."

He stopped, looked anxiously into her face and waited for a reaction.

"Is that so terrible?" she said, having heard the three over-used words many times before and spoken them herself on occasion as well.

"Yes," he replied instantly, "it is. You do not realize what it means. I have never said those words to any woman before."

She couldn't help smiling, feeling suddenly older and quite maternal towards him. "I think that's pretty obvious."

"Oh God! What am I going to do? I have fought and fought but I cannot control my feelings any longer. Nothing has worked! I love you, Petra. I love you."

"I fought too but I feel the same way."

"What way? Do not torture me, anymore. Say it, darling, say it."

She stared at the radiant, magnificent face above her, eyes still haunted, insistent, but imbued with gentleness, and she whispered, "I love you, Dev. I love you. You are the only person I need or want."

He knew then he could possess her. In fact, owned her already. To do with as he wanted.

He also realized she was as bound by contemporary morality as any girl in India and would be as vilified if betrayed. He knew because just this had obsessed him for months, almost since the day he first saw her, sweaty, her naive white face flushed pink from the tennis lesson, the innocence as blatantly obvious as the opposite was true of the streetwalkers on Broadway.

Or the boring sexuality of the woman down the hall whose nocturnal knocking on his door was now being ignored.

No wonder, he realized later, Baboo had wanted to protect her (and made his friends comply also).

She was a girl-child in the middle of a male adult world and completely oblivious of the danger. How ironic, he thought, her very naivete was the most powerful weapon he had ever encountered, which had subdued and tamed him as completely as if she had physically attacked and conquered him... the infamous, irresistible ladykiller!

But now, wary and fully conscious of the consequences, he assumed responsibility and became omniscient ruler in the relationship.

Kissing shut eyes, which melted when he looked into them (kissing them shut because he could not bear to see the innocent expression there without feeling overwhelmed), he whispered the promise which had been haunting him for months. "I will never take you no matter how much we both desire it. Not until in the future our marriage has taken place. I swear it."

His arms around her relaxed, and the relief of finally talking openly allowed an instant of surcease, then he frowned, cradled her against his chest and murmured, "But, oh God, what if we have no future?"

She kissed him to quiet the words.

"My love, my sweet, sweet love," he crooned, "do not leave me, please, please, do not ever leave me."

Chapter 28

"No. You stay here until I return," Prince Solomon the eldest of twelve (legitimate) grandsons of the emperor ordered, striding confidently towards the front door of his Park Avenue penthouse.

His lovely American mistress of the moment, auburn hair cascading over bare, pink shoulders, and familiarly naked in his presence, looked up from the sofa where they had spent the better part of the morning and pouted angrily. "But I want to go with you. I haven't been to a tea dance in ages."

He frowned, his dark, skeletal face suddenly animated and turned back to her.

"Wait here, dear. Restore your strength. You will need it for your work tonight when I come back. It may be Sunday for most people," he laughed, "but for you there is no day of rest. Nor a night."

Unlike her, he was fully clothed. He took her in his arms once more, kissed her and observed the reaction clinically as her eyes closed; expertly caressed her breasts with one hand while owning her most intimate parts with the other, then when she was flowing and whimpering abruptly released her, leaving her limp and panting, watching impotently, as he went to the bathroom, washed his hands, and walked nonchalantly into the vestibule to his private elevator.

Throughout the interlude he had not even experienced an erection, nor indeed felt his breath accelerate in the slightest.

His chauffeur helped him into the Jaguar, and the prince glanced at the diamond encrusted watch on his wrist. They would arrive at the I. House twenty minutes after the commencement of the music, insuring he would charmingly make the necessary "grand entrance," thereby infuriating most of the already present (and presently impoverished) male students while simultaneously stunning the young women with his elevated rank and the obvious wealth which accompanied it.

While the huge ballroom was already filled when Petra arrived, she did not find Dev. Disappointed, bereft, she waited near the perimeter of the dance floor.

Last night, after finally acknowledging his feelings and falling asleep, she studied his face and read the conflict etched there as he battled both their pasts and futures and watched as the pain gradually disappeared.

"At the tea dance," he whispered at her door but warned he had library research to do and might be late.

They realized they were inextricably involved in a relationship which had brought more joy than either had dreamed was possible. But were aware their happiness would not be cheaply bought...and still mutually agreed to accept the price.

She looked around the ballroom, noisy with laughing people and throbbing music, but without him there, it seemed huge and empty, its coldness tearing through her.

From the entrance Prince Solomon gazed around, a starving falcon searching for prey. And as always, he quickly found it.

She was lovely. Fragile and very fair, her hair the color of sunlight, her eyes he appraised from afar would be lakes of blue, hues he constantly found exotic and irresistible, having come himself from a world of exclusive browns and blacks. He was still not able to distinguish between beauty salon blonde or the real thing but he was fully aware he would have the answer to that question very soon.

He walked over and said imperiously, "Please dance with me."

Startled, she assented. Like everyone else, she knew his identity, had observed him at other social functions at the House, usually accompanied by several men and occasionally his red-headed "Queen of Sheba," but had not been introduced to him.

The band played a bolero.

He was so slender as to be almost cadaverous, the perfect features of his face, lean nose, thin lips, cheekbones protruding from his dark skin, all pointed to his aristocratic heritage: His bearing and assumption of authority over everyone screamed at the legitimacy of his birthright.

"What is your name?" he demanded politely and expectantly.

She told him, surprising him because he noticed her eyes were not blue, but rather dark green. Even more exotic, he rejoiced, and pulled her closer as the music continued its sexual cadences.

He was a superb dancer, effortless, moving fluidly as if he had no hipbones, the writhing, sinuous steps accompanied by provocative drumbeats flowed through his body as naturally as if he were constructed entirely of liquid.

Expecting no resistance, he pushed his torso into hers and was astounded as she recoiled, causing him to have an immediate erection. Delighted by his own arousal after the boring chilliness of his recent experience with his mistress, he pulled her even closer to his lower body.

Again she resisted.

He was not used to being rebuffed and found it excitingly unique. He felt himself growing ever larger, stiffer, and thought of the pleasure he would soon bestow and receive.

The music continued, he tightened the arm around her waist allowing no space between them, bent his knees and held her so closely she could not help but feel the thrust of his penis through her own clothes.

She flushed, the white skin tinged hot with highlights, took her free arm, gave him a hard push, which made him stumble backwards, and walked off the dance floor. Leaving him and his throbbing erection in the lurch.

Astonished and embarrassed, he watched her disappear among the students, recovered some of his dignity, asked someone less exotic to dance, but felt his royal prerogative had been breached and swore revenge.

Petra, blind with tears, renewed her search for Dev and found him standing in a corner with an attractive American girl, but with his eyes already long on her as she approached.

He had seen it all, missed nothing.

His oblivious companion was doing her best to attract his attention. She had a fashionable short haircut, was wearing a wine colored velvet dress with a low waist, the round neckline set off by a long single strand of pearls which hung well below her non-existent breasts. She looked as if she had just stepped out of the flapper age, and carried it off superbly.

"Wow, that Prince Solomon is really something. He knows every woman he wants is going to fall into his arms. Hmm, I wonder if he's searching for a new Queen of Sheba!" She swayed her body in unsubtle provocation towards Dev, laughing too loudly at her own comment.

Of course he noticed but did not react, said little, politely returned her smile, although his was completely superficial. Not that she realized it.

From across the room he glanced at Petra, nodded slightly and so beckoned her to his side. She wanted to throw her arms around him.

Meanwhile the "flapper" continued to make what she considered witticisms about everyone and everything, prattling on, apparently unconscious of the fact she was carrying on a monologue.

"Hello. Was it a bit difficult for you just now?" Dev asked mildly, angry but illuminated with joy when Petra joined them.

"What was difficult?" inquired Miss Flapper.

"Oh, I think Petra did not enjoy the last dance very much."

"Weren't you dancing with the Prince?" she asked, her eyes enormous with curiosity and mascara, and not at all cognizant there was no response, continued, "I wish he'd give me a few moments in his arms. I'd make sure he'd never forget them!" and again the chuckle at her own wit.

"By the way," she asked Dev, "do you dance?"

"Not very well," he answered truthfully.

"Oh."

They remained on the sidelines for at least fifteen minutes, watching the dancers, listening to the music, while Dev stood between the two women (holding Petra's hand). And the self-absorbed flapper, still unaware, played with the long beaded chain around her neck, swaying in time to the music, using her body to gain attention.

It didn't help. Dev had no idea she was teasing him and didn't react.

When the band played a slow number, Petra frantic with the need to hold him, to be held by him, still traumatized by Solomon's actions, turned to Dev and asked timidly, "Will you dance with me?"

Knowing her completely, he murmured, "Of course I will," took her hand, lay his face against her cheek and held her for a moment, unmoving in his arms.

Comforting, shielding, feeling her tremble. "It's all right, my love. It's all right."

She opened her eyes and saw "His Highness," angry, scowling, dancing past while a furious flapper snarled, "Well, there's nothing like the direct approach, is there?"

Petra nestled into Devs shoulder, safe, not ever wanting to be anywhere else or with anyone else.

He smelled her hair, inhaled its essence and felt the world was in his arms.

Neither of them heard any music but their own. And neither noticed the arrogant prince waltzing over to their part of the ballroom or realized he was watching them in wonder.

He gazed boldly at the boy with his beautiful luminous face, the tender smile that dimpled his cheeks, the happiness shining from his eyes as he held the girl in his arms. He marked the instant, so slight, so fast when the boy reached down and brushed his mouth quickly against her forehead, a caress as sweet and slight as a parent kissing his child, a caress Solomon noticed but assumed no one else had.

He saw the girl, her head resting against the young man's shoulder, a look of infinite peace on her face, and when she happened to open her eyes, the spoiled possible heir to an empire understood she did not see him. Indeed, she probably saw no one.

They were so beautiful together, these two, that his anger completely disappeared, replaced by regret no woman had ever looked at him with such trust. Nor had he ever looked at a woman with such love.

Passion?

Desire?

The constant needs of the flesh so easily assuaged? His money and his position had easily addressed such inconveniences...but the gentleness, the incredible tenderness which the young couple shared, the prince had no experience with anything even close and he felt a surprising admiration mixed with simultaneous envy and sorrow.

When the selection ended, he left his partner standing alone on the dance floor—just as he been left by Petra, nodded at the boy who looked at him suspiciously, defensively, bowed, took her hand and kissed it, saying, "Forgive me, please. I did not know."

She frowned, tried to smile, felt safe, loved, with Dev's arm securely around her waist.

She accepted his apology and silently pitied the spoiled prince with his insatiable, indiscriminate needs, who had never known the difference between love and desire.

And probably would not ever know it.

In the farthest corner of the room, Alan was talking with Parvati, an apparently intimate conversation because despite her horrible teeth, she was smiling radiantly. Moments later they were gone.

Dev, still holding Petra in his arms asked, "Have you danced enough?"

"Too much," she whispered. "I have seen too many people today and danced one dance too many."

Without saying goodbye to anyone, they left the I. House together.

Chapter 29

An entirely new relationship developed. Emotions deepened as trust grew, confidences were shared, and both found total encouragement from each other's friendship. In the great, glorious, heartless city they found constant warmth and support.

There remained one obstacle and it appeared insurmountable.

The Sunday evening dances.

No matter how many times she explained that dancing with someone and feeling romantic towards him were two completely different things, he just couldn't accept it. His culture and hers clashed head-on, mercilessly, endlessly, directly between the maracas and the sitars. There seemed to be no solution since neither understood where the problem was or why it even existed.

But of course it did.

On a Sunday evening return trip to New York (after a three-days-long weekend nightmare in Washington, which began when she told Sofie about Dev, naively assuming her mother would be happy for her child, and instead was threatened with immediate disownment), Petra made a decision.

She would not give Dev up, could not imagine anymore living without him and the happiness he brought her. The sacrifice was simply unthinkable.

Back in Manhattan, she changed into her usual dance outfit, the lace petticoats, ballet slippers, black jersey top, and was soon shedding some of the weekend's emotional destruction by moving to the uninhibited South American music.

By the time he arrived, looked around, found her and frowned, she was laughing and at least partially regaining her psychological equilibrium.

The trauma slowly fading.

Dev had no hint of what she had endured a few hours earlier, only witnessed the abandoned dancing and, despite his best intentions, became steadily angrier, not understanding it was saving her sanity. He settled on a sofa in the corner of the room and was instantly joined on either side by several women intent on befriending him. They perched beside him, giggled, turned the conversation to him and inched ever nearer, while he was increasingly limited in space and trying his best to ignore the self-made seduction trap.

Petra surmised what was happening and watched with unhappy amusement from the dance floor as he politely addressed each speaker in turn, thus charming her into further weakness, letting her think what she might of his actual intentions. Or hoping in vain.

But suddenly his tolerance level reached its flood-point, and he stared directly at her, unhidden fury on his face as if he wanted to strangle both her and her innocent dance partner who, ignorant of the dynamics around him, felt Petra go limp in his arms, while she missed several simple steps.

"Would you rather sit down for a while?" he asked, leading her to a seat far from the sofa's action, of which he knew nothing. She agreed and sat down, feeling completely miserable again.Emotions which Dev, even from afar, perceived at once. He hoped desperately the next dance would be one he could do.

As soon as the music changed to a rare foxtrot, he pushed aside the feminine bars that held him, escaped from his enviable prison, left his adoring wardens without explanation and quickly claimed her.

"I am so sorry. I know it means nothing to you but seeing another man's hands on you is torture. I must learn to adjust but so far have not succeeded. Will you forgive me, my love?"

She curled into his shoulder and closed her eyes. Dance partners were only instruments allowing her to forget the weekend horrors. But he, this kind, good man, he was the only real peace she had ever known. She lifted her face and quickly brushed her lips against his cheek.

From the sidelines Baboo watched, could do nothing to avoid what he had foreseen. But because he genuinely loved them both, he could help solve this insignificant problem.

Later? Ah, who knew about later!

"I have a friend," he told Dev the next day, "also an engineer. Married to an American lady. He is an exquisite dancer but his wife hates it. He would like to find a dance partner but without causing friction in his marriage, particularly since she is pregnant. Do you know of a solution to his dilemma?" he asked innocently.

"Thank you, father Baboo," the boy murmured. "Thank you."

The following Sunday, Petra was introduced to the Indian engineer who would from then on with unanimous consent, completely monopolize her, as they tangoed, merengued, cha-cha-cha-ed and waltzed. Dev, meanwhile, stayed on the sidelines with the young wife, or escorted her to the Waffle Wing for a cup of tea while her husband and Petra danced. The first night, he attempted to pay his countryman but was refused. "No, not necessary. We are actually helping each other."

Petra pretended to be ignorant of the arrangement, but had quickly guessed. If the man had been a clumsy oaf she would have protested, but in fact, he was easily the best dancer she had ever met. He in turn found her limber, easy to lead and musical. It wasn't the chore he had feared, he informed his wife, as they lay in bed and he kissed the slight, growing bulge on her belly.

They performed so beautifully that during a particularly strenuous Viennese waltz, he whirled Petra around at dangerous speeds, which meant they had to look into each other's faces with complete concentration, seeing nothing and no one else, or both could lose their balance and land on the hard floor.

"You are going to lose your husband to that skinny blonde if you are not careful. How can you sit here so complacently and allow such a thing to happen?" a "friendly" onlooker gossiped.

The woman calmly turned to the handsome young man at her side and asked, "What do you think, Dev? Is my marriage in jeopardy?"

Pretending to be deeply concerned, he redirected the question.

She retorted haughtily, "I am here. My husband is dancing directly in front of me. What is he doing wrong? What is she doing wrong?"

When the evening's music was finished, her partner brought Petra to Dev. "Here, my friend. Now you may have her back. Till next week, Petra."

Taking his wife's hand, he left the I. House while Dev put his arm around Petra's waist and took her upstairs to the lobby. Baboo watched them, waved "goodbye" and smiled benignly, but he felt helpless and deeply troubled.

Part Three
ALLEGRO

Chapter 30

NEW YORK

Over the weekend, winter gave one last, furious gasp and landed an overnight blizzard on Manhattan. Snow lay on the ground, at first immaculately beautiful, stilling the ubiquitous clamor of eternal traffic. Slowly it changed hue, ingesting the city's impurities and the remains of "doggy-walks," the piss-yellow remnants left by roaming stray cats, soot and grime from countless chimneys and incinerators, until what had begun as a pristine blanket became ultimately dirtier than the filthy street it covered.

But not at first. Not quite yet.

Dev, even a year after experiencing New York's arbitrary weather, was still unused to and enchanted with snow and reveled in it, throwing handfuls towards the sky, showering himself as it descended back down, a child experiencing it again for the first time. His face glowed from the cold wind and with the enormous joy which was a permanent aspect of his character.

In a totally spontaneous action, he ran towards Petra, picked her up in his strong young arms, twirled her around and around, roaring with delight. Then carefully, securely, set her down and embraced her while pressing her face safely to his chest, his natural exuberance tempered with tenderness, concerned as always not to injure her.

"So, I have had my cricket practice for one day. Now it is time for us to eat a steak dinner. Is that acceptable to you, my lady?" He bowed towards her so deeply his head almost touched the frozen sidewalk.

"As a matter of fact, you impudent serf, it is not all right! I do not remember giving you permission to feed me morning, noon and night. It's my turn to feed you!"

He pretended to be shocked, then burst out laughing.

"If you insist, you proud Jewess. But your budget does not allow for steak, only hamburger, and I am feeling an un-Hindu-like urge to devour good meat." And added, "My mother would be horrified! Oh well, if you must be an independent woman, how about a pastrami on rye instead?"

"Where did you learn about pastrami? Certainly not in Bombay!"

He stared down at her haughtily. "Madam. In Bombay, sandwiches are eaten only by foreigners who have never had true Indian cuisine." His eyes taunted her. "Beside, you are not the only kosher chicken in the pot!"

Petra decided not to investigate the topic further, not knowing where it might lead, grabbed his elbow and dragged him, sliding and symbolically protesting, into the nearest delicatessen. It wasn't a particularly good one, not like the excellent ones farther downtown but would suffice on this frozen day when transportation was problematic. The pastrami, greasy by nature, was even more so, but the rye bread, fresh, hard-crusted and crowned with caraway seeds was superb.

And the place was clean, warm and cozy.

Dev asked, "Would you like some coffee?" and still teasing added, "If you can't afford it, I'll pay. But only for one cup."

She swatted at him. "You'll only get tea and black coffee here. Without milk. Kosher restrictions."

"My God, you people make life difficult for yourselves. Ugh, coffee without cream. Undrinkable!" he complained, ordered a soft drink and continued to eat. Then he stopped chewing and frowned at her. She knew that particular expression always meant something serious was bothering him.

"My love," he said softly, "tell me. Are you Jewish or American?"

"What?" she gasped, but recovered enough to comment, "If you want to be so spectacularly specific, don't forget my Dutch birth! What the hell do you mean to infer with such a question?"

"Don't. Please don't be defensive. Only, if I am asked what I am, I say I am Indian. I don't specify Hindu, Moslem, Parsi, whatever. But when I asked some of my classmates what they were, instead of answering American, they said Jewish. And I do not understand what they mean."

Petra sighed. If he asked someone else, the response could be very different. "I'll try to explain, Dev. But only how I understand it." He reached across the table to grasp her hand.

"I am an American citizen, while my faith, if that is what I have, is Judaism. It is the religion my family has always followed. Just as yours has probably followed Hinduism for thousands of years. But you don't seem too involved with yours. Nor am I with mine."

"And," she continued, "you eat pastrami, which is meat, while I love lobster, both of which are forbidden to devout members of our faiths."

He nodded but still looked puzzled. "What about Israel? Do you have any emotions about Israel?"

"Of course I do. There must be a place of refuge for Jews. A homeland where there is no religious persecution. Dev, six million innocent, unarmed civilians were slaughtered! Among them more than one million little children. Don't you think we are entitled to a place where we can live in peace and safety just as everyone else on earth?"

"So, there actually is a place, a nationality...Jewish...as my classmates answered."

"No," she insisted. "If they were born in this country they are Americans. Period. Most people can delve back into their family histories and discover ancestors who came from Poland, Russia, Germany—or Ireland and Italy for that matter. Or were brought here on slave ships. For the Jews it was primarily to escape religious persecution. The point remains, eventually these diverse people all became Americans. Which doesn't mean they eradicated their heritage. And why should they have to?"

She thought her explanation was clear and he would be satisfied. But Dev was an attorney and by no means finished with the cross examination. "If that is so, if it is only a religion and not a nationality, then why do some people look typically what we call 'Jewish'?"

She was stymied, not able to explain where religion ended and race or nationality (if there actually was such a breakdown) might begin and vice versa. "Jews have been trying to solve that riddle for thousands of years. Please, just accept an answer, any answer, because we don't know either."

She bit off a chunk of her sandwich hoping he would let her finish it in peace.

He didn't. Or rather he couldn't.

Dev, joyously, overwhelmingly in love with a woman whose every thought and action were of major importance to him, was determined to learn as much as he could humanly absorb about her, her people and background, to experience her not only as a physical being but a spiritual and emotional one as well. He wanted to crawl into her brain, to comprehend what she was thinking, why she acted and reacted as she did. To know her as well or better than she knew herself. What he realized already was basic enough. If she was hurt he knew the pain would be every bit as intense for him. Perhaps more so, since he would also feel he had failed to protect her sufficiently.

They were inside each other's eyes, true, but their souls, invisible, were also tightly intertwined. Still, the eternal riddle perplexed him and her answer did not satisfy him.

She found it amusing to see a non-involved spectator struggling with the ancient question.

He shook his head, "I do not understand at all."

"No one else does, either. Someone once said, 'a Jew is anyone who says he is'

He nibbled pensively on his (kosher) pickle, took a long, deep breath and fired. "If Israel and the United States ever went to war against each other, where would your loyalties be?"

The pain she felt showed instantly on her face.

"You see," he cried in triumph, "you are Jewish. It is your nationality!"

"That's not true!" she retorted. "Besides, it's an unfair hypothetical question."

"Then accept it hypothetically. What would you do if you were asked to take up weapons in defense of one against the other?"

"My God," she mumbled horrified. "I don't know. I can't imagine raising my hand against either of them."

The hot pastrami was now ice cold, curled and drying against the crust of the bread. Not that it mattered. Her appetite was entirely gone, anyway.

"You must recognize your identity, my love. And you have run from it for years, haven't you? Choose, Petra. Know yourself."

"Why? Why is it essential we be uniformed into a niche, frightened of defying some artificial political or religious system with which we have only the slightest connection? Why can't we accept more than one ideology or nationality or whatever? Why must we be cubicled?"

"How expertly you are evading the issue! Again, my love. For whom would you fight? Israel or the United States?"

She felt him probing and jabbing at her deepest thoughts, her greatest confusions, and because she knew he loved her unconditionally, she attempted to answer the unanswerable.

Very softly, she murmured, "If it ever came to that, Dev, there would be two options for me. I could commit suicide (killing myself would be more tolerable than knowing I might have killed another American or another Jew). The other? I would request service in the Medical Corps...to heal rather than murder."

She was shaking, her eyes flooding but felt she had given a truthful answer. One he could accept.

He reached across the table with his handkerchief and carefully wiped away the tears. She did not realize he was fighting to keep from crying himself, aware he caused her distress. But feeling he was finally close to reaching her elusive core, he continued, "And on whose side would you serve?"

"Stop it, Dev! Stop it! Why are you doing this? Leave me alone!"

"Just answer. For yourself. Not for me." He took her hands in his, held them firmly but without hurting her and would not release her.

"To whom would you offer your help? The Americans or the Israelis?"

"What's the difference? Either way I'm a traitor. It's only a question of whether I betrayed my country or my family."

He released her. "There! That is what you needed to understand. It is more than a religious philosophy, is it not? There exists a much stronger bond than mere ritual. It is indeed a question of kinship. Now the rest of your answer."

She sighed, but was now able to finish the interrogation. "I owe my first loyalty to the country which saved my life. This one. America."

"Do you think you could live in Israel?"

"Not permanently. It would be too difficult for me to accept the religious restrictions," she answered.

"And could you live in India, where there are not only religious restrictions but women do not have the freedom you are accustomed to?" he asked timidly.

She did not answer because she had no answer.

***

They left the delicatessen and proceeded slowly towards Riverside Drive as the street lights were beginning to glow. Suddenly a woman impatient to get past them pushed into Petra, throwing her unexpectedly into Dev's shoulder.

She did not apologize but hurried by, turned for an instant to glare at them, her face livid, then winced when she recognized Petra huddling against Dev.

Nettie de Vos.

She walked quickly away.

Chapter 31

A separation, either temporary or permanent, would inevitably follow.

He was holding a letter in his hand when it became imminent. "My sister is getting married and the family wants me to be there. Besides, she is my favorite sibling and would be devastated if I did not attend."

A flash of hopelessness streamed across his face.

"When I am alone, I can think of nothing but our future and I am in despair. But when I see you again, I bless God we have found each other."

She knew, had known all along, one day, he would leave, but had made the choice to encapsulate the two of them from infringement by the world—eyes fully opened, conscious, aware their happiness would not shield them, but also unwilling to sacrifice even a moment sooner than necessary the joy they shared. Now the ostrich months were ending and reality was beginning.

"When?" she asked.

"During the summer. For two months."

"We still have time."

"It will race by us, my love. As it is I cannot endure even a weekend without you, anymore. Two months apart? It is an eternity I am unable to even imagine!"

He reached into his jacket pocket and shyly pulled out a small envelope. "Here. I managed to get these today. I hope you like them."

Inside were two box seat tickets to the Saturday evening performance of "Rigoletto" at the Metropolitan Opera House. She gasped, realizing it was a special gift for her

"I am expected to absorb something of Western culture while I am here. My parents would be justifiably upset if I didn't learn at least a little bit. So you are doing me a favor. Oh, and the evening before, we must attend an Indian dance performance at the Consulate. It's part of earning the opera evening, you see. The music will sound unfamiliar and the dance movements are standardized and symbolic. You may find it a difficult trade-off!"

"Indian music?" she replied. "I've been listening to it for years. And the dances? They're regular entertainment fare in diplomatic corps circles. Hell, there isn't much else to do in Washington except pursuing foreign relations or swilling from an illegal bottle in the after-hours clubs."

"Incorrigible child," he retorted, "such language for a lady! Now, tell me what the opera is about. I don't understand a word of Italian."

"Neither do most of the people in the audience." She reached up and kissed him quickly. "Jopie thinks you are 'obscenely handsome' but don't let it go to your head. The only males she's seen lately are lying naked on laboratory tables and being disemboweled."

"Petra? The story, please!"

"Oh, the story? Well, it's about a philandering nobleman who is also obscenely handsome and seduces every female in sight. Sound familiar?"

He laughed, "A bit. Maybe I should have chosen an opera with another plot. So what happens?"

"Well, this hunchbacked fellow who acts as the duke's procurer isn't thrilled to discover his only daughter (who nobody else knew existed and was raised in a convent) is the most recent conquest and the dad plans a murderous revenge. But at the end, his irresistible employer happily trots off singing that women are all fickle. Bit of Verdian irony, don't cha know."

"And the girl?"

"Oh, the girl. Well, like all enamored women who would instantly do the same, she makes the ultimate sacrifice, saves his life and dies stashed in a burlap bag. Nice neat ending, no blood on the stage, all wrapped up in a sack and unseen. Of course, before she beautifully and totally expires, she does have to sing one more aria, Dad unties the thing long enough to allow the audience to see and hear her last liltingly lovely gasp. Finis. End of story. There is no more!"

"And that simple plot takes how long to play out?"

"Usually three or more hours. But there are a few intermissions. I'll buy us each some champagne. Unless you prefer lemonade?"

"Champagne will do, thank you. Do I need to wear a tuxedo?"

"As far as I'm concerned, you can go stark naked. You'll still be the most desirable man in the entire opera house. But don't think I'm going to die for you in a dirty burlap bag. Silk, maybe. Linen, maybe. Burlap? No!"

"Brat!" he shouted, grabbed her hand and went laughing with her down the street.

Chapter 32

Their lives revolved around the time they could spend together.

With classes slowing down as springtime matured into early summer, Dev drove to her office building towards lunchtime, carrying sandwiches and coffee so they could sit in his car, perch on a bench in Central Park, be any place where they could avoid the senseless chatter of others. Often they ate only a bite, feeding the rest to the pigeons while the coffee became cold, brown dishwater, untouched and unappetizing.

They never even noticed.

He waited in the lobby downstairs, shifted nervously from foot to foot, watched anxiously while the elevators emptied, until finally he found her. In-between classes, hungry to have a moment's contact, he phoned, subsisting on the few seconds he had to say "I love you," hearing her voice responding softly before hurrying to the next one, sliding the coins in his pants pockets through his fingers and counting to insure he had enough money available, in anticipation of the following phone call.

They were ecstatically happy, alive when together. Insulated, complete only then.

He found himself smiling at strangers, feeling sorrow and compassion for the smelly, ragged alcoholics huddled on the streets, mumbling incoherent exhortations; the prostitutes hip-swinging, tightly clothed, meandering along the traffic islands on Upper Broadway; emotions he had never confronted earlier, because in his culture they were not expected.

Not of people in his caste.

She glowed, the once too pallid skin tinged with pink, eyes streaming with joy. When she looked at him, it was with amazement and tenderness, saw him only. Her aloofness to anyone else made her appear mysterious and intensely desirable. The men of Manhattan, jaded and sated, passed her on the street and were entranced, pausing to gaze after her, wondering, envying, recognizing the signs of a woman who loved and was loved deeply. She, in turn, was completely oblivious to her own new allure.

They shared every confidence, became closest and dearest, most trusted friends, knowing neither would ever willingly hurt the other. He finished her sentences, she unerringly read his thoughts before he uttered them.

Intertwined, braided stalks of bamboo, with time waiting to unbind them.

Baboo, sensitive, alert, watched with worried eyes and was not surprised. He noted the care and consideration that now shone from the boy's eyes, the naked emotions on the girl's face when she turned to speak with him.

One evening at the I. House, an arm around each of them, hugging their bodies close to his thin one, he whispered, "Be happy my dear, dear, children. Love each other. You cannot help yourselves in any case. But do not hurt one another."

Dev answered at once, "Hurt her, Baboo? How could I do that without inflicting pain on myself?"

Baboo nodded, "I know. I know. You have both grown older in the past months. But life is not as now it seems."

He kissed Petra's cheek, embraced Dev and left them to return home to Gita.

No, they would probably never share the intense passion he sensed burned between his two friends, but he and his brilliant, witty new wife were content together, had known each other since childhood and would consequently never suffer as much, either.

Baboo did not envy the young couple. Not for an instant.

Dev watched him hurry away, gazed down at Petra, his dark eyes reading her face.

"Follow me, follow me," he signaled mutely.

Without words she answered, "Wherever you choose to lead, I will follow you."

He held her hand, and slowly they went outside into the darkening night towards his apartment. He took her in his arms, and carried her inside, aware as always of the pledge he had made to her and to himself, a pledge he swore he would never break. At the same time he could not bear to let her return to her solitary room, leaving them both miserable, particularly when soon he would be going to India.

Towards morning she awoke and saw by the light coming through the window that he was still asleep. He lay with his head curved towards her, helpless and vulnerable. His eyelashes quivered occasionally as he breathed, the eyebrows arched upwards from his temples, giving him a look of aching innocence. She watched him a few minutes and knew only she did not want to live without him. Then, because she couldn't help herself, leaned over and kissed him gently.

He opened his eyes. "Good morning, doll. How are you? Can you imagine, I dreamed you would be here when I awoke and my dream has come true!"

"Ah, you silly, superstitious Indians," she teased him, "your dreams are not dreams. They are simply facts in the making! All you have to do is pretend you foretold them and manipulate the time until they become reality!"

"You think so, do you? Come here and I will show you some reality!" he teased back. "Now, before the situation becomes significantly more dangerous, let us get up, find a coffee shop on Broadway and have some breakfast. All this deep conversation so early in the morning has made me very hungry. You will learn I am not a pleasant man when all I can think of is my empty stomach!"

She chuckled evilly. "Just as long as you make sure my stomach and its environs remain empty, all will be well!"

He threw a pillow at her. She ducked just fast enough to land in his embrace.

Chapter 33

Alan picked up the phone and dialed, his fingers traveling automatically over the correct numbers, so accurately did they recognize the too familiar combination. He hoped for a response but didn't really expect one, put the receiver down for an instant, cursed in Hindi, shrugged indifferently, skimmed through his address book and dialed another number. One he had never bothered to memorize, and as he expected, Parvati did answer.

"Hello, dearie. I hope I didn't wake you, but you do sound as if I did. I just wondered if you'd like to accompany me to the Consulate to see the dancers this evening. Good. Try to get some rest meanwhile. Till later."

He placed the phone back in its cradle, feeling powerful, worthy of glorification, a knight riding courageously on his stallion towards the rescue of a helpless maiden. Unfortunately she was far uglier than the ugliest steed he had ever seen (having never actually ridden a horse but observed several). Hmm, he wondered, what if...?

He chastised himself for not facing reality but was determined to reinvent the future, obliterate the embarrassment of the past. Still, no matter how hard he tried, the memory of Maria continued to obsess him although he knew only too well she did not return his fascination.

Friends. Yes.

More? Absolutely not. Under no circumstances.

How dare she? How dare she? He fumed.

A woman like that! Whom he knew completely from the smooth, chignoned hair on her head to its dark, curled equivalent between her legs, legs which had opened for him at his slightest touch. And not just once. Many times!

Whose arms embraced him freely and who ultimately shouted in abandonment and delight at his sexual superiority as they chorused together.

But when he informed her after one not so perfect incident that she ultimately belonged to him and until he chose to end their affair (which, after all, as the master in the relationship was his decision to make) was his exclusive possession and, by allowing his sexual overtures, she had inadvertently forfeited any involvements (physical, emotional, even platonic) with other men without his consent, would indeed have thoughts of no other man and remain steadfastly faithful solely to him (as was only seemly and his prerogative as the male), she screamed at him in heavily accented English interspersed with Spanish scatology, to put on his trousers immediately ("with or without bothering to include your underwear, you medieval prick!") or she would throw him out on the street and them after him!

He had allowed a week to pass before calling her again, giving her adequate time to realize how much she had missed him, to understand how he had, of course, been entirely justified. But she never answered the phone.

A woman like that! He reminded himself in consolation, common, not particularly bright or well educated, who had allowed him secret privileges just like the Calcutta whores, who at least demanded a rupee or two for their services.

He did not even think he really loved her. No, he knew he did not. It was rather anger at her arrogance and the perceived loss of his manliness that so bothered him.

She, a lowly female, had embarrassed him.

Unthinkable!

Whoever heard of such a thing?

A man, by virtue of his inborn maleness and its exterior manifestations, could rid himself of a slut at any time. Or indeed any female, virtuous or not, for it was historical fact women were congenitally inferior to even the least manly male. Mastery and ownership over the female was the male's prerogative, always had been, always would be.

But she, that venom-tongued bitch, she dared to deny his omniscience and omnipotence after what they had experienced together!

He hated her and vowed revenge!

Unbidden and without warning, suddenly he would remember how lovely she was and wished desperately he could hold her, caress her, make love to her. "Maria! Oh Maria, come back to me," his soul mourned, and he forgave her immediately.

Tonight, however, he would not sit at home alone brooding, would seek surcease, make the most gentlemanly sacrifice and escort Parvati, allow himself to be seen with her by his countrymen, aware her dark eyes turned to puddles when she glanced at him.

He considered how ethical it would be if he seduced her and mused he half expected her to moo with pleasure should he caress her sari-concealed mammaries (which he assumed—and correctly—were as untouched as undoubtedly the rest of her must be).

He took her to dinner, Parvati dressed in a beautiful gown of crimson silk embellished with gold thread, and they arrived in the Consulate lobby just prior to the performance.

"Look, Alan. Baboo with his wife!"

Dev and Petra arrived a few minutes later; he in a dark blue suit and white shirt, which set off his brilliant smile. She, dressed in a short sleeved black dress almost funerary in its solemnity but for the tiny embroidered flowers scattered over the fabric.

Although thrilled to be with Alan, Parvati recognized that even by Indian standards Dev was extraordinary, an obvious direct descendant of the Aryan hordes which had swept from the Northern Caucasus and overwhelmed India generations earlier, forever relegating her own darker-skinned indigenous ancestors from the South to the lesser social positions and the poorer areas of the huge sub-continent.

"Those damned Aryans," she muttered while admiring him from a distance. And despite the endlessly-longed-for-never-to-be-realized-but-now-miraculous presence of her adored Alan next to her, she felt herself arching slightly, uselessly, uncontrollably, towards him, where he stood unaware of the effect he had on women, leaning familiarly against the girl with him, gazing at her, addressing every word to her, with infinite sweetness on his face.

Did she appreciate him, Parvati wondered, this too-white Jewess from a completely different culture than theirs? What power did she have over him? Could it be they were sleeping together? Was that the secret to getting and holding a man's love?

At the conclusion of the performance, the couples resumed their separate-joined lives. Baboo and Gita returned home, quietly contented.

Dev and Petra disappeared, after being glued to each other in the semi-darkened auditorium.

Alan took Parvati confidently by the elbow and led her to his car.

She loved the security of being guided by a man not a member of her blood family. It was a sensation she had yearned for, been told about in India since she was a child, and it felt as wonderful as she had imagined, allowing her to be feminine and vulnerable.

Would it continue? she worried. Would Alan ever want to be alone with her? Completely alone at some time in the future? Or was this gala, platonic evening the full extent of her relationship with Alan, forever a friend but nothing more?

The wily, successful businessman knew exactly what she was thinking.

As brilliant as she might be, dealing with the illnesses of children, she was herself an infant in his hands. He read the anxiety in her eyes, the slight trembling of her ugly mouth when she looked at him, the downward embarrassed turn of her head after she dared to gaze directly into his face and he caught her.

He made a decision.

They drove directly to his apartment and he invited her to enjoy some tea with him—if she would like that, he added politely, opening the door and guiding her expertly inside.

She was overjoyed! The evening was being prolonged! Oh wonder, oh paradise! She would see his home, the spacious rooms, the furniture he used, would not have to fantasize about his living quarters anymore but actually inhabit them, if only for a little while, with the man she adored.

As promised, he brewed tea, tea from home, from India. The familiar taste made her feel nostalgic, at ease. They chatted and he casually placed an arm around her, the natural male gesture of protection.

She did not object.

Another pot of tea and genuine English biscuits to accompany it.

They continued to talk, his arm drawing more closely around her shoulder, reaching casually down, loose, a slight touch here and there, an accidental brushing against one breast.

Nothing of concern.

By the fourth cup of tea she asked where the lavatory was and rose to leave him. When she returned, he had changed into casual slacks and wore only a sleeveless undershirt.

"Ah," she thought, drunk on what she saw, "how magnificent he is! His skin set off by the white cotton and sprigs of black, curly hair emerging above the round neckline."

"And," she exulted, "he is smiling. At me!"

"Another cup, Parvati, dear? The water is still hot."

"Yes, thank you." She would joyously attempt to drink the Indian Ocean dry if it meant being allowed to stay with him even ten minutes more.

He poured carefully, an expert who spilled not a drop (she noticed with ill-placed pride), waited until she had taken a sip and placed the cup safely back on its matching saucer, then reached forward and took her in his arms, fervently kissed her cheeks, the nape of her neck, licked the exposed skin around the front of her blouse, which sent shivers of unexpected pleasure through her, pulled her closer and fitted her expertly against his own partially aroused body, furtively then more boldly stroked her breasts (which had never felt a man's touch before), found no resistance and immobilized her as he increased the strength of his caresses, finding the nipples through the fabric, kneading, pinching first gently then more harshly as they reflexed in response, listened with satisfaction and cynical amusement as she began to moan in virgin-awakened uncontrolled desire, and when he knew she could no longer resist in the slightest, unwrapped the purple sari and watched clinically as the too long restrained butterfly emerged from its cocoon.

She said nothing, desire had made her as mute and powerless as if she had been drugged.

Her body, still clothed in short-sleeved blouse and underwear, would probably be lovely, he guessed, and with her silence as consent continued to undress her, kissing the newly exposed skin repeatedly as he removed the silk top, then unclasped the confining brassiere beneath it, glanced initially somewhat indifferently at the Indian doctor's now (not quite publicly) exposed secrets and, to his own surprise, gasped in admiration. Her brown breasts, perfect, firm, waited for his caresses, the unmarred skin glowed like beige sateen, which, when touched even slightly, shuddered awake and molded innocently to his hands, the nipples coaxed quickly into erection.

For him. Exclusively for him!

She reclined prostrate on the sofa, completely helpless. A helplessness he had induced, and the knowledge soothed some of his badly bruised masculinity. But there was more to do before he could legitimately reclaim his assertion of manhood and hold his head up among his strutting peers and colleagues.

Again he fondled and teased, causing even louder, more frequent moans, then coolly reached for the ultimate prize, felt her flinch immediately, but had already ascertained she was ready to receive him and wordlessly removed the rest of her clothing.

She lay against the sofa cushions inert, no longer enshrouded, breathing shallowly, her eyes half-opened, but wondering if this man, whom she loved completely, approved of what he scrutinized so calmly, well aware of her physical impairments, praying she compared favorably enough with other women he had known to beg his forgiveness for the ugliness of her face or any disfigurements he might find elsewhere.

Alan gazed down at where she lay, motionless, meek, cognizant he was undoubtedly the first man who had seen her so and, despite his experienced callousness, caught his breath (and hoped she had not noticed it).

Parvati's naked body was the most beautiful he had ever seen. And he had seen many since his initiation into manhood at age fourteen!

He couldn't help himself, kissed it, stroked it, unconsciously murmured his adoration, was enthralled with its perfection and enchanted with her childish reactions as she moved towards and away from his ministrations, involuntarily, unschooled, innocent still.

He recognized she was unique, divine, and bowed in adoration at the altar of her womanhood.

Patiently waiting for the perfect moment.

Finally no longer able to control himself, his penis frozen and jabbing painfully at nothing, he tore off the rest of his clothes, threw himself on her, thrust forward and erupted.

She gave a shriek, just one, while silent tears streamed over her face, tears he did not notice because he had purposely avoided looking at her. Had not once kissed her on the mouth, and would not do so now.

He got up, went to the bathroom, returned with a wet washcloth, calmly inspected the damage he had inflicted between her legs, approved of his handiwork, wiped a little blood away and tossed the soiled cloth in the laundry hamper.

The divine had been made flesh and was no longer worthy of his servility.

"So, now, Parvati, you belong only to me," he announced peremptorily, knowing she would understand, be grateful for his exclusive sexual attentions, unlike that Latin American slut.

"Yes," she whispered, "I am yours."

"Good. Then you must obey me. I have given you great pleasure. You will do the same for me."

He took her head and guided it downwards. When she hesitated, he released it, assumed she had learned enough for this initiation and said as gently as he could, "Well, then, perhaps not tonight. Now you must go home. I know you are a bit sore but the pain will soon disappear. I am sorry, dear child. But I am very tired."

He phoned for a taxi, did not offer to pay for it, gave her a quick fraternal hug and kiss on the cheek and sent her off to the utilitarian room she inhabited at the I. House.

Parvati lay awake most of the night, carefully cleansed the wound, soothed the ruptured orifice, crooned maternally to herself, content as she bathed and balmed, aware she was now irrevocably elevated to womanhood.

Alan had assumed he had given her "pleasure" while in fact she had only felt pain and warm blood dripping, at first rapidly, then waning slowly between her legs, combined with a burning, subtle sensation where none had been previously.

Pleasure? Was the definition of sexual gratification the palpitating discomfort she had experienced? The violent, invasive spear of pain which tore and wounded and then withdrew as suddenly and painfully, just when she had begun to accept it? Was that defined as pleasure?

She loved him totally, unendingly, had done so for many months, but she was puzzled, a little disappointed. Still, convinced after tonight she and Alan would never be parted, she finally dozed off, dreaming of his caresses and the hours they had spent together, while the evening's insults to her body began to heal.

Alan also slept, almost as soon as she was gone, in fact. He dreamed about his conquest, how she would be enslaved to him forever, to keep or abandon as he willed.

To service him as he chose.

He took her ugly, overly-willing face between his hands and pushed it down, breathing deeply in happy anticipation, while she, at first appalled by his instructions (as was proper for any recently deflowered female) but obediently aware he had taken her virginity and thereby accepted him as her unquestioned master in all things, eventually complied and opened her mouth as widely as she could, although he noted her front teeth did prove a momentary impediment to fulfilling his sternly specific command.

Almost immediately, as she obeyed and seized, he groaned, gasped, shouted, and attempted unsuccessfully to escape from his self-imposed imprisonment—the pleasure palace he, like Kubla Khan, had desired and decreed—while she, misunderstanding, grasped him ever more firmly, wanting only to please her lord, cognizant that since she was finally and very expertly deflowered by him and he had labored so diligently (and successfully) to make the experience magnificently memorable for her, there now followed certain necessary preliminary proceedings which would insure the next unanimously desired copulation and, by her certainly desired bathing of her lately (but thankfully no longer) arid innards, thereby undoubtedly culminating in even greater elation.

For him.

(And probably for her, too, although that was irrelevant.)

At last screaming, "Aaaghhhh. Let me go! You bitch! Let me go!" he awoke; in panic, hurriedly felt between his legs to ascertain if his penis was still where it should be, was relieved to discover that while hugely engorged and straining futilely against his too-tight pajama bottoms, all appeared hunky-dory. Nonetheless, he sleepily expected to see bloody gashes and the deep imprint of two front teeth on the sensitive skin of his blue-pink stalk, then noting there were none visible but he was indeed feeling quite some discomfort, staggered half-awake to the toilet where he voided most of the tea he had drunk earlier. His emptied bladder and member shrank back to their normal, not particularly impressive, proportions.

"Well" he vowed to himself, "I must never order Parvati to perform that particular favor!"

And as he remembered the magnificent body, which he had been the first to invade, conquer and now would eternally possess, he felt himself grow hard again, grasped his pulsing organ and labored to satisfy himself.

When he was finished, he picked up the phone and dialed the familiar number. As usual, although it was the middle of the night, there was no response.

***

Fast asleep in her own apartment, Maria dreamt she was being driven through deep snow drifts in a horse-drawn sled decorated with noisy bells, which tinkled in tempo.

She partially opened her eyes, realized she had been listening to the phone, reached over and slid the switch to "off" without picking up the receiver, dimly aware she had forgotten to do so earlier this evening and immediately fell asleep again.

Chapter 34

Dev couldn't stand it any longer, stared around his shadowed room, haunted by its singleness, gazed outside where morning light was dancing on the sidewalks, noticed a few dandelions peering through the cracks, and pink dogwood beginning to bloom, bees flying into a sky of azure blue.

He wanted to shout his exultation to the world, embrace everyone and everything in it, tell them he was the most fortunate man ever born, loved by the woman he loved.

They had parted only a few hours earlier, and already he missed her.

She had become a part of him, perhaps the most important part. He felt empty without her, hardly recognized himself from before they met, but when she nestled in his arms, knew he could overcome any obstacle created by hordes of humans or the entire pantheon of divinities.

And now, recognizing the new day in all its beauty, he wanted to take her into the sunshine, feel again alive and affirmed.

But it was only 8 a.m. and Missus refused to answer the phone before nine.

He dialed anyway.

A tired, cranky woman replied she would get Petra, and whined that in the future he must refrain from calling so early.

Then he heard the soft, sleepy voice he loved and whispered into the phone, "Get up, my love. This evening we go to the opera but now it is glorious outside. I will come in fifteen minutes to take you to breakfast. Then, if you like, we can visit the Cloisters."

"How did you know I was dreaming about you? And now I don't have to close my eyes to see you again. Yes, yes, yes to all your questions."

She stumbled into the bathroom, showered and dressed. Usually on the weekends Ellen would have been moving around but this time Petra heard nothing.

"Well," she thought, "I guess Salmi has abducted her for the weekend. I wonder if they've finally found a time and place to be alone without Kerim."

When Petra emerged from the building, Dev ran open-armed to embrace her, kissed her with renewed longing and tenderness but also possessory confidence directly on the mouth, in front of the International House on a morning-bright sunlit Riverside Drive, indifferent as to who might observe them, and crooning, guided her head with one hand to his shoulder and held her, his carefully schooled British-cum-Indian reticence completely forgotten.

His family would have been scandalized!

He didn't care.

The only person whose opinion mattered was that of the fragile girl in his arms, where he wanted her to stay forever, for whom he would give his life willingly to keep her safe.

He wordlessly considered the irony! She had brought him to his knees but he had never imagined he could feel such happiness at relinquishing his traditional control!

They wandered into a coffee shop on Broadway, ordered breakfast, gazed at each other, held hands and barely spoke. Suddenly the door opened, and Jerry Roth, the young math professo, entered, greeted them unenthusiastically and joined several colleagues at another table.

"Are you finished, doll?" Dev asked, looking at the plate in front of Petra.

She nodded, he paid, and they left the restaurant, took the short subway trip to Fort Tryon Park, and entered the Cloisters.

They strolled, enchanted, through the lovely French Gothic building filled with medieval religious artifacts, paintings, sculptures, executed in every medium.

"I know you admire them," Dev stated, "but don't you find them a little offensive?"

"I've thought of that so often," she answered, "but the Da Vinci and Raphael holy family paintings are glorious. I don't know whether Jesus was the Messiah or not. But I do know his life inspired magnificent art, music, literature. To me, the beauty of the work transcends the conflict. I love Bach, but some of the texts he used are virulently anti-Semitic. I ignore them and concentrate on the genius of his music."

"Ha!" he noted, observing a famous tapestry of the unicorn trapped within its circular enclosure. "Look, it's just like me. Fenced in by a powerful fiendish force, a sacrifice to love!"

"Oh really?" she goaded back, "and who do you think erected the fence around you?"

"A blonde witch from a faraway very low land. And you know, her magic is so potent I cannot begin to think how to extricate myself. You see, I am simply another pitiful entrapped male, imprisoned and as helpless as the poor beast up there!"

"Hmm. Well, if that's how you feel, I'll give you both the key and the boot any time you want them and find myself a less demanding unicorn!"

"You will never find one as wonderful as I am."

"Probably not. But if you keep complaining about your terrible mistreatment, we both might find out! Do you dare to take such a risk?"

He kissed her cheek, then led them towards an exit which opened to a gravel path overlooking a valley filled with formal flower beds.

"Let's go down," she said, "walk among them, smell them. I used to come here during the war with my family. One of the first havens I remember from those years. Every weekend unannounced, it became the favorite gathering place for the refugees. An ice cream cart and vendor always stood over there," she continued, "just off the main path to the museum entrance. I don't think he had many customers even on the hottest days. Most of the people had no jobs. Everyone was living on whatever cash they had managed to save as they fled—and when that was gone?"

She shrugged. "Who dared to waste money on ice cream?"

"And did you long for some?"

"Oh yes. I remember staring at the blue popsicles painted on the sides of the white cart and the treat they represented seemed unattainable, a delicious melting treasure. Most kids didn't expect to get one, though. They were little realists, very aware of why they were forced to leave Europe. When a parent said, 'no,' usually no one cried. Except maybe the poor vendor."

"Is there one here today?" he asked and ran down the path holding tightly to her hand.

"Yes," she answered, pointing in the distance, "over there."

"Then, today, doll, you shall have your popsicle or dixie cup, or whatever else you choose."

He became very serious. "You will never be denied anything ever again when I am with you. I swear it."

"Thank you," she answered and frowned, "but this time, I want to pay. For both of us. It's maybe a bit silly, but it is symbolic. Don't be insulted. Let me do it. Please."

"To show you survived? Thrived?"

"Yes," she replied so softly he could hardly hear her, while silently she exulted because he understood.

He stood aside after she told the vendor what they had chosen and watched as she took out her wallet and paid, kissed her on the forehead to thank her, finished eating and announced they had to leave, to get ready for the opera.

"Six o'clock. The Bentley and uniformed chauffeur will pick you up," he teased.

"Oh sure! A Bentley! More likely a tandem bicycle and you in Brooks Brothers!"

He laughed, "Far more likely!"

***

Petra always felt transformed into a delicate nineteenth century ornament ensconced amid a classical red velvet, gold embellished jewelry box, when she was in the Metropolitan Opera House. It was furnished exactly as an opera house should be furnished, with its huge crimson-draped curtain, deeply plushed seats, and on either side of the stage the many elaborately gilded tiers of boxes, extending like the subjects of a Victorian Period painting upwards towards the ceiling.

Dev found their box, and they watched as the seats below them began to fill up.

"How many wonderful evenings I have spent here," she mused, but never in such expensive seats.

She winced, remembering a "Tosca" featuring the world's reigning prima donna, for which she'd saved up for weeks, skipping breakfast, wearing torn stockings, walking instead of taking public transportation, until she had enough to buy a ticket. But when the day of the sold-out performance arrived, she discovered her seat was directly behind a pillar with no view whatsoever of the stage. Because there were absolutely no other seats available, she received a refund before the curtains opened, but left the theater in tears.

The Metropolitan Opera House was unique but by no means perfect. But there would not be an "obstructed views" problem this evening.

"Rigoletto" had never been her favorite opera, its most famous aria having become not just a cliché but a particularly ugly one, evoking memories of Italian organ grinders on the streets of New York, playing the same tune endlessly, while their helpless little Capuchin monkeys (dressed in braid-trimmed costumes) looked up at their masters with expressions of fear on their faces, doffed their red caps and begged continually for pennies (or risked being exposed to a sharp yank on the leash around their tiny bodies).

When Dev obtained tickets for it, she was thrilled at his thoughtfulness but not overwhelmed with his choice and had few expectations about how much she would actually enjoy the performance.

It was glorious!

The music transported her to where there were no wars, no children being murdered, no innocent men and women suffering. Her elation was not due to the plot—(the usual operatically dramatic, ill-placed passion followed by blood, murder and perhaps retribution)—it was much more, the music, the lovely environment, or perhaps a new vulnerability emerging from the emotions evoked by her companion.

Even the over-played aria sung by the duke wasn't unpalatable; more credit to the tenor, she thought.

Once she glanced at the boy next to her and saw his face mirroring her own, eyes glowing, a hint of a smile around his mouth, shaking his head in amazement.

After the curtain calls he said, "Why did no one ever tell me about this before? My first opera but this will certainly not be my last."

He helped her into the car and drove directly to his apartment, knowing it was no longer necessary to ask, anticipating her answer. When they were in each other's arms he murmured, "You are so good. You do not realize what the world can do to us. How evil and wicked reality is."

"I don't care," she answered, "whatever happens I'll never regret having met you."

She suddenly laughed, "And you are so gentle, a lamb in a beautiful wolf's coat."

"Me? Gentle? But mademoiselle," he continued, "I am not really so soft. Did you know, back home in Bombay I am a big athlete? Yes, really, I have a shelf full of cricket trophies. Sometime I will show them to you. Then you will see I am a very tough person."

He shook his head. "Only with you, when I touch you, I am so afraid I will hurt you. When I gaze into your eyes I am awed at what I see. You must not look at me like that. As if I am a god."

He paused for an instant and then whispered, "But I know if ever you should stop, I would not want to live."

Chapter 35

Several weeks later, on a Friday afternoon, Dev stood on a platform at Penn Station rubbing his eyes as he watched the train to Washington disappear into the tunnel, then took the subway back to his apartment, finished packing and taxied to the airport. He was beyond feeling forlorn, tried to read a newspaper and failed, wandered from the Sabena gate to the men's room and back again, and when at last he was seated and the plane circled Manhattan in preparation for its long journey he looked down, blessed the city which had brought him so much happiness and wondered how long it would be before he could return. Or would return at all. On the way home to a home which was no longer his home.

And then he hid his face against the window, pulled a blanket over his head and cried like a little child.

Chapter 36

Nettie had dressed carefully for this evening, choosing a white linen sheath, smoothed her hair until it shone and lay at least moderately flat, strapped on black sandals and began to assemble keys, money, a Swiss embroidered handkerchief, and whatever else she thought she needed to stuff into the Italian leather handbag. She glanced at her watch and took a breath. Still ten minutes before Pieter would arrive.

The doorbell rang.

Impatiently she called out, "Who's there?"

"Registered letter."

She signed and took it, shrugged when she read the return address from yet another law firm, but for a moment delayed opening the envelope, dreading the message inside.

It was not the first notice she had received from various areas throughout The Netherlands—Noord Holland, Zuid Holland, Brabant, Friesland, Gelderland—naming her the beneficiary of insurance policies (from people she had never heard of or never met), or bank accounts with balances of various amounts (including the pitiful few guilders carefully and proudly saved, pennies at a time, by the little children murdered along with their parents), the pragmatic lugubrious reminders of Germanic genocide.

Scattered increments of impersonal cash...all that remained of her father's side of the family.

"Who this time?" she wondered as she tore open the envelope.
"Dear Dr. De Vos,

It has come to our attention that you are the beneficiary of the estate of the late Israel DaSilva who passed away several years ago. Our research confirms you are his grandniece and there are no other surviving heirs or claimants to the assets. Since there is considerable real estate involved, we recommend you come personally to view the properties and notify us as to their disposition.

If you will inform us as to the date of your arrival we will be happy to make hotel reservations and meet you at the airport.

We welcome the opportunity to tender the necessary legal advice and to be of service to you during your stay.

  Hoogachtend,

  NOTARISSEN RIDDER, DE ROOIJ & HEER

  Arnhem, The Netherlands"

Nettie gasped!

Her mother's extended family! The Sephardic DaSilvas, whom she had never met although she had known their names.

Sephardic Jews had lived in The Netherlands since they were expelled from the Iberian peninsula (first from Spain by King Ferdinand and the fanatic Queen Isabella in 1492, followed in 1496 by a semi-expulsion from Portugal when King Manuel I, eager to marry their daughter and rule (eventually he assumed) over both nations, was forbidden the marriage until the Jews were expelled from Portugal as well. Aware his country's economy would suffer irreparably he issued an Order of Expulsion and had the Jews converted *en masse* instead.

In the 16th Century, the *de facto* Inquisition was installed in Portugal and the Jews were again forced to leave their homes. Some, with many trusted commercial contacts in Northern Europe, traveled directly to The Netherlands, the small Protestant country on the North Sea, (which in 1555 had initiated its own revolt against its Catholic Spanish rulers, resulting in the Eighty Years War...the first nation founded on the successful revolt of its people against its hated overlords).

The religiously-inspired expulsions culminated in the Iberian Peninsula impoverishing itself of its intellectual giants, greatest poets, philosophers and physicians, and the visionary merchants who had originally helped Spain and Portugal to expand (many of whom had financed the lucrative colonial explorations throughout the world) and relegated it ever afterwards to the status of a dusty, unimportant, economically distressed, second-class geographical wasteland.

But The Netherlands welcomed the refugees, and the Jewish minority and Protestant majority cultures co-mingled, thrived, and lived together peacefully and prosperously until the invidious German occupation.

Nettie's mother was born Alicia DaSilva, a direct descendent of one of Holland's most brilliant Sephardic families.

Until this letter arrived, Nettie had simply allowed the previous unimpressive bequests to accumulate in a New York bank, drawing interest and partially paying the rent for her apartment, allowing her a bit less financial stress as she continued her residency on an almost non-existent salary. But even when totally combined, they would not even closely equal the annual income from the DaSilva inheritance.

When Pieter arrived, he found her trying to focus on the letter, tears flooding over her face, unable to squelch them, then she cried, " I would so much rather have known my uncle than to receive his money! What good does the money do me? I want my family back! Where is my family?"

Ironically, although they disliked each other, in that outcry, Nettie and Petra might have understood each other.

Pieter put his arms around Nettie as she sobbed, the veneer breaking, troubled by her agony but relieved she was finally allowing him to know her, to witness her vulnerability.

It meant she trusted him.

"It's all right, *meisje*. Go ahead and let it out. Cry as long and as hard as you need to, cry it out, talk about it, whatever you feel you must do."

She did try to stop but failed, shaking with anger and grief, chronically infected with the syndrome named *'familie ziekte'* by the Dutch, which could never be cured, because there was no cure, the desperate, hopeless search by the few Jewish survivors to belong to a family, one which no longer existed.

The family of which only life insurance policies, bank accounts, legal notifications, such as the one she had received, remained to prove it had once been strong, numerous, poor and rich, included vendors barely hawking out a living in the produce and junk marts of The Hague as well as wealthy industrialists and honored professors knighted by the Queen, who resided in the huge, imposing mansions of Wassenaar and Het Belgischpark in Scheveningen.

And of course, the DaSilvas who had lived in Arnhem.

Once she had sworn never to return to the country which had allowed its Jewish citizens to be decimated, ultimately culminating in one of the highest percentage of holocaust victims among the European nations.

A fact which the Dutch authorities preferred not to publicize, instead concentrating the attention and solicitude of the world on the story of Anne Frank, one little child-genius betrayed along with thousands of other anonymous forgotten children. Among whom undoubtedly were other geniuses.

Or to glorify (justifiably) the handful of Christian citizens who felt it their moral duty to rescue their innocent suffering compatriots, who had, after all, given the world the Ten Commandments.

On the whole however, most of the nation's Jewish population was deported without much public protestation, their assets stolen and distributed, and they were soon murdered.

And forgotten.

Nettie realized her vow would be broken, she would have to return at least once more to face the obscene results of German generated horrors, be educated in family data, marital situations, places and dates of births and deaths, learn the names of still more Polish concentration camps. To absorb facts she had tried to ignore but now understood were essential so she could temporarily at least, transform the anonymous mounds of ashes which were her family into personalities once more, give them names, dignity, inform the calloused world they had indeed lived and would be remembered!

"Tomorrow, I'll inform the hospital. Perhaps they'll allow me to continue my residency but grant me a leave of absence. I have to do this, Pieter. As soon as possible."

"Do you want me to come with you?"

"No. I have to adjust. I need to cry by myself. But write to me. And I will try to phone you."

"When you return, Nettie, I will ask you to marry me. First bury your dead, mourn them, honor them. But *lieveling*, don't let them claim you, too. You must somehow overcome what is ahead of you and think of a better future. If the horror is too overwhelming, contact me and I will come to you. Immediately."

She didn't answer but reached up and kissed the earnest young Dutchman (as he had dreamed she would), of her own accord.

A few nights later, they stood together on the roof of Columbia-Presbyterian Hospital, watching the lights sparkling across, around, through the George Washington Bridge as it united New York and the Palisades of New Jersey.

Above them, the sky glowed rosy pink near the span, becoming gradually darker, denser, the farther they gazed north, away from its eternal daylight, while to their left the clouds hung, smoke filled, above the skyscrapers of Manhattan.

Tomorrow, early, he would drive her to the airport, help her get settled, manage somehow to control his dismay, while he watched the plane take her away. And, with it, all he cared for and aspired to, for the rest of his life, but not yet, not yet...not for a few more hours.

Daybreak, madness, hauling suitcases, driving through rush hour traffic to the airport, checking luggage, showing passports and tickets, finding the correct gate, his flowers wilting in her arms, a café open even this early in the morning. A glass of *tot ziens* wine. No kisses or displays of affection.

She, busy, nervous, her kinky hair unwilling to be tamed, writhing in every direction around her head. He, solemn, pale, but as usual carefully groomed, speaking with difficulty, his throat swelling around the urgent words, gagging him.

"Remember, if you need me. Don't hesitate. Not an instant. If you want to write, I'll answer promptly. Here is my family's address in Amsterdam. Use it. I have phoned to tell them about you."

"That I am Jewish?" she asked, expectantly, warily.

"Everything about you. They want to meet you. Welcome you."

"I'm not sure how I'll react to what's ahead, how much I can absorb. It might be too much and I may just want to run away."

"Nettie. Let me come with you!" he begged, aware of how fragile she actually was, despite the hauteur of her attitude, terrified she might harm herself.

She was cognizant of what he was feeling. "It's all right, Pieter. Really it is. I am stronger than you think. Knowing your parents are there and I am not completely alone is already a huge support."

"My mother said to tell you the coffee is always ready for you, the *appeltaart* is warming in the oven although she's still whipping the cream and might need a moment to remove her apron after you ring the bell. But she said to insist you wait."

Nettie replied, "If I ring the bell, I will wait. I promise."

"And I will wait too. When the plane brings you back, I will be here to meet you."

Then he added," But please don't bring a windmill with you. I can't get it into the car. Besides, as you discovered at Halloween I am perfectly capable of constructing as efficient a one for you right here. Aside from that, you can haul back whatever you like. Plus a *gemberkoek* for me, please."

"And *zoutedrop*?"

"Uh, all right, if you have space."

The doors swung open, she walked away, waved. He threw her a kiss and watched the lovely silver plane as it glided into the sky and disappeared, tiredly got into his car and went to find solace and traces of her at the I . House.

Chapter 37

Loneliness pervaded everything. She saw a man who walked like him on Fifth Avenue, recognized his smile on the face of a French movie actor, his dimples on an American one, heard songs they had listened to together, winced but sang softly along.

Dev was not present but not in the remotest sense at all absent.

Petra gazed at her uneaten salad—fragrant sweet strawberries, chunks of brown-eyed pineapple, melon in shades of palest orange, green and vivid red, creating a multi-hued halo around a mound of white cottage cheese—resting on fresh curly lettuce and endive leaves. The heavily laden plate was so beautiful it should have been painted.

And she couldn't eat even a mouthful.

"*Hallo meisje. Mag ik bij je komen zitten?*"

"*Ja hoor, Pieter, natuurlijk.* Sit down. But I'm not very good company."

"Me neither. We can be miserable together. Talk or not talk if we choose. How long still?"

"I don't know. His sister's wedding is next month. School starts soon after and he only has a few more months to finish here. Then he'll probably clerk somewhere in India or England."

"And what about you?"

She shrugged. "Who knows? *Wie dan leeft wie dan zorgt.* Did you see Nettie off at the airport?"

He nodded.

"You've become a good friend, but she is always cold to me. It's difficult to be nice to her."

"I know. But maybe this trip will force her to banish some of her ghosts or at least teach her how to live with them. Then maybe she'll forgive the rest of the world for what happened. Petra, try to understand. She appears stone hard but she isn't. It's all veneer, defensive machination. She's terrified of being hurt and I can't fault her, can I?"

"Still, I've never done a thing to her and she hates me!"

"Envies, probably. You didn't experience the family separation, the misery, the feeling of being 'different.' And you don't know what anti-Semitism is about."

"Not the way she does. But right here in New York I was restricted from joining the local tennis club or taking dancing lessons and I couldn't join the Girl Scouts."

"But the Girl Scouts is international. How can that be?"

"The troops are run locally and make their own rules. When I was about ten, a classmate invited me to one of their meetings, which was held at a church about three blocks from our apartment. Really convenient, particularly during the winter when it's cold and the snow is deep. Everyone was very polite at first, then I heard the adult troop leader (probably someone's mother) telling my friend she had been thoughtless. Had she forgotten? Jews were not allowed! The bitch made no effort to be discreet, intended for me (and all the other girls) to overhear. But I was only a little kid who had already fled Europe for the same reason. I understood what she said but not why."

"What did you do then?"

"Asked my parents why Jews were hated. They ignored the question. Ironically, we didn't belong to a synagogue and I felt isolated among my Jewish classmates, too. Later, I learned there was a 'Hebrew' troop, which met at a synagogue about three miles away from my house, too far to walk in bad weather. Besides, I didn't know any of the girls who were in it."

"I bet every year you buy lots of Girl Scouts cookies."

"Rooms full!" Petra sneered.

"I got back at them, though. Another classmate invited me to a Camp Fire Girls meeting. I asked her if they took Jews and she didn't know what I meant. Remember, we were both children. Anyway, the troop leader, a Mrs. Van Tassel, immediately made me feel at home. She never asked about my religion or raised the subject. I was a member for many years. It was a great organization."

"So, joining a rival group was your revenge," Pieter wondered.

"No, it was much better. We peddled donuts (not cookies) and one year our troop sold a lot of them. Mrs. Van Tassel was asked to escort several of us to Campfire Girl headquarters in Manhattan so we could receive some unnamed recognition. We had no idea what to expect and then, suddenly, Eleanor appeared, accompanied by a photographer."

"Eleanor? THE Eleanor?" he asked in amazement.

"There's only ONE Eleanor. Photo appeared in *The New York Times*."

He chuckled, "I wonder if those bigoted little brats and their mouse-brained troop leader saw the picture."

"I'm sure they did, because I brought the paper to school to show my teacher. They simpered a bit, pretended not to be jealous but undoubtedly told their other friends, and so on and so on. But I didn't understand the underlying reasons for the prejudice. And still don't."

"Neither do I, *meisje*. In Holland we allowed a hundred thousand of our citizens to be murdered. I live with the guilt."

"You were helpless, your people under occupation with no way to defend yourselves, much less try to help the others. And Holland is on the sea, making escape almost impossible."

"My people?" he repeated incredulously. "Don't you understand? Petra, the Jews were my people, too. And had been for centuries, were decent citizens, sent their children to school with us. Many had intermarried with the rest of the population, and the great majority were completely assimilated. THEY were US and WE were THEY. "Others," you said. What OTHERS? We were one people who observed different rites, Catholic rites, Protestant rites, Jewish rites. But we were all citizens of The Netherlands. Full citizens."

He stared at nothing and mumbled, "We could have done more. Only Rotterdam openly resisted."

"And was heavily punished for it," she interpolated.

"But the Rotterdammers can hold their heads up now, since the *rot moffen* are defeated. They know they tried. As for the rest of the big cities..." He shook his head in dismay, then took a deep breath as if he had been temporarily relieved of his anger. Abruptly, he changed the subject. "If you're not going to eat the salad and will only let it get warm and slushy, I'll fight you for the pineapple."

"Go get your own, you cheap Dutchman." She promptly forked a chunk and gobbled it down.

"Guess I'll have to." He stood up, "Don't run away. The conversation can only get more optimistic from now on."

With a fair amount of gusto, they managed to finish a complete meal, surprised their appetites had returned.

"More coffee?" he suggested, took their mugs to the never-empty pot in the corner and greeted Parvati and Alan, who were just entering. Alan glanced at the two Netherlanders with a knowing grin, but Parvati simply seemed confused and began to walk to a distant table.

"Please join us. It's so long since we've seen you," Petra insisted. "Bring two more chairs and come sit down."

As they complied, Petra observed the shy radiance which encircled the doctor, her shining eyes, the glow of her skin, the bend of her neck as she heeded Alan's words, the smile slight and mysterious, teasing her mouth, all knowing and tolerant. Only when she suddenly laughed aloud did the unnerving ugliness return, her teeth protruding like yellow enamel shields to protect her lips and the soft open vulnerability beyond.

Her demeanor was so obvious that no one needed to guess. Alan, who continually smiled his affable, brilliant smile, laughed about everything with vulgar guffaws, and to everyone's astonishment blatantly exposed his proprietary conquest by encircling Parvati's shoulder with one manicured hand and letting it accidentally glance across and around her breast, removing it quickly after insuring it had been adequately noticed.

After the slight shiver of surprise she felt, Parvati appeared not at all disturbed, continuing her diffident radiance, dreaming no doubt of the night ahead. This accidental intimate gesture meant for her alone had surely not been noticed by anyone else.

"There's a single showing of 'Camille' at the Thalia Theater this evening. Does anyone want to come with me to see it?" Pieter asked and was delighted the other three decided to accompany him. Wordlessly, Alan and Parvati agreed to act as chaperones, guaranteeing the two blond Netherlanders would have no time alone together. Parvati supposedly to protect the absent Dev. Alan, to protect Alan and any unformed plans he might make for the future.

"Do you miss Dev," Alan asked innocently but loudly enough to insure Pieter had overheard. Petra didn't answer. There was no reason to confide in this man whose intentions she never quite trusted. She smiled vapidly at him and remained silent.

The Garbo "Camille" was luminously lighted, fragile, unearthly, poetically doomed. It was also a seat-squirmingly embarrassing performance, and Petra realized the legendary Swedish beauty had wisely withdrawn from the film industry before she would be inevitably exposed as one of its worst actresses.

As they left the theater, they saw Ellen and Salmi (with the perpetual appendage). Salmi greeted Petra and, being a true gentleman, held the door open for her, while he gestured for the others to wait.

She assumed it was the exit and walked blithely through, smelling its stink before she even saw what was inside, whirled around and faced an audience of hysterical people (those she knew as well as complete strangers) who had witnessed the faux pas. Red-faced, she joined in with their boisterous laughter. What else could she do? Salmi expected tears or maybe a horrified flight from the theater, anger, bewilderment.

But Petra would NEVER let Salmi defeat her!

"Well, thank goodness," she informed her friends and enemies, "my education is being supplemented again. I was under the arrogant impression I knew absolutely everything! But tonight I've learned how the interior of a urinal looks. I find the white-yellow tiles uninspiring but the perfume does have a lingering quality, doesn't it? It's probably because of the high alcohol content!"

She graciously turned to Salmi and asked, "Will you join us for a nightcap, Salmi?"

The surly Turk agreed. Ellen, hanging onto his arm, pulled them all out onto the street.

Chapter 38

On Friday, late in the afternoon, Wilson Burken, in his normal, pompous manner, announced his presence was required in Brussels for an urgent meeting and therefore he would be absent the following week. She, however, was expected to remain in the office during regular hours each day, write the usual news releases and distribute them to the appropriate media and without his omniscient guidance be held totally responsible for any errors they might contain.

In addition, there was a possibility he might extend his European visit and would notify her accordingly, since she would then, the great man ordered, be required to take her annual vacation during the extra period he was absent...and upon his return they could both go back to work without any prolonged interruption.

He had not bothered to give her earlier notice of the impending trip, and she had no time to make extensive plans for the unexpected workless days ahead.

Feeling somewhat between a caged bird set free and one about to be imprisoned again for the weekend, Petra took the evening train to Washington, tired, anxious, lonely, apprehensive.

And was greeted by an effusive Sofie, "Darling! Welcome home! Put your suitcase down, dinner is waiting for you. I have wonderful news!"

Petra kissed her parents, sighed, obeyed the joyous commands and joined them at the dining table.

"Guess what? Dad's retiring in February and we're moving back to New York. You'll have your own room and won't have to pay that awful woman rent any more. If you want to, you can give us a little money every month but we'll settle it later."

The news shocked the girl. Living conditions with Mister and Missus were hardly ideal and in spite of heavy searching, to date she had been unable to find another affordable room.

But moving back with her parents, having her mother in complete control, appeared even worse!

And the nights with Dev! Oh God, would they be over now forever?

Then she remembered!

Dev?

Perhaps he was never returning anyhow. In his letters he wrote eloquently of his loneliness, how much he missed her but never mentioned when he was flying back to America.

Sofie would not be denied, however. Far more perceptive than her dreamy-eyed daughter suspected, she had been aware from the beginning about the danger of losing her, horrified by the obvious depths of Petra's emotions for a man she had never met, nor personally approved.

At night as she lay awake in bed next to Sam, she imagined her blonde child thrown among a multitude of dark strangers in a foreign country, unable to speak the language, alone and unshielded.

And she unable to help!

Sofie's maternal instincts screamed at her not to permit this mismatched, potentially tragic relationship to continue any longer. To stop it now, to rescue her gullible, innocent child. Petra would eventually be grateful, she knew, for the role her mother would play in saving her from certain disaster. As she had done before!

At the moment, Sofie knew he was far away, home in India and hoped he would stay there but dared not gamble. She could not risk losing her daughter.

And Albert!

More than a month ago, she had begun to harass Samuel, long piteous speeches about the reason she saved their lives, convincing him of the foreign-tinted threat to their small family, until gentle, compliant, he concurred with her endless arguments, and exhausted, calculated their assets, relieved to determine they could easily make the move, and he would never have to work again. The stock market and banks would work for them instead.

Sofie was ecstatic!

Her plans were not dead, and she could carry on with them in New York just as well.

Albert might have to work a little harder, of course, but could still prevail. Manhattan was not so far from Washington, he had a new car and plenty of money to pay for a train ticket if he didn't want to drive, knew how to read and write, could lick postage stamps and dial a telephone.

And. of course, she would help him. As she always did and had done, just a few days previously.

As promised, she contacted him when there was news, informed him Petra would be coming for the weekend. No, she was not currently involved with anyone else and it would be a good idea if he consulted the newspapers to see if any cultural events were being offered on, say, Saturday evening. A concert, for instance.

Yes, she was aware classical music bored him, but he should make a sacrifice, for once. Try to act as if he was becoming interested, since Petra had said he only liked going to western movies, which in turn bored her. After they were married, he need never go to a concert again.

Sofie hung up the phone, feeling she had done them both a great service and hoped they would appreciate her efforts on their behalf.

Petra was too worn out and lonely to fight this arranged tête-á-tête but when he called to confirm it, reminded Albert very firmly she would only consent if he understood they were friends.

Nothing more.

He assured her he understood.

Saturday evening was cloudy but Washington-warm and humid, typical weather for early August. Albert had discovered a culturally acceptable event that suited him perfectly, light, easy music, which he might even have heard before. Petra would love it, he knew. It seemed a sacrifice he could manage.

The Watergate Concerts, offered during the hot summer, tonight featured a well-known soloist who would perform a melodious, familiar piano concerto (to Albert none were familiar but when he mentioned its name to an acquaintance learned it was one of the staples of the musical repertoire, easy to endure, even for non-lovers of music).

Thank God!

Better still, the performance took place in an outdoor amphitheatre. This feature suited Albert perfectly since he had allergies and frequently suffered choking attacks from breathing stagnant air in confined areas. Although the malady never manifested itself when he attended yet another of his beloved, endless, mindless, plotless cowboy films, where the air reeked of buttered popcorn and cigarette clouds wafted around the screen

People nodded in tempo as the overly familiar first section ended and the quiet music of the second movement followed.

Accompanied by muted rumbling in the distance.

By the beginning of the last movement, with its renewed crashing chords and intermittent rests introducing one crescendo after another, cool drops were falling on the unprotected listeners, many of whom immediately fled for shelter under a bridge.

Others remained seated, but when the rain finally erupted full force, accompanied by searing lightning flashes and the boom of thunderclaps, the rest of the audience scrambled to join them, leaving the soloist and the full orchestra continuing to perform before a soaking wet amphitheater filled with unpeopled metal folding chairs.

From beneath their relatively dry places under the bridge, few onlookers actually left, preferring instead to listen and watch as the music continued, wonderfully and coincidentally synchronized as lightning bolts and racing clouds streaked across the sky, while terrifying thunderheads, their infuriated roarings multi-seconds long, subsided and started anew.

Petra, huddled with Albert under the bridge, and until the storm hit, snobbishly bored, was simultaneously frightened and jubilant, never having expected a performance this passionate or unique. She became transformed, her eyes which had been tired and dead, bloomed alive. "What a miracle! A marriage of nature and art!" she thought, embracing the phenomenon ecstatically.

She glanced at Albert and saw his face was petulant, not at all reflecting the exultation, the passion, the freedom she felt. He hunched deeply into his dampened jacket and whined, "I'm really getting wet. Can't we leave now?"

"No," she whispered immediately, not willing to miss even one note. "It's magnificent."

A few minutes later, the soloist waved to the people under the bridge and gestured towards the piano, ran one hand over the keys and held it up.

His fingers dripped with rain water, but a few placid bars of the concerto actually still remained to be played, a melodious flute interval to signify the Grieg-composed storm had passed. However, the real one at the Watergate concert had no intention of quitting.

It was time for the remainder of the performance to be halted. Loud applause from the semi-sheltered audience under the bridge erupted for the musicians as they walked off stage, carrying their dripping instruments if they could, escaping to the dry interior of the barge.

The soloist left last, thanking the people and bowing. The silent piano only remained on stage, accepting whatever music nature chose to compete with it.

"This is the most extraordinary concert I've ever heard," Petra murmured as they sloshed through the deluge towards Albert's car. She wasn't surprised when his only response was a sniffle. He didn't understand, and she had known he would not, then flinched as she remembered Dev's first experience with grand opera, his face transfixed by the music and the action on stage, his voice whispering, "Why didn't anyone ever tell me about this before?"

And, as quickly, another memory flooded over her.

A few weeks ago, when New York's young springtime light only hovered for a little while at dawn and the rest of the day appeared grey, wet, depressing, hunger forced them into the street to forage for an early morning open restaurant.

The rain fell blindingly thick, and she blinked against its ferocity, shivering with the unwelcome chill. But Dev lifted his head to catch the torrents of water full on his face, drinking it in with open eyes and mouth, raising both his arms towards heaven to receive it, dancing in joyous circles.

"You're sopping wet, you silly thing. Come on, over there is a coffee shop. Hurry! Let's get inside and warm up. I'm frozen!"

But he just continued to dance. "No, not yet. I want to enjoy the touch of it. I love the rain and I don't care if I get wet. Do you know each year we wait for it, endlessly it seems. And every year we are desperate, convinced it shall never return again. When finally the water clatters against the roofs, everyone rushes outside to praise God. You don't know what it is to ache for the monsoon's waters, to cleanse and refresh after the heat and the dust, to fear daily minute by minute there will never be relief." His arms raised in benediction, he gazed with exultation up into the dark, pouring heavens.

"You idiot! This rain is very different. It is cold and dangerous, and personally I find it not at all exhilarating. On the contrary. It depresses me."

"No, my love. It is never depressing. It is a blessing, and its coldness does not alter it. When I feel it like this, pouring into my mouth, I know it is really there. Do you understand," he pleaded, "a little bit?" while the water streamed over him.

With maternal dismay, she watched the drops accumulating and splashing over his clothes, turning them instantly into sodden messes. Unperturbed, he radiated health and joy.

"Yes, my wonderful, beautiful little boy," she said, "I understand. But I do not sympathize with the idea of you catching pneumonia. Now, come on. Let's have coffee."

Petra had taken the deliriously giddy boy by his elbow and pushed him towards the dry comfort of the restaurant and out of the rain.

Now she waited while Albert searched for his keys, opened a door for her and got into the driver's seat. She had been smiling but now frowned, wondering if she would ever see Dev again.

Albert, with his usual inability to read her moods, immediately attempted to kiss her. Disgusted, she pushed him away. "No. No. You promised!"

Still oblivious and convinced she would eventually return to him, he responded blithely, "Until I see a diamond on your third finger, left hand, I'm going to keep trying. But I won't force myself on you. Want to stop at a Hot Shoppe for a midnight snack? They have terrific hot fudge ice cream cake."

She declined, preferring to relive in solitude the passion of the music and its unexpected accompaniment.

And to imagine a dusty land she had never seen, where rain was a blessing, and a young man with the face of an angel danced around in it, his arms raised in thanksgiving.

Chapter 39

As promised, on Wednesday, Wilson Burken, the epitome of both efficiency and consideration, notified Petra via a secretary housed in an upstairs office that he would indeed extend his Brussels sojourn with an additional *'semaine'* in Paris. And reminded her to take one week of her annual vacation during his absence.

She welcomed the idea of a break but didn't know where to spend it.

An acquaintance suggested a resort in the Catskills, which suited her limited funds, and she booked a room for seven nights beginning on Friday. She had never been to the Borscht Belt before and had no idea what to expect.

Immediately, she was surrounded by predators (whose workweek frustration would be assuaged—they assumed—by the many desperate women encountered at the long bar...women who would gladly do anything to find a few hours of affection with whoever offered it at whatever price), males who considered Petra prime, eligible, available meat. Since she was tired but not at all desperate, her languor made her even more tantalizing. The men, intrigued by her reticence, badgered her continually to join them in their rooms. She was not in the mood for physical or psychological joining, however, but was eventually convinced to attend a huge party that one man insisted she simply HAD to attend. She doubted his sincerity and, dubious but curious, knocked on his door and heard loud music and people giggling.

"Just open it and come in," someone shouted.

She did and was faced with the "host" lying on an unmade bed, wearing only his bulging underpants and embracing an aging nude female with each arm.

"Welcome. Join the party!" he invited, gesturing with one semi-occupied hand to a bottle and some glasses on a bedside table. "There's room for one more," he said, glancing towards the foot of the bed. The two women, ugly and whiskey-unintelligible, sprawled over his compliant torso and covered it with kisses. He nibbled agreeably at each needy face and lay back, closed his eyes and, sighing happily, allowed them to minister to him.

Petra walked out as he protested, "C'mon. We're having fun here. Don't leave!" She didn't bother to respond, hurried to her room, showered and went to sleep.

Alone.

If Friday could be called disastrous, Saturday evening was catastrophic.

The nightclub/lounge was packed with singles on the hunt. She ordered a soft drink and was approached by a burly man in his early thirties, fair haired, athletically built, stocky and strong, despite the glasses he wore. He introduced himself as "Randy," informed her he was a lawyer, pasted himself on a barstool adjoining hers and discouraged anyone else from getting near. She found his conversation boring and approach too aggressive, tried to get away from him several times, but he playfully blocked her way with his arm and stood sturdily in front of her.

Towards midnight, people were leaving. Randy informed her that he would escort her safely to her door but as soon as the elevator closed with them inside, lunged at her. She recoiled, suddenly aware that her room had no telephone and was located in an area where daytime renovations were being made. It had not bothered her earlier, because like everyone else, she was rarely there anyway.

But now, to her horror, she recalled she had not seen even one other guest in the remote third floor hallway, and it occurred to her there might in fact not be one!

Her mind instantly went into survival mode and her instincts were screaming "danger!" The elevator left, and they were now quite alone. Maybe she could out-think him, she hoped, not wanting the "friendship" to progress an iota further, although she accepted quickly that if he chose to overpower her, she had absolutely no chance against this bull-physiqued brute.

They were at her door, and he confidently demanded the key. She held on to it and said, "I'm sorry but my roommate wouldn't approve," and smiled up at him, although she was trembling with fear.

"You have a roommate?" he replied, not at all convinced.

"Yes. Remember? The lovely brunette in the red evening gown at the other end of the bar talking to the man in the blue blazer." Petra had indeed seen someone of that description first on the dance floor and then later seated a few stools away.

He took his fist and banged heavily on the door. Of course, no one responded. "Well, she's not here now. So I can come in for a little while. Until she comes."

"No. It's not a good idea."

"I think it's a very good idea. Give me the key."

Petra sensed telling him outright she would never go to bed with him, actually wanted him to disappear, now, immediately, would only infuriate him and perhaps excite him even more. Trying to reason with him would be wasted effort.

She had to outwit him. Or be raped. Or perhaps worse.

She felt every nerve in her body tingling, warning her, each heartbeat pulsing inside her chest, behind her eyes, but her brain was functioning perfectly. Honed by desperation.

Taking a deep breath she sighed, "All right," watched him relax and labored to keep her voice steady, "but only for a few minutes. I just want to look inside first to make sure she didn't leave the place in a big mess."

Petra turned the key in the lock, and had the door opened and closed in his face before Randy realized he was standing in the hall.

By himself.

For the next three hours or more, he screamed at her to let him in, pleaded, entreated, assured her he would not hurt her, pounded continuously on the locked door. No one heard him because there was no one to hear him.

Or to help her, either.

She urged him to go away, reiterated she would not let him in, but he refused to leave. Finally, tired of the useless argument, she turned off the light, said, "Good night, Randy, see you tomorrow," but remained fully clothed seated on the bed, holding a high-heeled leather, lethal sandal in each hand, wide awake and ready, should the door splinter open. And if it did, she would fight with all her strength and, before eventually losing, wound him badly.

Guaranteed!

In the darkness the light from the hallway showed her exactly where he was standing directly before the threshold of the room, where the door and the floor had not quite connected, clearly revealing his shoes.

Just a few inches away.

She stared at them, trapped, helpless but for now still in temporary safety from behind the locked door.

Watched those shoes.

He walked away, noisily, saying, "Well, so long," making certain she heard him leave, whistling as he left. But she looked down and saw the shoes again. There, on the threshold, quiet shoes, not meant to be seen or heard. But noticed just the same.

Was he hoping to fool her into turning the light back on, into perhaps foolishly opening the door to see if he was really gone?

Whatever his motives, she did not move from her place on the bed, did not undress or lay down for an instant the only weapons she had, still firmly clutched in each hand.

Both of them waited.

He, sometimes loudly begging or pretending to leave but always returning, his telltale shoes showing plainly. She, absolutely silent.

As daylight appeared, he finally gave up, convinced she was actually asleep and his efforts were useless. But she had not slept at all. By 7 a.m. when she heard the workmen down the hall beginning to saw and hammer, she was at the front desk, complaining loudly, demanding another room on a lower floor where other guests would be staying, insisting on having a telephone.

No! Not later. Immediately! Or she would not remain for the rest of the week and complain directly to the media about the terrible security in this so-called resort!

The desk clerk, a startled, middle-aged woman, stared at her, raised her eyebrows and complied, meanwhile assuring Petra the remainder of her stay would be very pleasant, the situation would not happen again, management was really sorry, an oversight. Please, another chance?

Later, by the swimming pool, Randy approached her again, greeting her as an old friend. She got up, took her things and walked away before he could reach her. Towards early afternoon, along with most of the other weekend-only guests, he left the resort. That evening, in her new room, with the telephone close by, she pondered what Dev's reaction might be if he ever was made aware of what had happened. Dev, oh Dev, where are you? she wondered and mourned.

Chapter 40

When he stopped for an instant to consider the last few years, how they had transformed him, he was amused and amazed. Looking at himself in the mirror would be the first indication of the changes. The dark, strong face with its straight nose and full mouth was unfashionably devoid of the necessary Indian mustache. In fact, when he first succeeded in growing one (just as all his contemporaries did) it had seemed a necessary puberty rite, the proud symbol of his manhood and mature virility. Now he was conspicuous, because he was clean-shaven and despite continual pressure from both the male and female members of his family, stubbornly refused to grow it again.

As third son of an upperclass Punjabi and his devout Hindu wife, Dev's childhood in Karachi consisted primarily of school, prayers, cricket games and the close traditional, extended family relationship. Both his married, older brothers, their wives and children lived within the family compound. But Dev was the pampered youngest brother and adored elder one. His little sister always considered him her best friend, and he was her prime protector.

It appeared his own future would continue in normal tranquility, but suddenly in 1948 India, freed from colonial rule, was thrown into a bloody, religious, civil war. A war politically fomented between people who had lived harmoniously for centuries, who were the same race, spoke the same languages, shared the same culture and proud ancient history.

With horror and cynicism, he recalled the embarrassing orders for all males to lower their undergarments so they could be inspected. The victorious, circumcised Moslems retained the area, which would be renamed Pakistan. The Hindus were murdered, or if fortunate enough to have escaped by whatever means (as Dev and his family), left everything behind and fled, while only memories of their Punjabi homes and Muslim friends remained.

They settled in Bombay. The older brothers soon found suitable wives, joined and expanded the family businesses. Ultimately, partition seemed to have had little effect on their financial and social status. Although he could not drive himself, the patriarch's garage held Bentleys, Jaguars, and Austin-Healeys to be used by his sons at will, while he and the women had the full-time services of several chauffeurs. The new compound was enclosed by a thick wall, which effectively separated them from what lay beyond.

Which didn't really interest them anyway.

Dev's beautiful mother, devout and sincere, convinced her husband to let her endow the building of a temple school nearby. A truly good woman, who believed the impoverished people on the streets of the huge city had committed some evil deed in a previous life, she considered their suffering a punishment from God, to be endured in silence and with humility. By accepting it and learning from it, they too would ascend to a better life in the next cycle of reincarnation. In the meantime, she and her family would benefit from the blessings they had earned as a result of their virtue in the past, while the school she envisioned would assuage some of the difficulties for the children (innocent or not) in the challenging present.

As soon as his sister's elaborate wedding festivities were finished, Dev's mother began the search for a potential bride for her one remaining single child. And what a child! There were plenty of willing families ready to send their most beautiful daughters, arms laden with flowers, coffers filled with jewels and money, for the privilege of marrying the handsome, wealthy bachelor. And, since it was known he was studying abroad, he would of course take his bride with him to learn the sophisticated and exotic ways of the West firsthand. In all, a wondrous future awaited her!

Dev tried his best, wanted to please his well-meaning parents, was polite to the eager young women and their families, but was not interested. Their beauty stirred his senses deeply, their giggling compliance bored him even more. Months ago, he had surpassed the need for simple sexual satisfaction, used now to the stimulation and challenge of a partner who always instantly defied him, made him laugh aloud with delight, and sometimes even succeeded in conquering his best arguments. And then taunted him shamelessly when she won!

He remembered the first time he had seen Petra, her cheeks bright red against the fair skin, the blonde hair curled in wet wisps around her face. Most explicitly, he recalled how suddenly his stomach had churned and he acted without even thinking of the consequences, intent on meeting her no matter what.

Not one of the lovely women who his mother brought to him caused the same effect...or anything even resembling a slight stir. No matter how hard they tried. Or he did.

And he did try.

His mother watched, absorbed, understood, but remained silent and waited for him to tell her.

In good time, she knew he would.

She was wrong.

Chapter 41

By Wednesday, bored with being the eternal deer attempting to escape from the penis-weaponed hunters who made the week-long vacation more into an eternal flight from potential unwanted impalement instead of a time to relax and recuperate from the stress of being Wilson B.'s flunky, Petra left the resort, spent the next few days in Washington listening to her mother enthuse about the impending move to New York, returned to her ghastly little room with Mister and Missus and, on Sunday evening, finally wandered into the I. House.

Pieter was sitting alone, reading a letter limp from folding and re-folding, when she slid into a seat across from him. The happy look in his eyes instantly revealed who had written it. "She's fine. And, thank God, discovered she misses me. *Meisje*, perhaps, perhaps after all, there is hope for her. For both of us."

"Oh Pieter, how wonderful it would be if you finally found the way to reach each other. After what she has suffered and your patience, you both deserve a lot of happiness."

Pieter nodded. "And Dev? Have you heard from him?"

"He writes but doesn't state when or if he is coming back."

"Nettie plans to be here in a week or so. She must finish with the legalities and then will never have to worry about the future. Even though she'll still earn a resident's salary, she'll be able to afford a decent place to live. Eventually set up her own practice if she wants it. Her life will be far easier now."

"Maybe she'll decide never to practice; after all, medicine is not an easy life.."

"Nettie? Not practice medicine? *Kind ben je gek*? Medicine is her heart and soul! Her refuge, the only place she has been able to show the other side, the compassionate gentle one, without being terrified she would get hurt again. No, she'll NEVER sacrifice that. Besides," he added proudly, "she is absolutely brilliant at it, both the intellectual and emotional aspects. The patients trust her, love her and she reciprocates. I've seen her hand-feed recalcitrants who wouldn't allow anyone else near them...who refused food for days and meekly swallowed as much as she offered so as not to disappoint her! And a patient with a brain tumor who everyone thought was paralyzed and mute held out her arms for an embrace when Nettie came into the room, and although the words were garbled, the woman tried to talk to her! She is a healer, Petra; giving it up would negate the best part of her character!"

"Then here's to you and Nettie," Petra responded, lifting her coffee cup, "and to your future."

He clinked his cup against hers, "Together, I hope, *meisje*. Because apart from her, mine will certainly be miserable."

"Oh stop mooning like a goddamned teenager in heat!"

"I AM a goddamned teenager in heat!" he laughed.

The following morning, she returned to the office and found an envelope from Brussels containing insignificant information for creating more inane news releases, which Burken expected her to transform into somewhat legible English (and for which he would receive praises and raises while she remained stuck forever at the stultifying sixty-per, dependent and desperate).

Before his European excursion, he had informed her (in an extraordinary moment of democratic communication with an inferior) that at one time, he had been attached to the American Embassy in New Delhi. She was immediately impressed (not by the knowledge of the appointment...who in the State Department was responsible for recommending such an arrogant fool to represent the rest of the Americans?) but by the name of the city. Eagerly, she plumbed him about his experiences, impressions, insights, starved for news of Dev's country and its people.

"Climbed a few mountains," he bragged, pointing too humbly at a black and white print of a Himalayan peak with no human beings in sight.

"Did you get to Kashmir? The beautiful valley of Kashmir?"

He stared at her in confusion, disturbed perhaps that his lowly servant had ever heard of it.

"Yes, I did. Lovely. Nice temperature. Better than Delhi."

"And were you curious about Indian culture? Did you absorb some of their philosophy?"

"Ha, ha," he chortled, "at the embassy? Really, Petra, we had no time for such trivia."

"No. Not during working hours. But in the temples, or talking to people on the street. Were you able to touch ordinary Indian people and learn from them? Could you understand a little of their lives? Their religion? Surely they must have taught you something."

The sneered laugh breezed haughtily across his spoiled, cupid-bowed mouth.

"The Indians themselves? A filthy, stupid people. I did my best to avoid them as much as possible. I really couldn't waste my time making friends with such rabble. Made quite certain I only mixed with the European colony."

She stared at him with disgust. Simultaneously, she mourned silently for the Indian people who had been exposed to Burken and his man-child arrogant authority! And, she jeered mutely, did he insist they call him "sahib," instruct them to bow in humble respect and scrape the ground at his feet?

Mentally she spat at his stupidity and cursed the old-boy network social system that relegated her to labor for such an idiot. She found his triteness elephantine, his depth miniscule. And the mountain of badly written garbage he threw at her did not diminish, nor had he even once voiced appreciation for the work she did to clean it up for him.

Each week she pleaded for the promised (and earned) byline or some acknowledgment which could lead to a position as a copywriter (with greater status and salary), particularly since she knew the Belgian Government Account intimately. Born to the Dutch language and fluent in French, the acquaintanceship with what was required had been easy.

But no surprise, Burken's response (just as everything else in his life and vision) would be now and in the future predictably clichéd.

"Copywriters are a dime a dozen," he pontificated. "I need a good secretary a lot more. But maybe next week."

Next week could easily become next month, next year, next decade, next century, next life.

Her IQ and budget railed silently and insanely at him.

***

Enough! She scolds herself! Right now he is in Paris, supercilious and undoubtedly pretentious but for a few more days I am free of him.

Petra has finished with the monotonous day's work and writes her frustration and despair, the catharsis which saves her sanity and replenishes her squelched spirit.

"The hotel is on the Place Vendome," Burken informs her in a dialogue which never happened.

Well, obviously! Did the arrogant bastard assume she thought it would be on the Rue d'Antin?

They continue their fictional conversation.

"Too bad there are so many French people in Paris. A dirty, stupid bunch, the French. Don't like the dark, ugly little men and their squat, rat-haired women. Filthy wastrels most of them. Must be quite certain to get vaccinated against them before I leave New York."

"Obviously again," she types and then...

"I dream of days in Paris," she writes, "Of cafés near the Rue du Rivoli where people laugh and dine among the fruit-vined doorposts. Chansons in French and English, ubiquitous bottles of fragrant wine too much to drink, too good to waste. Paris, lovely, lovely Paris. God has taken the most beautiful things in the world, gazed at them with tenderness and placed them here, beside the Seine, a glorious gift for the world to succor and appreciate. Paris where even the most unhappy can find surcease albeit for only a drugged moment.

"The office is empty, my work for today quite finished. While Burken struggles with Harvardian French somewhere between Brussels and Lyon my typewriter stares at me. I insert fresh paper and the words of my days and nights spill automatically on it.

"This is being written for the future, for the time when life will no longer resemble the gentle womb which presently encases me, yet urges me to catapult outside myself, take flight, but defies me to break the walls with which infinite tenderness envelop my soul. When each day will no longer encompass this terrible, overwhelming happiness, turning me instantly from a thinking human into a sensual, melting, amorphous being, an expanding entity without shape or form. This exquisite spectrum of emotion, stronger than my negativism, forcing in one instant, tearful joy, the next a peace not known before. I bless my mortality, my humanity and greatest limitations, grateful, bewildered. My daily world comprised of greys and whites is non-existent, and I no longer fight, for deep inside me resounds eternal music."

The phone rings.

"No, I'm sorry. He'll be back next week. You're very welcome."

She replaces the receiver and watches as the door opens. A small man dressed in a rumpled brown suit enters carrying an aged leather briefcase. "I'm doing a customer survey, miss. If you could choose three magazines from this list which would they be?"

"I am not interested in buying a subscription," she answers aware they are alone in the office.

He persists, pushes the list under her hand. "You don't have to. It's only a sort of opinion poll. Go ahead. Just pick any three."

For a little while, her thoughts still half on the sheet in the typewriter she is taken in and glances at the list searching for *'The New Yorker,' 'Réalité,' 'National Geographic,'* knowing they will not be there. And indeed they are not.

Only the usual contemporary, bland men-germinated and published magazines geared towards keeping women in their assigned places at home, wearing frilly lace aprons and robotic smiles, thrilled to clean toilet bowls and share with each other the name of the most effective products to eliminate bathroom odors, to joyously cook three meals a day (and serve them on time), launder endlessly, bear children without discomfort and act uncomplainingly as legalized prostitutes. Only without being paid for any of it. Not one cent.

All contain the same "Ladies Magazines" garbage, pages of recipes, fictional sob stories, directions for being chicly married to interior decorating musts and must nots (this month aquamarine and pale blue are THE colors). And in all of it nothing which interests her in the least little bit. Just one gross compilation of journalistic junk scattered over dozens of magazines.

He sees her hesitate and jumps in, "Quickly now, Miss. Pick three. Certainly there are plenty to choose from. Here's my pen. Just circle the ones you like best." Arbitrarily, she circles three titles, not even actually aware of what they are, anxious to get rid of him so she can return again to her writing dream-world.

"Wonderful choices, Miss. And those three, fortunately for you, fall under a special promotion campaign. Because you assisted with the poll you can have all of them for..." and he quotes an astronomical sum.

"Remember, little lady. It only seems expensive because it's for two full years! Calculated per week it comes to less than four dollars. For such truly excellent magazines. With marvelous information geared expressly towards your personal interests. A small enough amount for so much wonderful entertainment."

He shoves the pen back in her hand along with a subscription form and points to a line for her signature. Hypnotized, she stares at it, confused, brainwashed. Again, he notices her wavering and softly continues coaxing, saving his trump card for last. "Very smart decision, miss. All the girls upstairs are ordering them, too!"

He has overplayed his hand.

At once, images of the high-school-educated secretaries, spike-heeled and cheaply glamorous with their tight skirts and carefully applied make-up, flash into her consciousness. She hears their inane conversations during lunchtime, sees the rows of grey machines (like hers) shackling them forever to someone else's demands, grimaces as she recalls their pitiful preoccupation with movie stars and television programs, their laughably naive obsessions with baseball games and sports heroes.

Her equilibrium has returned and she says firmly, "Thank you. I do not want them. You might remember also this is an advertising agency. We have access to all the print paraphernalia free of charge."

His eyes flash angrily and he looks ready to strike her, when blessedly the door opens again. One of Burken's colleagues marches in, greets her with some condescension and violates the great one's vacant inner sanctum. She does not protest, delighted to see him. A miracle in disguise!

The magazine peddler disappears rather suddenly and, some moments later, after riffling through several papers on the desk and quickly grabbing one, so does the colleague.

She returns gratefully to her inner world.

"A strong yet infinitely tender hand, masculine, the long, fine fingers perennially warm, thawing my winter-frozen limbs, probing the untouched mystery of my soul, holding strongly and carefully my dark newborness to gentle light.

"So, so, do not be afraid, my love. My only love. Come, come and walk with me by the shimmering, by the rippling, come here to the warmth and find shelter in me. Follow me, Rhada. Follow me, little one. Come, my happiness and my hope. Here, to me."

"Follow Rhada, follow," slowly at first for sanctuary is an unknown thing. "Follow Rhada and embrace the supreme joy, which only he, who knows and knows, only he who is forbidden to you can give. The ecstasy of his love is a sheltered thing, its shaded light burns long, its hooded beam burns calm and long, enduring, abiding."

The door opens abruptly, startling her.

"Petra, are you busy? Can you type this letter for me? As long as Wilson isn't here anyway?" Another junior executive colleague but a very nice one.

"Sure, Richard. Bring it here."

"Thanks a lot. I really need to get it in the mail. I tried to do it myself but made a real mess of it. Say, what are you working on?"

"Nothing. Just bored. Wasting a little time. Give me your letter. I'll do it immediately. Service while you wait!"

"Hmmm. He doesn't really appreciate you, does he?"

She shrugged and began to type.

Chapter 42

The summer heat receded gradually, and autumn descended on Manhattan, transforming the dried green leaves into brilliant reds, golds, yellows, which soon pillowed the streets and sidewalks with a soft carpet of foliage.

Students from all over the world arrived at the I. House, their faces echoing the terrifying newness which every one of their predecessors had felt as strongly. Suddenly they were startled awake, forced to adapt immediately to a new language, school and culture and the realization that they were now completely anonymous residents of the most vibrant city in the world (which did not accept weakness or homesickness and would do little to help alleviate either). Additionally, although they might have been outstanding in their home countries, in New York they were absolutely nothing extraordinary and would not be cosseted.

For many, it would be the first time away from their families, for others the voyage itself had already been the farthest from their immediate environments. Lonely, frightened, they found empathy among their dormitory mates at the I. House and clung to each other, learning to share the mistakes they made, laughing at themselves, learning together, adjusting. Loving or hating the enormous city where they now resided.

Pieter wandered into the lobby, oblivious to anyone and anything, staring with joy at another letter he was reading and bumped unchivalrously into Parvati. She stumbled backwards into the wall and moaned softly.

"Oh God, I hope you aren't hurt," he gasped, reached out to catch her, embarrassed at his own stupidity.

"It's all right, Pieter. A little bruise. Don't be alarmed, please." She rubbed her elbow quickly.

"What a sweet lady she is," he thought and apologized again, looked into her face and winced.

If at all possible, she was now uglier than before. Her cheekbones gated the rest of her features, which were sharper, more pointed than he remembered. The hand she used to hold the aching elbow was skeletal, and even beneath the blue sari, he saw no trace of the slightest female softness. The short, midriff-baring blouse she wore covered non-existent breasts and, where it ended her ribs stuck out like matchsticks covered with mottled, wrinkled brown paper.

He was shocked but dared not ask her what had happened. However, she was not so reticent and asked, "Is that from Nettie?"

"Yes," he answered.

"And is she well?"

He nodded. "Yes. She'll be here next week. Thank God. I don't know how I survived without her."

The Indian doctor answered, "I understand how you feel. True love can lead to intense suffering."

Now he dared to speak. "And you, Parvati, how are you? You look a little thin."

"I am quite well, thank you," she replied formally. "Work at the hospital has become quite heavy." She glanced away from him and murmured, "It is not an easy thing to watch a child die. Particularly if she has been your own patient. I will never get inured to it."

She hoped he would be satisfied with her response and since he didn't ask more questions, she said goodbye and took the elevator to her room, dialed Petra's number and waited. "Can you meet me for lunch today, please?"

"Of course. Do you know the Delmonico Hotel? On Park Avenue? At one o'clock?" Petra replied at once, surprised by the phone call since she had seen little of Parvati for several weeks.

She recalled the last time vividly, how despite the gaping hole between her teeth, Parvati appeared almost pretty, laughed easily, was more poised and even came out of her neurotic self-consciousness long enough to jibe at someone in a friendly argument. And although she still doubted his motives, Petra admitted Alan had performed a minor miracle on the uncharacteristically insecure physician-recluse. A shy doctor. Whoever heard of such a phenomenon?

She noticed immediately the new change in Parvati, the obvious weight loss, the dark eyes continuously unable to focus on one thing for more than an instant. But Petra also admired how she ate her lunch, with graceful, lady-like motions, her hands careful and certain. Suddenly Parvati put her dining implements aside and gazed at Petra strangely, nervously and then said very deliberately, "Are all American girls immodest?"

"What are you talking about?"

"Alan had a party a few nights ago and one of the guests simply disrobed so he could take a photograph of her."

"A nude photograph? In front of a room full of people? I've never seen it happen."

"I did not say she was nude. I said she disrobed. All she had on was a black camisole."

"And what else?"

"A black skirt and petticoats."

"And I suppose the blouse she discarded was lace? And you could see the camisole right through it?"

"Yes, you could." Parvati suddenly realized Petra hadn't found the situation particularly shocking.

"So Alan wanted to see a little more skin and some neck. So what? Who was the girl?"

Parvati picked up her water glass, took a quick sip and whispered, "Maria."

"Oh! Are you not seeing Alan anymore, then?"

"Yes. Often. But he seems detached. He used to look at me with tenderness. There is little now. He is much more in control of his emotions." She sighed. "What few emotions there are. That is why I wanted to speak with you. I don't know what to do."

Her thin starved face bore the expression of the clichéd jilted lover. The lunch she barely touched lay on the plate unwanted, becoming with each second less appetizing.

Poor thing, Petra thought, her happiness has lasted for such a short time.

"How do you keep a man in love with you?" Parvati demanded.

Petra replied slowly, "I don't know. And I don't know what motivates a woman to remain in love with a man either, even if he badly abuses her. The feelings are just there or they aren't."

"You have dated many men. You can have any man you want. What do you do to keep him interested?"

"You're exaggerating, Parvati. I have dated a lot of men, but usually it means no more than a solution to the boring alternative of spending the evening alone. It doesn't mean they are in love with me or I with them."

"And Dev then? Is he also such a solution?"

Petra gasped. She hadn't expected such a bitter comment, and it hurt. A lot! At the same time, she realized Parvati was lashing out because she was desperate for answers.

Scowling, she remembered asking the same questions as a teenager, when boys had suddenly become different beings...unknown creatures apparently choosing specific girls to spend time with, based on various exotic formulae whose secret ingredients were unwritten. Why, she had wondered at the time, were some perfectly nice ones always ignored while others were consistently desired and pursued?

And now she was being asked to dissect the amorphous something termed "attraction." She accepted that sometimes she liked a man (and he her) or both realized friendship was the only recourse. But how to explain to a physician, the confused and brilliant woman sitting across from her at the linen bedecked table, who expected a scientific response, which, like the experiments she had performed in medical school could be proved or disproved?

The dark anxious eyes bored into Petra's face, seeking a reaction, an answer to her search. Her sheltered Indian background could never have prepared her for a man like Alan, a predator who took the gift she gave him of herself and indifferently shattered it.

Petra didn't ask for an explanation. She had guessed weeks ago what happened between them was far more than a friendly kiss or a civilized handshake. She was furious at Alan and pitied Parvati.

It must have been obscenely easy for him, knowing he had no rivals and she was an innocent. Morals and ethics? She doubted he cared about either. But Parvati could never resolve a casual affair (despite her physical liability, trained as all Hindu women to chastity and total fidelity to one man). Her exuberance around Alan revealed their secret so blatantly she might as well have worn a billboard which screamed in huge, block letters, "I am doing it! Look at me! Someone wants me!"

"Are all American girls immodest?" she had asked, preoccupied with her own situation, seeking justification, psychologically saturated with the inversion of what had been her past life and the horror it had become in the present.

"No, Parvati, we are not," she finally answered. "You knew the answer before you asked the question. And what Maria did was not even immodest, no more so than Indian women showing their bare midriffs, which you do all the time. As for Dev being a simple solution? What do you mean?"

"Well, he surely was the solution to avoiding lonely evenings, wasn't he? And now Pieter is fulfilling the same function, isn't he?" she wheedled in the lovely sing-song accents of Indian English.

"What? Parvati, what are you thinking? Pieter and I went to a movie once...along with a lot of other people. We have coffee now and then and share a background. But dating? Of course not! He and Nettie belong together. At least he thinks they do. I don't know how she feels. But our conversations are usually about her. Not about him and me!"

"And what then is Dev's place in your life? Suppose he does not come back to New York?"

Petra thought, "Dev? He is the inspiration I never missed but cannot now live without. The reason I see and hear and feel with an intensity I never guessed existed. Or I was capable of. Even now, despite the separation because of what he has taught me, I am totally alive."

She remained silent, not willing to share, but Parvati stared at her, willing a response.

Finally she answered, "I don't know what the future holds for us. But whether he returns or not, I am grateful to have known him at all."

What was the sense, she thought, of trying to elaborate? Parvati would not understand.

Petra realized how stunned she must feel, a woman "ruined;" despite her excellent education, actually just a child, isolated until for one brief instant she had actually touched life and love, then watched helplessly as it callously paraded right past her.

She reached out her hand and took the thin one on the table. "Baboo and Gita, Pieter, Jerry Roth and I are going to see a play this evening. Why don't you join us? The diversion would be good for you."

"I will not be in the way?"

"Of course not. All of us love you, Parvati."

"Then I would be very pleased to be there, too. Except I don't know if Alan will want to see me later. He has not called yet today. You will excuse me if at the last minute I shall cancel?"

"I understand, Parvati. You must do what gives you happiness."

Chapter 43

Alan gazed at the photographs he had taken a few days earlier, his emotions as unstable as if he were experiencing his own deflowerment. She was looking up at him, her lovely, oval face meeting the camera's lens clearly, perfectly, her half-smile teasing him, the lips opened partially to hint at perfect, white teeth. Her shoulders were bare except for the wide straps of the black lace camisole, the rest of her body not visible, just as he had envisioned the shot, so the miracle of her beauty, its perfect symmetry would have no competition.

He gasped and felt himself swelling: Even he had not expected such an instantaneous reaction. She had tentatively agreed to see him again. TENTATIVE, she emphasized, when she accepted the invitation to his party. Tentative, she declared again, when he called today and invited her to accompany him to an art gallery opening, with dinner afterwards. He knew he had to move very slowly if he had even the remotest chance of winning her back. Tonight, for instance, only a friendly good night kiss on the cheek at her door, which surprised her. He desperately wanted to caress, kiss and probe the woman whom he had in the past completely possessed but was astute enough to realize she would have the power to reject him. At this point, he would allow her to think she was actually in control. Besides, he knew she would relent soon enough. He would wait. Probably not for very long. Another dinner or two and then the inevitable. A carafe could hold only so much liquid before it spilled over. Maria would spill over quickly.

Later that same evening, as he lay alone in bed, stone hard, sexual desire coursed through his body, rampant and unfulfilled; clutching his burning hot penis, he reached for the phone again. "I need you now. Get here immediately. I will leave the door unlocked. Just hurry up."

Parvati, who had just returned from the theater, didn't bother to unbutton her coat and obeyed Alan's summons. Weeks earlier, she had quietly accepted the unavoidable reality. She belonged to him completely and would never refuse anything he asked of her.

Her identity had faded and been totally absorbed into his desires.

Chapter 44

Pieter recognized her instantly, black, curly hair carefully hidden beneath a blue cloche, a familiar frown splitting her face into dissatisfied halves, the mouth curled downwards, a semi-circle of discontented repugnance, and his stomach lurched. What had she endured during this trip, he wondered, as again she had been forced to relive the horrors inflicted on her innocent family? How often and for how long would the nightmare be repeated until finally she would be able to heal, mourn the dead but regain her own life?

He took her in his arms, felt her body resist and did not force her, giving her time to adjust. And then she rested for an instant against his shoulder, feeling its strength, knowing suddenly he would be there for as long as she wanted him.

"You've lost weight," he murmured. "Isn't the Dutch food agreeing with you?"

"Oh yes! It's wonderful! The *maatjes haring*, the wonderful *gebak*. But I had so much to do, eating was not a priority. I did remember my promise. Here is your *gemberkoek*!" and she thrust a package at him.

"Nettie, how did it go?"

"Same sad stories. But I think there won't be many new discoveries. Some of the family died at Auschwitz, but most at Sobibor. The remainder who have just disappeared...we'll probably never know what happened to them. I'm finally able to realize how lucky I am to have escaped."

"Did you see the people who adopted you?"

"Yes. I thanked them, treated them to dinner one evening, a strained conversation. We have very little in common now. It was a necessary purging for me. I don't think I want anything else to do with them."

"Did they agree to return the balance of the money your father left for you?"

"It wasn't mentioned. They can keep it. After all, they risked their lives to save mine so they've earned it. But I think if they had talked about it, perhaps offered, I would have respected them more. As it is, there's no need for further contact, unless I choose to initiate it. Right now I just don't."

They hailed a taxi and returned to Manhattan, Pieter feeling for the first time in weeks his life had meaning and was complete again.

Over dinner, he asked her. Her sad, dark eyes gazed into his blue ones, seeing the love, the honesty. And now she was ready to acknowledge how she felt. The separation and its trauma had achieved some good, besides just the financial security.

"Yes, Pieter."

"Nettie. You mean it, don't you? I couldn't bear it if you changed your mind."

"No. I will not change my mind. I've had time to think. I do want to marry you. Very much."

She stopped, looked off past him and said, "Nettie van Hoorn. Sounds much better than the name I have now."

"I have been thinking *meisje*. If it makes things easier, shall I convert?"

Nettie looked at him in astonishment. "No, of course not! Why would you choose to make your life more difficult? Besides," she added, "you have one of those wonderful, non-committal Dutch last names. Would you change it to Levie or Cohen, along with becoming a member of the tribe? Oh, and by the way, are you circumcised?"

"Stop it!" he admonished her. "I am serious! If you think we will be happier both being Jewish I will do it!" and added, "The circumcision isn't necessary, Doctor! That was taken care of long ago!"

"Well then, *schat*. You've already experienced the most painful part. The rest is entirely up to you. But you don't have to convert for me."

"Nettie, Nettie, stubborn Nettie. I love you! I want to tell the world we are getting married."

Part Four
TENERAMENTE

Chapter 45

Jerry Roth, carefully holding a dangerously full cup of coffee in one hand, glanced around for an empty table, saw none, but noticed Petra sitting alone and joined her. They shared the usual "how are you's" and then were both silent; she, looking at nothing; he, frowning, staring into her face. Moments passed, and he could no longer restrain himself. "So, where is he?"

"Still home. In India."

"Is he coming back?"

"I don't know. I haven't heard from him in a while."

"Do you really love him? A man from such a different culture?"

"Yes." A simple, three letter-reply.

"And if he returns and wants to marry you? What will you answer?"

Silence.

"What about your family? Have you told them?"

This time her face contorted into grief.

He continued, "You have discussed him with your parents?"

She nodded. "My mother threatens to disown me, hates him although she has never met him. Soon they are coming to New York and want me to move back in with them. I don't want to, but everything I earn goes into paying for the cage I live in now. Even if I pay them something each month, there'll be enough left so I can save a little."

She stopped and sighed. "I feel trapped. No matter what I do, it's wrong."

He feigned sympathy but was, in fact, elated. "Your mother is right, you know. You cannot continue the relationship with him. And as for marrying? Impossible! Too much has happened and you owe your people a debt. One you absolutely must repay."

She gasped. "What are you talking about? I owe no one a thing!"

He decided to avoid an argument and try another tactic, one less confrontational but perhaps more effective.

If she would cooperate.

"Petra, do you have plans for this evening?"

"No."

"It's Friday night, *sjabbat.* Will you come with me to services at Temple Emanuel?"

She considered the novelty of the experience, and agreed. "But I won't know what to do. I haven't been inside a synagogue since I was a child."

"Most of it will be in English. No one cares if you know Hebrew or not, and the Friday service is usually led by young adults. Finish your coffee and let's go."

They were just leaving as a radiant Pieter and Nettie (for once smiling) arrived. Nettie embraced Jerry, indifferently acknowledged Petra's existence and then the couple joyfully announced their news.

"Do you want to join us at shul?" Jerry asked. Nettie started to decline but Pieter stopped her. "Yes. That's a wonderful idea! I want to learn everything I can about my soon-to-be-wife's heritage. We are definitely coming with you. Besides," he added, "we need all the blessings we can get from now on!"

Nettie mumbled an "okay," and decided to let him win this particular battle, took his arm, and they all caught a bus on Riverside Drive to carry them to the lovely Reformed Temple on Fifth Avenue.

Chapter 46

When was the last time she had been inside a synagogue? Petra couldn't really remember. Possibly more than a decade ago for the bar mitzvah of a family friend's son, when she herself was not quite a teenager. The Hebrew she had learned to read and write as a young child was entirely erased from her memory, and she had felt very much like an outsider even at that long-ago event.

The interiors of and services held at local Protestant churches were actually more familiar and far less intimidating. She knew the lyrics and music of all the Christmas carols, had sung hymns in the choir and, like the other kids in their Jackson Heights neighborhood (both Protestant and Catholic), attended the popular dances held every Saturday night at the Methodist church around the corner. Everything was comfortable and in English.

At thirteen, feeling she would never be completely safe from anti-Semitism until she broke entirely with Judaism and could fearlessly wear a cross suspended from a gold chain around her neck, with the indifferent consent of her mother, she had even been converted and confirmed. Her father, raised as the eldest son and favorite child in an Orthodox family, was too shocked to disapprove but understood the underlying insecurity which prompted it, said nothing and quietly continued to love her far more than he hated the deed. He shook his head, stayed silent and in his heart he mourned. Even today, she remembered the pain on his face, devoid of any anger.

Neither of them came to the confirmation ceremony or ever set foot in

No, she corrected herself, that wasn't actually true. Several years earlier on VE Day, she and Sofie had gone together to pray for a few minutes, to beg for the success of the campaign and an end to the bloodshed. Together they sat on a wooden pew among all the other people who had come for the same reason, as the sun came through the windows and shone on their bowed heads. In the stillness they could hear soft murmurings and the stifled sobs of a woman in front of them. There was no minister present and no formal service, but like all the other religious institutions, the Methodist church was open on that day to anyone who wanted to enter.

Somehow, despite the comfortable assimilation, the weekly Sunday school classes and teen social contacts, the dinners and dances, the Christmas trees which her father had silently, reluctantly allowed into the house (admitting against his will their colorful decorations did, in fact, make the winter darkness more bearable), even the realization that she was an accepted part of a very vibrant Christian community (and could finally wear the gold crucifix around her neck), intrinsically none of it even partially succeeded in convincing her she was anything except Jewish.

Bible studies were the most problematic, because she continually asked questions which were always answered with, "You just have to have faith, to believe." But such evasions led to more doubts, still more questions, more confusion and more responses, which she couldn't accept no matter how sincerely she tried.

The desire for teenage acceptance, which drove church attendance and conversion, was superficial. She nodded agreeably as if she understood (although she didn't) because she genuinely liked the minister, the congregation, the stories, and most of all, the music.

And, of course, as she openly admitted, going to church was a legitimate excuse to be close to the brilliant high school senior, newly named Merit Scholar, who sang bass in the choir (she sang thin soprano), expertly played the trombone (she struggled to learn the rudiments of viola), although he half-heartedly pretended to ignore her un-subtle adoration (but was simultaneously annoyed and flattered by it) and rarely acknowledged her existence. The Saturday evening he asked her to dance with him (once) to "Moonlight Serenade," courtesy of a Glenn Miller record, she lived on the memory for weeks. She never dared to ask him but, based on his last name, suspected his father was also Jewish and realized she felt a kinship with him which fed the attraction. But never questioned why she needed the kinship.

When they moved to Washington, D.C. and she attended its largest Methodist church (which was segregated, although she couldn't understand the rationale for it, and when she questioned the hypocrisy of the 'whites-only' custom was ignored and smirked at), again a stranger, again needing acceptance, the alienation she experienced was not just physical, it was theological as well.

One hot, humid Sunday, after a particularly grueling, fire-and-brimstone, long-winded monologue by a well-intentioned cleric (with whom she felt nothing in common), and who preached in the accented drawl of his Southern Methodist upbringing, she tried to stay interested, failed, and decided she didn't believe a word he was saying.

Or shouting.

Or singing.

Or forcing his listless herd to accept!

That was the last time she pretended to be anything except what she had found the path back to her identity completely unfamiliar, decidedly frightening, and it had—until Jerry's invitation to *sjabbat* services resulted in being branded an outsider.

Again.

Discouraged, she had left the road to organized religions and remained unaffiliated, assuming at times she eventually might have to take it. One hesitant step at a time, perhaps culminating tonight, after many years of denial and assimilation with an unplanned exposure to the traditional religion of her entire family.

What family?

A young man met them at the entrance to the beautiful building (oblivious of course to the conflict in her head) and guided them through the interior of the synagogue, past its multi-pewed sanctuary (erected to seat and comfortably accommodate the largest, wealthiest congregation in New York), now dark and chilly, and into an exquisite side chapel, small, intimate, decorated in pale blue and gold, warmly lit, a miniature jewel.

Perfection.

As they entered, she looked upward and around, enchanted by the beauty of the little temple and immediately determined that should she ever marry, this would be where she wanted to have the religious ceremony.

Simultaneously, the face of the only man she even considered flittered across her consciousness.

Dev, a Hindu, here?

They found seats towards the middle of the chapel, joining several people who introduced themselves and welcomed them.

Petra was suddenly paralyzed with shyness, apologized but explained she wanted to sit in the last pew by herself, assuring the others she was fine, thank you, no, didn't feel ill, and would join them at the *oneg shabbat* afterwards.

She had no idea what prompted her reaction.

The service was, in fact, as described by Jerry, mostly in English, led by a newly bar-passed attorney and his fiancée. It was completely non-threatening, all-encompassing, easy to follow, and elicited immediate camaraderie among the thirty or so participants.

Actually, Petra smiled to herself, it was similar to the Methodist rituals she knew so well.

Without the inclusion of Jesus as the Messiah, of course.

Maybe after the years of procrastination, the road back would be easier than she had feared.

Suddenly, the language switched to Hebrew, as a few people rose and mumbled the Kaddish, the ancient prayer commemorating the death of a family member. Then she understood why she had chosen to isolate herself from the others, while shadowed memories of her childhood in Europe, suppressed and long denied, swept violently through her senses: shades buried, embalmed and uncorrupted for decades, their forgotten realities resurrected, unsought, burst forward into her full consciousness.

She cried, inadvertently, eyes wide open, silently without sobs, tears flowing steadily across her cheeks, unstoppable, endless, noiseless.

She recognized herself, a child of perhaps three or less, climbing the staircase of the shul on the Wagenstraat in The Hague (the shul her family had helped to build generations earlier and where her grandfather—for whom a service was in progress although she did not understand it at the time— the rabbis until his recent death), separated with other female congregants in a balcony above the enormous sanctuary, while far below, the men, tallis-clothed, heads covered, chanted, bowed, and faced the lovely, ancient, carved *bimah*, behind which were stored the sacred Torah scrolls.

She saw her gentle father, his back towards them, body swaying back and forth, and called out loudly above the hushed murmuring of the prayers in her clear, childish voice, afraid he might not be aware she was up there with the women, so far away from where he stood.

"*Daar is mijn papa! Ik zie mijn papa!*" she cried excitedly.

"*Papa! Papa! Ik kan je zien! Papa kijk eens naar boven! Hier ben ik!*" and as he finally turned around, no longer able to ignore the urgent anxiety in that beloved echoing voice, looked up and of course immediately found her, she watched the unaccustomed sorrow on his (for once unshaven) face replaced with tolerant amusement, while he raised one hand and waved quickly at her, then placed it to his lips and threw her a kiss.

The women, laughing softly, tried to constrain her misplaced exuberance, smiled indulgently at her, and some offered the blonde, dainty little girl a sweet, not at all annoyed at the child whose voice still echoed singularly through the cavernous temple, drowning out and interrupting the pious ministrations of the dovening men below, disturbing their prayerful concentration, as their supplications accompanied her grandfather's soul to heaven where he, beloved and compassionate, would sit eternally among the angels and watch paternally over them.

She did not remember this grandfather, had not been aware of him when the only surviving photograph showed him, already an old man sitting outside on a patio in a rattan chair with a walking stick balanced next to it, holding her, a squalling newborn infant with unrecognizable features, in his lap.

He must have been remarkable, according to the obituaries clipped and saved from the newspapers of The Hague. Even her volatile, passionate mother referred to him with respect and admittedly something close-to-but-not-quite-full-fledged affection.

"*Ach ja*, he was a good man," she would say condescendingly when his name was mentioned, *"zacht, net als je vader.* (Gentle, just like your father). And he had a very difficult life. But he was always kind to me. Not like the rest of the family!"

Family?

What happened to all the people who attended her grandfather's funeral?

How many had been her relatives? What were their names? How old were they? Did they have children? Perhaps her age? Or older? Younger? Boys and girls? Perhaps cousins?

Those nameless, faceless children, had they been her friends playing hopscotch and marking the squares with colored chalk on the sidewalks or shouting to each other as with one foot they pushed their wide-tired scooters, skimming joyously, recklessly across the streets of Scheveningen? Had she been to their homes, eaten meals with them, been spoiled as the youngest member of the "family"? Could they perhaps have been her cousin-classmates in kindergarten?

The children? Where were they? Confidantes by virtue of blood relationships, who could never be replaced by strangers?

How many members of that long ago congregation who might have been her uncles, aunts...or no, not how many...had even ONE of those innocent people survived the murderous Teutonic barbarity?

WHERE WAS HER FAMILY?

She screamed in anguish, introverted, unheard, asking if she too should have risen to say the Kaddish in their memory, thoughts which remained raging, unsaid, inside her skull. As the prayer ended and the congregants in mourning resumed their places on the soft, pale blue velvet pews in the exquisite Temple Emanuel chapel, blinded with tears, she opened her purse, took out a handkerchief, silently dried her face and assumed an expression of complacent control, although her knees were shaking when she rose to leave.

The others seated towards the front of the chapel had not noticed, greeted each other with hugs and "*shalom sjabbats*" and walked slowly down the aisle towards an ante-chamber to enjoy coffee, pastries and become better acquainted.

Somehow she managed to add a civil sentence or so to whatever topic was under discussion but declined quickly when someone suggested going to The Plaza for a drink and further conversation, hailed a taxi and retreated to the safe, impersonal sterility of her rented room.

A light shines beneath the threshold of Ellen's door but Petra doesn't want company. She knocks softly, mumbles, "Hello. Forgive me. I'm really tired. See you in the morning," glances listlessly at the envelope lying on the mat addressed to her with the familiar Indian stamp, picks it up, and goes inside.

She leaves it closed, afraid of its contents or her own reaction.

Not tonight, no news good or bad, she knows she cannot handle any more tonight, washes, brushes her teeth and climbs onto the hard little bed.

And is asleep.

Petra dreams she is in the lovely blue chapel, its non-existent spires reach high above her, colors muted, intonations meaningless, a hymn played weakly on a guitar... "Holy, holy, holy, God is three persons," a young voice reading scripture in English. Then Kaddish. Again. Kaddish.

She cries in her dreams. And sees...

The sunlit corner of a huge room. A tall, proud man of around sixty, his dark, intelligent eyes encircled with wire-rimmed glasses, throat enveloped in a stiff, old-fashioned wing-backed collar, black suited, carefully bow-tied, sits at a desk watching two silver-haired children at play.

Suddenly, the boy trips and falls to the ground and his sister, directly behind him, cannot stop and also tumbles down. Both of them begin to cry, not so much from pain as shock.

But the old man rushes over to them, inspects their minor injuries, picks them both up, places his rambunctious grandchildren on his lap and instructs them to search through his pockets. They find a roll of peppermints and he gives one sweet to the little boy, another to his sister.

Their mother, hears them crying, rushes from the kitchen but all is peaceful by then, the children cuddling against their beloved grandfather's chest, and the girl plays with a tiny gold watch fob in the shape of a wild boar, suspended by a chain from his vest pocket. "A good luck charm," he informs her, then turns to Sofie and thrusts a brown, leather briefcase into her hands, stuffed with Dutch money. His life savings.

"Now, daughter! Now! Don't wait any longer. They've entered Poland! Take the children, get out while you still can."

The scene changes, concrete prison grounds, greys, blacks, leather knee-high boots, the salivated, obscene shlshing sounds of German and two uniformed soldiers heavily armed, holding the tall, aristocratic man between them, shouting orders in their harsh, guttural language, unaware of how incongruous they appear, ignorant peasants commanding a direct descendant of the Spanish nobility!

At length they lecture him about their glorious German victories, their own elevated status as Aryan *ubermenschen*, the unavoidable glorious conquest and reorganization of the world, the classification of the Jews as beneath-human.

He stares them down, defiant, and spits out, "*Vuile rot moffen! En toch gaan jullie verliezen!*" He speaks in Dutch, although as are most of his countrymen, he is fluent in several other languages.

Including theirs.

Someone translates, a rifle shot and the old man slumps to the ground.

She gasps, cries aloud, opens her eyes, recalling dreams that are not dreams but recurring memories just beneath her consciousness. Memories which emerge when she is not awake, not asleep, somewhere between reality and suppression, where she is helpless and cannot control or deny them.

Petra, half-asleep, gets up, stumbles to the sink and gets a glass of water, gulps it down, returns to bed. And blessedly blanks out until morning.

Chapter 47

The next day, she opened Dev's letter, which basically repeated the same things. He loved her, was terribly lonesome, still had to stay in India a few more weeks to attend the opening ceremony for his mother's temple school.

He was obligated to attend.

After the turmoil of the Friday evening service, the subsequent overly realistic dreams, she was too stunned to react and held the thin airmail paper in her hand, staring at it, at his neat, inked penmanship, the "I love you, doll" closing, then carefully folded it and returned it to its envelope to store in a dresser drawer.

When she went to the I. House for an early hamburger-and-fries dinner, Jerry was sitting in a booth, alone as usual, and gestured towards her to sit down with him. "What did you think of the service?"

"Just as you promised, short, lovely, in English. Thank you for inviting me."

He answered, "My pleasure," gazed into her face and suddenly realized he was falling in love with her. Immediately, he tried to pull back. A relationship was not in his plans. Teaching, research, finishing a project he had committed to, those were his priorities. The only ones!

And of all the foolhardy actions, to fall in love with a woman who was deeply involved with someone else. Total idiocy, he chided himself. "Any news from you-know-who?"

"Yes. A letter yesterday. I guess he'll certainly be back next month to take the bar."

"But he didn't specify?"

"No."

Despite his reservations, Jerry calculated quickly (a few more weeks, perhaps there was still a chance). "Do you think he'd object if you came to Carnegie Hall with me tonight? Jascha is playing the Beethoven and Arturo is wielding the baton. Want to go?"

Although the invitation was tempting, she managed to decline.

Chapter 48

She slept late on Sunday but towards lunchtime bought a *New York Times* and a cup of coffee in The Waffle Wing, settled into a booth and attempted to unpuzzle the weekly puzzle.

"Excuse me, Miss. Is this seat taken?"

Startled, she looked up, and within seconds was in his arms, the coffee cup and its entire contents splattered to the ground.

"You wrote next month. Your mother's ceremony. You...you..." She didn't even know the words she was babbling.

"I didn't want you to be disappointed if I missed a plane or an emergency kept me home, or God knows what else might have delayed me. So I decided it would be best just to surprise you. Do you mind? Really?"

But she just stayed buried in his embrace without answering, a non-response he surmised meant she was probably pleased to see him.

Dev knew how desperately he had missed her. Almost from the moment he arrived in Bombay, his life had consisted of meeting one eligible girl after another. Most were very beautiful, educated as he had been in private English schools. All were wealthy and ready to share the family's money via an enormous dowry with the handsome lawyer.

Their willingness to appear like animals at an auction for his discriminating scrutiny he found demeaning. Their cotton candy sweetness and desperate desire to please annoyed him.

Back in New York, he knew irrevocably he, too, wanted to get married. But not to them.

"Come, my love. Home with me. I cannot kiss you here in front of everyone and if I don't do so within the next few minutes I know I shall die of misery."

"Yes" was all she could say and took his hand.

They barely released each other for an instant once they were finally alone, and as they murmured their love for each other again and again, the clichéd age-old declarations were new for them, never uttered or heard before.

"Darling. I have to tell you something."

"Not now, Dev. Please. Just let me stay in your arms a little longer without having to think. I want to look at you. Make certain you're really here."

He kissed her again but continued, "I have been accepted at an international law firm for a year's clerkship."

"Oh Dev. How wonderful. Congratulations!" Then she realized the implications. "In India, you mean?"

"No, doll. Not India. Here in New York."

"And when does it begin?"

"They will let me study for the bar, take it and expect me to begin working in two months. Next year they plan to transfer me to their San Francisco branch office."

"San Francisco?" she echoed.

"Will you accompany me?" he asked, swallowing his words, as tongue-tied as he had been the first time he'd told her he loved her.

"Accompany you?"

"Marry me in a year. Join me as my wife."

"But your family? What will they think if you bring home a Jewish bride?"

"They'll get used to it. My mother and father want me to be happy. Believe me, you will have more trouble adjusting to their Indian ways than they will getting adjusted to yours. So I have come up with a plan. After the clerkship is finished and I am offered a partnership in the firm (I hope), we can spend six months in San Francisco and six months in India. Or if you prefer, split it up so we can be in Europe for three months also. Or rent an apartment in New York. You choose. So, Petra my love, my life, will you marry me? Please?"

"What do you think my answer will be?" she replied, and when she saw the sudden pain in his eyes, quickly kissed him and whispered, "Yes, Dev. Yes, darling. Of course I will. "

Chapter 49

She began to steep herself in Indian culture, inquired at the Consulate if there were classes available for learning Hindi.

Dev gave her a copy of the *"Bhagavad Gita,"* not to convert her but because she requested it, as determined now to grasp the core of his background as he had previously clawed into hers. She studied it with pain and pleasure on the way to the office.

Immersed in the lovely Oriental music of its language, which sang in her brain even after she closed the little book, it was always a shock to suddenly find herself sitting at the grey, metallic desk being ordered to transcribe pompous letters and type numerous vacuous press releases. Usually it took a while before she could disengage herself from contemplating its one pure world and force herself to plunge unwillingly into the shallowness and oil-slickedness of the advertising game puddle.

"Day dawns and these lives that lay hidden asleep

Come forth and show themselves mortally manifest;

Night falls and all are dissolved

Into the sleeping germ of life." *

From the simple beauty of the "Gita" to "Fly Royal Belgian Airlines, the world's most efficient route to Brussels, which welcomes you aboard its newest,

---

* "The Song of God," Bhagavad-Gita, translated by Swami Prabhavananda and Christopher Isherwood, The New American Library, New York 1954.

most modern, speediest, super-de-luxe-non-stop flights from New York, featuring authentic Belgian breakfasts, superb luncheon and gourmet dinner menus, served with pleasure by multi-lingual ready-to-accommodate-your-every-whim beautifully groomed and uniformed stewardesses."

She actually loved Belgium (where her mother was raised and which she herself had often visited as a child, splashing in the waters at Spa and riding in a little flower-painted goat cart, while Sofie's numerous Belgian relatives lovingly taught her French songs, pampered her and showered her with endearments and presents) and had nothing against its airline (which she had never flown but assumed to be as good or better than any of its competitors) and sincerely wished it the success and prosperity it undoubtedly had earned.

But—oh God—Burken (Wilson Lloyd to his friends, of whom she obviously wasn't one, too far below him, don'tcha know) back in New York, more arrogant than ever, who now had a new modus operandi.

Although Petra was required to be seated and waiting eagerly for his slightest word at eight each morning, he jounced in whenever he chose.

As a superior being (had he ever read Nietsche she sometimes wondered? Of course he had. After all, he was a graduate of Harvard, wasn't he? Had he ever understood Nietsche? Of course not, but that wasn't Harvard's fault), he could commence the workday whenever he chose, and since every evening he was laboriously wooing General Woodward's daughter and planning to propose marriage very soon, he announced grandly to Petra (who disdained the entire kill-them-for-a-living-profession and was tempted to ask innocently, "Who the hell is General Woodward?" because in fact she had never heard of him but knew enough from having lived in Washington, D.C. about the military to realize that generals and admirals were as numerous as mosquitos near a swamp), sometimes her beebusyboss could not quite make it into his office on time and might start his workday at 11 a.m. or later.

Then he would order her to make lunch reservations for him and a friend, waltz out for a-many-houred banquet and return towards four in the afternoon (the time she was actually supposed to go home), talk wildly into a dictaphone machine, make some scribbles on a legal pad and throw the whole mickmack at her. She was expected to have everything grammatically cleaned up, put into advertisement-lively English, typed and ready to be mailed before she could leave.

At first she didn't mind, but soon it became habitual for him to insist on rewrites, more rewrites and still more rewrites, until quitting time became six o'clock, seven o'clock and his superiors were enthusiastically impressed with his willingness to stay after hours (unaware of his playboy schedule but stopping by now and then at the remotely placed office, finding him still hard at work, not noticing she was still imprisoned there also (like him, they assumed classified employees were invisible). He got the praises and the raises, and she got headaches, lost her appetite, and received neither a cent for all the overtime nor even an acknowledged "thank you" from him.

Eventually she figured out the real reason he chose to begin his workday so late—he had nothing to do before picking up his date for the evening's hoodoo and didn't want to wait around by himself.

Dev noticed how nervous she was becoming, overworked, tired, almost unable to eat from exhaustion, and he couldn't help her.

Not yet.

One Tuesday, he phoned to tell her he had been able to get tickets for "La Boheme" for the next evening's performance, which would also feature the debut of a young Italian soprano. They would first have dinner at the Russian Tea Room.

Immediately she informed Burken that she could not stay late on Wednesday and told him about the opera. He mumbled something, which intimated he understood. But the next day it was the same thing. He returned from lunch well after four, threw a stack of raw copy at her and demanded she edit it for him.

She looked at it and knew.

At four o'clock, Dev called to say he would come by for her in half an hour. She told him to wait till a little later, she would call him when she could leave.

The rewrites kept being sent back. One had to be completely retyped because Burken decided to indent a sentence which was not indented earlier. Another did not meet his demands since the margins were not where he wanted them although they were exactly as they had always been. The stack of news releases did not diminish in size.

She was frantic!

Six o'clock!

Dev called again. "I'm doing my best. Just have dinner without me," she informed him, and he heard the fatigue and discouragement in her voice.

"Bastard," he fumed silently, "son of a bitching arrogant bastard!"

After still another hour, Petra picked up the phone, asked Dev to meet her downstairs in the lobby, went to the Ladies Room, washed her face and applied fresh makeup, slithered into a new pair of stockings (still a luxury on her salary), took off the sensible shoes she wore in the office and put on the high heels she had in the desk drawer, stormed into Burken's office and let loose.

"I warned you I had to leave on time today," she announced, tossed a paper on his desk and added, "This is the final rewrite I am doing. If it's not good enough, correct it yourself. Good night!" and she lifted her head high, turned around and walked out.

He sat in his leather rocking chair and gazed in astonishment as she slammed the office door behind her. For an instant he considered firing her but then recognized (although thankfully she did not) he would never find anyone with her unique multi-language facilities.

"Quit, love. Tell him to go to hell," Dev whispered as he held her for an instant in his arms.

"I can't, Dev. I have bills to pay, the rent, other things. But the next time he decides to go abroad I'm going job-hunting." She laughed cynically, "Unless of course he's already fired me."

By the time they arrived at the Met, the first scene was in progress and they weren't permitted to enter the hall until it ended. Even so, they could hear Puccini's lovely melodious arias clearly being butchered. In fact, after being shown to their seats they had to work hard to stifle their laughter, although many others in the audience could not restrain theirs. The nervous soprano, far too well fed to be believable as a tubercular flower seller, her voice distinctly thinner than her non-existent waistline, flatted, sharped, wobbled and slurred. Everyone agreed they couldn't wait for the pasta-princess to succumb! In good time or not, Mimi died to minimal applause.

Outside, happy just to be together even at a disastrous debut, Petra and Dev stopped on Broadway at an all-night restaurant.

"Next week, my love, is the Halloween Eve Festival. It's been a year since we met. Do you remember?"

"Yes, Dev. Of course. You sneaking me into the Indian show. Baboo telling my fortune. How could I forget?"

"I will not participate this time. Too many other things, the bar, soon a new job." He paused. "And I think I might have other distractions also but cannot remember what they are. A blonde demon who keeps me on tenterhooks, perhaps. Or something like that."

"And I am not doing anything with the Dutch group either. I'm just too tired after working at a job I absolutely love and trying to keep an insistent suitor in line whom I absolutely hate."

"Oh good," he countered, "in that case we are both free to be observers with lots of cash to spend. The I. House will certainly welcome us."

"And your money! This year I won't be so shy about spending it!"

Chapter 50

As usual, the Halloween Festival was thronged, but this year Dev held Petra's hand with familiar confidence, not concerned he would lose his grasp on her, and even if he did, he knew she would return to him gladly, as happy to be with him as he was to be with her.

They knew there was not enough time to see all the shows but there were two they could not miss; the Dutch one , where Dev purchased a huge slab of Edammer cheese, freshly cut and wrapped in thick, white paper, bowed and presented it to Petra—but she had no refrigerator and asked the costumed seller to cut off a slice, which they ate)- and they donated the rest back to be resold; and the Indian performance where they were welcomed by Baboo, Gita and Parvati (who was this year's official ticket-taker and gleefully insisted that no one—with no exceptions, absolutely not—could get in free).

"Parvati. You look wonderful!" said an astounded Petra to the radiant pink-saried doctor, who uncustomarily reached forward spontaneously and embraced her. She appeared far healthier than when they had shared lunch, had gained enough weight to no longer resemble a walking cadaver. What had happened? And if Alan was the reason for the transformation, where was he?

"Thank you. Ah Dev, how are you?" Pavarti replied.

"So, I have news," said Baboo. "We are moving to Schenectady. I have been offered an excellent position, and Gita can attend graduate school in the vicinity."

"But I thought you wanted to work in India," Petra said.

"That would be ideal, but dear child, at the moment there is no technology advanced enough to fit my expertise at home. Therefore, no work for me, either. Until India catches up, I shall remain in this country. In the event, we are leaving in a month."

"We will miss you terribly, you know," said Dev.

"Well, we will share a farewell dinner soon. Afterwards you will write and I will write and we will stay in touch. But now let us see what the other countries are offering." He gestured to his wife and waved goodbye, instantly hidden by the crowd.

"Look here. They are selling bells of Sarna! Petra, I will buy you some. Every time you feel sad you must ring them, so tung, tung, tung, and then you will soon feel cheerful again." Dev paid for a string of the brass bells and gave them to her. "We too, will see what else there is upstairs," he told Parvati and headed with Petra towards the staircase to explore further.

Standing by herself in front of the Indian booth, Pavarti watched them leave and was neither jealous, nor lonesome, just smiled her sweet, ugly smile as people began to gather in front of her, gave her tickets and entered the auditorium where in a few moments another Indian wedding would take place.

Chapter 51

"Breathe! Now!" the voice in her head commanded. "Do it! Breathe! Damn it!"

Parvati, somewhere between infantile awakening and the depth of sleep, heard it clearly but couldn't obey, something had clogged her nose shut and prevented her from taking even one breath. "You've got to live! Now breathe!" the voice persisted, becoming more desperate as the seconds of nothingness continued and she began to feel herself suffocating.

Still, she could not manage to force her own breathing process to restart, could not pump air and life into her lungs even as she struggled feebly and felt herself giving up, slowly accepting the darkness, mentally and physically experiencing every conscious second of its horror.

"You are going to die! After all you have suffered, you stupid woman. You are going to let yourself die!" the voice repeated, furious, helpless. "Breathe! God damn it! Fight back!"

Parvati knew the voice was right. Somehow she must take a breath, but the insidious progressive weight on her chest and the shuttered openings into her nasal passages prevented it. She was steadily weakening, tiring, submitting. The voice too was receding.

With one enormous desperate force of will against the paralyzing inertia, she managed to move her head slightly, just far enough to one side of the pillow to free her nose. She inhaled tentatively, a tiny initial whiff followed by a loud gasp, as fresh air flew into her throat, her lungs and emerged again.

Trembling but now semi-conscious, she forced herself to take yet another breath, and another, until she lay on the bed wide-eyed, fully awake, frightened but alive, realizing that she had almost died.

And more than ever, she wanted to live.

Rounds were early this morning and she arose quickly, took a shower, dried herself off, applied lotion to her body, and gazed for a newly vain precious moment at herself in the full-length mirror. She saw a naked woman, glowing and beautiful; her breasts, round, firm and perfect, the waist long and slender tapering to gently sloping hips.

And for the first time, she recognized her own value and gloried in her sexuality.

Even her face was lovely, the soft dark eyes, thin regular nose, mouth closed but warm, knowledgeable, set into an almost perfect oval and surrounded by a knee-length veil of silk highlighted hair.

Parvati knew she was beautiful.

As long as she didn't smile.

Quickly she dressed in a plain cotton everyday sari, twisted her hair into a chignon, applied kohl to her eyes, fastened simple gold jewelry around her neck and in her ears, and went to the hospital, still somewhat traumatized from the near-death experience of this morning, grateful she had survived.

She guessed Alan was tiring of her, using her solely as a convenient outlet—his personal toilet, she grimaced—when he needed one, but quietly accepted the situation. Women in India were accustomed to infidelity in their men, accepted their suppressed life roles, continued to function normally, as if this were simply inevitable.

Parvati decided to behave accordingly.

It was not difficult to assume who her rival could be. She had even heard Alan whispering her name as he lay assuaged next to her, frowning, smiling, remembering some incident of which she had no knowledge.

It didn't matter. When he needed her and she was available, she would help him. If he should decide at some future time to throw her aside, she would accept rejection, as well.

Gracefully, she hoped.

None of it was important anymore.

Just a few days ago, the lab at the hospital had confirmed her self-diagnosis, the rabbit had indeed died. Perhaps later she would tell Alan, or if she felt he would be displeased, keep her entire pregnancy a secret and handle the situation in her own way.

But she would certainly not die an old maid, alone, unloved, having no proof a man had ever lain between her legs, and she had given and received pleasure.

And borne a child.

She had thought it through carefully. Her residency would soon end and she could return to India (with experience and an excellent education as buffers), inform the curious that her Indian husband had met with a fatal automobile accident (the fact Alan had survived this long without one was a miracle in itself), and although shocked and in mourning, she wanted to have and raise their baby at home, to work among her own people (who needed all the Western trained physicians they could get).

Female pediatricians, in particular.

Eila, her sophisticated sister, would, she was certain, support her in every way, delighted no doubt to finally have a little child in the family, devoid of any illusions herself of ever marrying or bearing one.

Parvati knew that no matter how badly Alan might treat her in the future, whether he accepted or rejected her, a part of him would never be entirely separated from her again. The child nestled in her womb, secure, loved and definitely wanted. Its radiant mother was beyond happiness.

Chapter 52

Sunlight gleamed beneath her eyelids, waking her.

Beside her, Alan was still asleep, and she glanced quickly at him, gagged with spontaneous revulsion, shook her head in dismay, noted the deep pockmarks drawn on his face, the black streaks on the pillow from the dye on his thick, straight hair, observed without emotion the naked body, which she alternately despised but had not quite denied, and looked at his flaccid penis, which presently rested harmlessly, shrunken to unenthusiastic proportions against one pudgy thigh, then afraid to rouse him (and it) stirred quietly and attempted to escape.

Instantly, his hand reached out to stop her. "No, Maria. You may not leave. You stay here with me. I need you. Just look!"

She didn't have to, knowing blindly what he wanted to show her. But Maria hit him hard with her other hand, and the blow surprised him enough to free her.

"We've had this discussion before, Alan. You may think differently but you don't own me, even if I did sleep with you last night. I want to go to my own house, right now, without you and I am leaving. You cannot stop me!"

"Oh, indeed I can! After the way you performed? How you serviced me in ways no decent woman would? Not another man in the world wants you now. You belong to me, Maria, irrefutably. Get used to it! Do you understand? If you leave, I will smear your reputation all over the I. House, tell everyone about your sexual calisthenics. And I shall notify your superiors at work you are no better than a prostitute. I will ruin you, Maria. Count on it. From this time on, you will obey me in all things. And you will NOT leave until I allow it. Understood?"

To his astonishment, she got off the bed and calmly dressed herself. Then she went to the door, opened it and walked out, knowing that naked as he was, he couldn't follow her. Furious and unbelieving, he threw his shoes at the closed door and emitted a loud primitive bellow.

"You bitch, you stinking Latin bitch," he screamed, totally aware she couldn't hear him and even if she did, would not have reacted. "Goddamn you! One day you will obey me. You will beg for my forgiveness. You will need me and I will trample on you."

Even though it was early in the morning, he reached for the phone. "Get over here. Instantly. You can shower afterwards, but I want you to drop everything else right now! I'm in bed and will leave the door unlocked. If I'm asleep, don't wake me. Otherwise, I'll tell you what I want you to do."

He was swollen to excruciating hardness from anger, frustration and desire when she arrived fifteen minutes later. "Hurry up, you slut. Get out of that shroud and come over here," he ordered.

Silently but gracefully, because every movement she made was graceful, Parvati unwound the sari, removed her underwear and went to him. In all things she would obey him until he chose to cast her aside.

She smelled the ammonia odor of sex, saw an empty opened condom envelope, noticed a long dark hair on the rumpled sheets and when she attempted to kiss Alan's neck (he would never allow her to kiss him on the mouth), she noticed another woman's exotic perfume.

And she knew it was Maria's.

Parvati had been horrified and bewildered as she sensed the change in her relationship with Alan, when he no longer asked but demanded, called infrequently and then always at the last moment, forced her to perform acts which revolted her, made no excuses, gave no verbal balm to soothe her emotional wounds, did as he chose and, as in everything he desired, she became accustomed to his whims, accepted and acceded without protestation.

While untouched by them, Alan also recognized the physical changes in Parvati.

The last time he had summoned her, several weeks ago (when he was overwhelmed with joy at having Maria again but dared not push their newly reborn relationship too quickly, yet demanded a more exotic and satisfying sexual favor than she would perform), Parvati looked as if she had a terminal illness, skeletal, tired, her normally lovely balletic posture reduced to a head-faced-to-floor stumble as she walked towards him, ministered to his needs and, when he dismissed her, went directly to the hospital for rounds.

He tried not to contact her often afterwards (not from pity for Parvati but his own precious emotions were, after all, limited), waited for Maria to accede completely to his requests (she never did), and assumed eventually he would get his way there, too. Besides, the core distance she maintained against him was a challenge. No woman had ever challenged Alan before.

And after a night of romance (for once he had convinced her to remain in his bed overnight), when he fully expected her to obey his one simple request and she absolutely refused to consider it, he was not only bewildered by her continued resistance to his undeniable male charms and attributes (no matter how provocatively he dangled them in front of her), her ice cold indifference to their undoubted uniqueness humiliated him as well!

It was definitely time for Parvati to ease his sufferings. Too bad if she was hurt, or sick, or would go home crying (it was obvious to everyone he simply did not love her, and the silly woman wasn't stupid!)

Therefore, whatever minimal kindness he showed Parvati was all she would get from him.

Ever.

So that when she arrived, he was amazed to see how lovely (for Parvati, of course) she actually looked. Her face smooth, the skin lustrous and golden warm, her eyes soft brown, the whites not yellow from crying over him, but healthy, blue-white. He was used to her body by now but it thrilled him anew when he observed it, the lovely round mounds, the long tender lines of her torso.

"I am almost tempted to order her to quit medicine altogether and tell her to walk around here naked all day for me and my guests to admire!"

He grinned at his own fantasy and foolishness.

He could just picture how Maria would react!

Maria! Damn her!

"Parvati. Do it fast. I have an important business appointment this morning."

Obediently she leaned over him and got to work.

Chapter 53

Maria wasn't sure at first and waited another two weeks, but then she knew. She loved him, completely, deeply, and probably eternally. As soon as they were apart, even after they had just spent hours together, she missed him, ached for the sound of his voice on the phone, heard unsung music in her head, and danced on tip-toed emotions.

She was miserably happy, and happily miserable.

Without his presence, her existence was imperfect. When she saw him rising to greet her at a restaurant, or standing on the threshold of her apartment, she ran into his arms and felt a completeness she had known with no one else.

He, too, recognized he loved her, admitted he would never want anyone else, hoped she would end other relationships that she might still have and, when timidly he asked, she complied at once.

"Will you marry me, then?" he repeated hoarsely, barely a month after they had met, held out a small velvet covered box, let her open it, watched with indulgent amusement as her dark eyes widened, waited seconds (which seemed much longer), and reached inside to place the sparkling jewel on her accepting, engagement ring finger.

The next time Alan phoned, she informed him, and he exploded, "You did what? How could you? I have not given you permission Maria, to do such a thing! Does he have any idea what kind of woman you are? I will tell him! What is his name? Tell me at once! Maria! I mean it. You belong to me and only to me, until I choose to break up with you!"

Without responding further, she hung up the phone and rejoined her fiancé, who had overheard the hysterical tirade, but simply took her in his arms.

Chapter 54

For whatever reason, Alan had been particularly brutal to her this evening, screamed at her continually, although she could not remember having done anything to warrant his cruel behavior. Well then, she would adapt and manage to get through this bad-boy mood, too, she thought, grateful he had called her at all.

But when she had done everything he demanded and more, to show him how much she truly loved him, demeaned herself in ways she could not have guessed a human being could be demeaned only to please him, had begged him to tell her what else she could possibly do, and winced when he labeled her a filthy slut, she still stayed, called him her love, crooned to him with sympathy for who knew-not-what he was suffering, and tried to caress his face.

Sexually drained but emotionally an infuriated bull, he grabbed her by the hair with one clenched hand, punched her numerous times in the face with the other, breaking her jaw and her nose, kicked her in the stomach, opened the door and threw her out of his apartment.

"Stupid bitch. Stupid, silly whore! Get out of my house. I never want to see you again!" he screamed at her.

She lay in the hallway for a few minutes sobbing, tested the bone in her chin, instantly diagnosed the damage, crawled almost sightlessly to the elevator and managed to take a taxi to the hospital. Despite the painful injuries, she had hope, determined to heal quickly, aware the tiny seed in her womb would sustain her forever.

If he actually meant it, and she never saw Alan again, she would always have his child. And that was enough.

The emergency room doctors treated her, taped up her shattered face, soothed the swollen eyes, let her rest in a clean, private room.

Her shocked and angry colleagues brought flowers, kissed her, assured her they were praying for her and missed her, needed her back on the wards when she was better.

Asked who had attacked her.

She said nothing and kept her secrets.

Within three hours, one became evident, when the bleeding and contractions began, and the fetus was expelled. Her friends, in tears, informed her she would not be able to conceive again.

Three days later, she was released from the hospital.

Parvati went home, looked in the mirror and saw the black and blue bruises, the misaligned jaw which might heal in time. Through the pain, all she saw were the ugly front teeth—not dislodged, despite the beating the rest of her face had endured.

She opened her dresser drawer, removed the lovely green and gold sari and dressed herself.

Then she went out.

She gazed up at an azure sky where two birds soared. The larger, perhaps a falcon or an eagle, spread its wings beneath the other, infinitely smaller, which flew above it. And as the tiny bird moved ever higher, so did the larger one, always together. At first she was enchanted by their apparent camaraderie and the symmetry of their duetted flight—until she realized the raptor was forcing the other ever higher, flying beneath it if it tried to escape, its huge wingspan blinding the prey, until from exhaustion, eventually it fell and the predator scooped it up in its talons.

When she hadn't returned to work or phoned to explain her prolonged absence, no one was worried at first. She had experienced a series of traumas and certainly was entitled to adequate recuperation time.

Her beautiful, slender body, still wrapped in the heavy, water-logged silk sari washed up near Riverside Park a week later.

"Indian Doctor Suicide" screamed the headlines in the daily newspapers.

Alan, surprised and momentarily feeling slightly guilty, wondered why women were so irrational. Then forgot about her and wandered idly into a downtown cocktail lounge to see if he could pick up a prostitute.

Or even better, a woman who, gratis, would appreciate his manhood and respect it.

Chapter 55

A group of Parvati's acquaintances gathered at the I. House for a short memorial service, brought bouquets of violet roses, recited poems or shared stories of how she had touched their lives. Several of the other doctors recalled her sweetness and the way she related so naturally to the children in her care, comforting them, easing their fears.

Baboo, as always, the accepted leader and patriarch, emerged from the music room with Gita, supporting Eila, who stumbled between them, her usually jovial face transformed into a mask of numb despair.

No one had actually considered the self-inflicted death of a friend. Friends, by definition, were young, alive, happy. Perhaps older people were suicidal, had psychological problems too difficult to bear.

Parvati, of course, did also, but they went unrecognized. Or were ignored, considered temporary lapses of balance in a life which was professionally so successful.

Even as the disquieting facts presently haunted the mourners, some began to recognize an additional cynical truth.

Tomorrow Parvati, at eternal peace, would be returning to India, accompanied by her traumatized sister, while the suicide and its assumed terrible provocation (did you hear she was pregnant?) could be put into proper perspective by the other residents in the I. House, (i.e., she was simply an overly neurotic, hypersensitive misfit, who got herself into an embarrassing situation), after which time she would be discussed (for a day or two), with less sympathy and more pragmatism (she took the easy way out!).

And be forgotten.

An evening of shared grief and horror, then the marimbas would play again, the dancing continue as carefree as before, classes would resume, exams (oral and written) had to be endured, their lives would go on as usual.

Outside, the beautiful, imposing building, ancient oak trees grew even more ancient, drinking in the winter snowdrifts, knowing spring's sunlight would inevitably return, observing the ageless flow of the Hudson River, nothing altering or obstructing its everyday magnificent monotony.

The building, the trees, the river, immune to everything but their own existence, would endure long after the young people experienced their own multiple tragedies, their private battles with past and future lives. Where humans destroyed, nature within a decade would cover the destruction with grass, wild flowers, waters feeding the poisoned ground, sunlight giving light and new life.

Parvati's death had taught them momentary sympathy.

No more, no less.

Parvati, the ugly, was gone, obliterated, never existed, shadowed in life, not even alive in death, to be cargo carted in a box on an airplane, skimmed across the ocean to her homeland among the dark-skinned Dravidians. And suppose she had been born a light-skinned Aryan? Outcome, the same! Still neurotic, intolerant, bitter, haunted, desolate, deserted, death-longed-for-annihilated. Dead, intrinsically unimportant, done-away-with.

Finished!

And the stethoscope, then?

Oh God, her friends mourned, what a terrible, terrible waste!

Chapter 56

Christmas arrived with its seasonal giddiness, while the shock of Parvati's absence gradually receded. Presents were exchanged, parties attended, traveling between cities increased, lines at the stores were longer. New Yorkers again experienced the annual relaxation of hostility.

Petra gave Dev a briefcase with his initials to carry the scattered melange of research which papered his room. He chose a gold compact with an embossed flower on its cover for her and a tiny, diamond ring charm, which she wore on a thin chain around her neck, beneath the collar of her clothes, completely out of sight.

They decided not to disclose the promise of their next-year marriage to anyone yet, preferring to wait until it was closer to the actual time, giving both families a chance to meet their future in-law children.

On New Year's Eve they attended their second Masquerade Ball at the I. House. She, dressed as a Greek nymph in pale blue chiffon; he, wearing the silk embroidered coat and trousers of an Indian prince, his dark hair covered with a gold lamé turban.

But this year, everyone recognized them as a couple and no one attempted to separate them (in fact, Alan had not been seen for weeks), and as midnight approached, they were already in each other's arms, while the public kiss that followed was deep and emotional, a pledge, a promise, gratitude for having found one another.

There was a sudden blare of trumpets in the hallway, and the double doors were thrown open. Four pages dressed in silver, blowing on pennant-covered trumpets moved slowly into the ballroom, followed by a dozen young women in harem costumes carrying baskets and tossing flower petals which soon formed a springtime carpet. Behind them came a troupe of female dancers, arms encircling their heads, faces hidden behind short veils.

In-between them, tall and majestic, strode the Sun King himself, gold feathers protruding from the enormous mask, which totally covered his face and extended two feet from either side of his head, his body dressed in a gold and silver suit that clung to his thin frame, while a huge semi-sun formed the collar framing his face and shoulders and fell as a shimmering mantle behind him to the ground, where it was held up by young pages.

In his hands, which were enclosed in elbow-length silver and gold lamé gloves, he carried several gilded roses. As he proceeded regally towards the front of the ballroom, nodding graciously to the astonished students watching him, he suddenly paused before Dev and Petra, took one of the jeweled flowers he was holding, inclined his head quickly, bowed, and presented it to her.

"Thank you," she murmured, recognizing him then, accepting the gift and understanding its intent as an apology.

Prince Solomon!

Chapter 57

As the aging winter begrudgingly bowed to warmer weather, the frozen filth which had for weeks covered the city's gray streets gradually receded, and cold puddles of accumulated water and ice sloshed next to the curbs, sometimes as much two feet in depth. As each centimeter of dry sidewalk re-emerged, cleansed by the melting waters, the people began to hunger for springtime, their faces turned spontaneously towards the strengthening sunlight in a hundreds-of-thousands-years-old gesture, they no longer recognized as symbolic of all living things.

For utter misery, this had been one of the cruelest winters in years, but Petra had no memory of its wrath. Within her there was overwhelming gratitude, softness, tenderness for every aspect of nature. Nothing negatively touched her for very long. If she had ever been in the least bit pragmatic (which was questionable), pragmatism was totally banished, and she relished being alive in the present, loved by the man she loved.

It was more than a gift...an ephemeral blessing, temporarily shielding her from the rest of the world.

But that was hardly true of Ellen.

Even in her own love-induced, insular stupor, Petra eventually noticed her roommate's withdrawal, the lack of seeking company, even for a hasty cup of tea or coffee, indeed any sort of communication, whatsoever. Not that Ellen was consciously impolite (she wouldn't have known how to be), but she was experiencing an inner trauma, grappling with a desperate need for solitude, as if the wretched, cold weather had triumphantly succeeded in making an aged recluse of her.

Salmi was the only one who could drag a few words of conversation from her, but even with him she was turned inward. After a few weeks of attempting to reach her, he realized he had failed (but it didn't really bother him very much, which was in character). And when Petra announced she would be moving in a few weeks to an apartment in Riverdale to live with her parents, Ellen's reaction was a mumbled, unrecognizable babble.

One Saturday morning, Ellen knocked on the door between their rooms. She held a cigarette in one hand, a hand which trembled uncontrollably.

"Want one?" she offered, knowing Petra didn't smoke.

"Thank you," Petra said and accepted one, causing the grey eyebrows to fly into Ellen's forehead.

As soon as Ellen helped her light it, Petra began to choke, and her friend exploded into noisy, effortless, laughter, the kind Ellen had not experienced in many weeks. The two women coughed and guffawed and tried to stop the hysteria suddenly enveloping the dreary, virginal little cell.

"I'm sorry about having ignored you lately. I realize I've been unfriendly. But it's not you. Suddenly, for whatever reason, I just can't stand the fuss, the noise around me. I want peace! No, *want* isn't even the right word. I need peace, desperately."

No laughter now.

Ellen blew smoke from her nostrils, shook her head in bewilderment and gazed at nothing, her face reflecting an uncharacteristic innocence, despite the grey hair and the gouged wrinkles, which seemed to have multiplied around her neck, her eyes, on her cheeks.

She sighed and said, "When you move, I'm moving also. I want to go home. To Massachusetts. I don't belong among all the money-seeking, ruthless vampires here in New York. Can you begin to understand? I dream of the dunes on Cape Cod, of their silence and the reflections of sunlight on the Atlantic Ocean. When I remember the coastline, the roar of waves crashing against the rocks in Marblehead I want to cry. And I think of them constantly. So I am always on the verge of tears!"

She frowned, and continued, erupting finally.

"I used to resent the shingle summer houses. They were symbolic of everything I wanted to escape. The tourists with their vulgarities and noisy drooling brats, the ever-open hands of the townspeople. Their wheedling attempts to make a few fast dollars, taking advantage of the ignorant visitors, seemed like seasonal prostitution to me. But I don't think it would bother me anymore now. Besides, the tourist are only around for a few months and I can always go somewhere else until the season subsides."

"Have you ever seen the ocean in autumn? With the clouds, thick, grey, terrifying and the swirling sea as it breaks on the shoreline? The waves, endless, constantly changing, accompanied by the screeching and dancing of the seagulls above them?"

"Oh shit! What the hell am I doing in this overpriced mud pile of carbon monoxide and endless misery?"

Her blue eyes were suddenly wide with fear and loneliness.

"Has that sardonic Turk been giving you such a bad time? Why doesn't he just go back to his reticent, subservient wife?" Petra burst out, certain no amount of homesickness for Massachusetts, as beautiful as it undoubtedly was, could cause Ellen, always controlled and poised, to bend so completely, and even become poetically sensitive!

Salmi, she knew, had to be part of the breakdown.

"How did you know he was married?"

"Open secret. Everyone knows it. To be expected, isn't it? After all he's old enough and apparently not poverty-stricken. It was just logical he had a family back home."

Ellen's voice was softer now. "Don't be too hard on him. He warned me at the very beginning. For a long time I thought it really didn't make any difference to me. I am here with him, and his wife and children are thousands of miles away. And not only geographically. Living in this country has alienated him from her in other areas. Anyway, if she really knows Salmi, she must be aware he is hardly material for serving as a paradigm to celibacy or the priesthood."

Petra had grown more expert at hiding her aversion to smoking, and feeling unrealistically competent managed another drag from an ash-burdened butt before it completely disintegrated and fell in various sized lumps across her blouse. Still, saying nothing, she brushed them off and gazed with full attention at Ellen.

"Actually, I'd adjusted to the idea of not ever allowing myself to become emotionally dependent on a man. But suddenly I need the security of knowing he'll be nearby. And I hate myself for it. Don't laugh, Petra, but I'd like to have a child with him. Ha, imagine me getting pregnant while also experiencing the symptoms of menopause! Poor me! Poor baby!"

"Does he know how you feel?"

"Well, he may not be the most sensitive man born this century but he does realize something is off center. Last night he asked me why I was so moody.

Moody? I'm terrified he's going to board an airplane one cloudless day, wave a fez at me and disappear forever into the wilds of Istanbul. Period! It will happen sooner, of course, if I continue being 'moody,' but I can't seem to think beyond the constant panic in my mind. I've decided to beat him to the inevitable and leave while I still retain some dignity. When you move in with your parents, I move in with my brother—empty or full-wombed. Enough of my adolescent problems. A shot of vodka will trivialize them quickly and thoroughly."

"But only for a little while. You're going to have to face reality, Ellen. I really do understand."

Ellen smiled slightly. True understanding extended only as far as actual experience. What possible experience could this child have to compare with the struggles she was enduring every minute of the day and night? Struggles so intense they burrowed into her unconscious and she awoke almost every morning curled tightly into the fetal position, every nerve in her body trembling, her heart beating violently, while her brain screamed, "Jesus Christ! What is going to become of me?"

Still, she managed to thank Petra and, forcing herself to be more cheerful, went into her room and returned with a half-empty bottle of vodka. "Join me?" she invited. "I've got you smoking and now it's time to lead you all the way to hell! Oh, and by the way, don't think I haven't noticed: Often, you don't sleep here anymore."

She grinned evilly, poured a tumbler partially full and handed it to Petra.

"Far too much. I'll pour my own."

"Never mind. I know you hate the stuff. No sense wasting it. I'll just drink this one alone for both of us. Toodledoooo."

"Ellen. Remember, if you need me, I'm here!"

"Yeah. Good. Thanks." She clutched the glass and the bottle, lurched out of Petra's room and into her own and closed the door behind her.

Petra gazed at it for a moment, then picked up a basket with soiled clothes and took it to the International House laundry room where she would spend the rest of the morning.

Towards the end of April, she moved to a spacious bedroom in her parents' new apartment. As agreed, she contributed to the rent, less than had been charged by Missus and for a much more beautiful place, with an unobstructed view of the Hudson River and a swimming pool.

Every month, after she received her daughter's check, Sofie deposited the full amount in the savings account she had secretly opened in Petra's name. Accepting money from their child was anathema to everything she and Sam believed in, but she rationalized to herself, it was an investment in the future.

"When she and Albert get engaged, I'll give it to them as a wedding present," she promised. Meanwhile, the little account grew each month with interest and small extra deposits she hoarded from the household expenses. Eventually she told Sam, who had never been comfortable charging his daughter rent in the first place. He approved at once, and consistently contributed dividends he earned from his stocks.

Once a week, while Petra was at the agency, Albert phoned to gauge the status of his suit, to learn if his reluctant potential wife was still available, or had indeed succumbed to the charms of the Orient and might be wearing a diamond ring on her finger or through a pallid nostril.

Sofie reassured him all was proceeding satisfactorily; now, with Petra again under her control, it would be much easier to push her in the direction of the waiting chuppah. Summer was approaching, and the Indian would soon go home, and after his vacation he would be transferred to San Francisco.

"Wait, Albert, be patient. Wait and all will be well," she repeated weekly, and he smiled into the black phone, assured he would eventually win.

Willing to wait patiently until then.

Chapter 58

The days and nights of being in love, shutting out the rest of the world, insulated and needing no one and nothing became shorter and more frantic, as both Petra and Dev recognized that people around them were intent on sabotaging their relationship.

One afternoon, as she was returning from another uneaten grab bag lunch with Dev and rushing to an office lobby elevator, a woman suddenly screamed, "Petra! What are you doing here?" and Petra was immediately embraced by Janet Spiro, a former college classmate.

Within minutes they realized they were employed by the same agency, although neither had known the other was in New York, and agreed to meet for cocktails directly after work the same afternoon.

Later, Petra watched as Janet lifted her martini glass, and the lovely diamond solitaire on her finger sparkled brightly, overshadowing the wedding band behind it.

"Phil's a banker. Well, that is, he's in training to become a manager at Bowery Savings. We got married last spring and moved here soon afterwards. What about you? No rings? No boyfriend?"

She told Janet about Dev and watched helplessly as familiar frowns creased her friend's face, cognizant another person was joining the many who already disapproved.

"Is it serious?"

"Very."

"Marriage?"

"We've talked about it."

Janet leaned across the table, "You can't do it, you know. He's not Jewish. You can't marry him."

"But we love each other," Petra responded simply as despair overwhelmed her. "Everyone says the same thing. 'You can't marry him.' In fact, my mother adamantly refuses to discuss his existence when I mention bringing him home to meet her and my father! They won't even give us a chance!"

Janet, shocked by the suffering on Petra's face, suddenly relented. "All right, then. Phil and I will give you a chance," she said at once. "Would you like to have dinner at our house Friday night? For Shabbat?"

Petra hugged her. "Neither of us will know how to behave. Is that all right? I can't remember what to do and Dev won't be a bit of help!"

"Just come. Don't worry about the rest. And it will only be the four of us. No pressure."

Friday was cold and rainy, typical New York almost-weekend weather. Dev, grinning nervously, met Petra in the agency lobby, helped her pick out a bouquet of flowers for Janet and together they went to the West Side apartment for dinner.

"Welcome!" Janet exclaimed, took the flowers and introduced a rather tall, brown haired but dissatisfied-faced man who shook hands with Dev, relieved them both of raincoats and a huge umbrella and led them into the living room.

The furniture was comfortable but hardly lavish, plain, utilitarian, the necessities that young people would throw away as they progressed farther up the social and economic ladder. For now, Janet and Phil had what they needed, and the place looked cozy and clean. More important, it was theirs alone.

Janet placed a white embroidered kerchief on her head, lit a candle, circled her arms above its flame and intoned the prayer to welcome the Sabbath bride. She turned to her husband, *"Shabbat shalom."* He answered with a quick kiss, faced his guests and hugged them each in turn.

The evening was perfect.

Dev immediately felt at home, was completely relaxed, the laugh dimples grooved deeply into his cheeks, his eyes dancing with mischief as he teased the others or told them stories which had them laughing at and with him. Exactly as he had intended.

"Help me carry the coffee cups, will you, Petra?" Janet called from the kitchen.

As soon as they were out of earshot, she grabbed Petra and said, "If you ever look at another man, you're absolutely crazy. I was wrong! For God's sake, marry him."

She noticed the tears in her friend's eyes and embraced her, "It's not easy, is it? Being so in love and having everyone against you? But I'm not anymore. And neither is Phil. Or, if he still has any reservations by tomorrow morning, they'll be gone. But I suspect Dev has won him over also. You're right, Petra. And so is he!"

She handed Petra a tissue and they returned to the living room.

Dev sensed instantly that she had been crying. Keeping any emotion hidden from him was as impossible as keeping his hidden from her, but he said nothing, took her hand as she sat down next to him on the sofa, and soon she was smiling again.

It was still pouring towards midnight when they headed home, and Dev opened the umbrella, put his arm around her waist and pulled her close for protection.

Not quite a block away, the Juanitos, a Puerto Rican street gang were also wandering around in the rain and coming directly towards the couple. Their leader spotted them at once, elbowed his lieutenant. "Easy pickings, a girl, a guy, nobody else near by, you decide..."

There were some mutual mumblings about a plan and then the decision. The gang would split into two rows, immediately surround the oblivious victims, ensuring there could be no escape. Maybe a quick rape, certainly some cash, who knew what else the snared rabbits could be worth? Stupid gringos, rambling around this late in the rain.

Had it coming!

The umbrella-shielded couple never noticed the young men heading confidently towards them, just kept looking at each other and stayed close for warmth against the chilly wetness. Even when they were surrounded on both sides by the leering, grinning gang members who, seeing she was a pale, fragile blonde, already had dreams of violence and violation, the girl reluctantly tore her gaze away from the boy next to her and faced them.

To their astonishment, she was smiling. A smile so innocent and gentle, without either fear or malice, full of compassion and love, it totally stupefied the gang's leader.

This was no broad, no cheap babe walking the streets with her latest paramour. She was a child, completely without rancor, absolutely pure, and probably for the first time in her life in love with the dark, beautiful boy who smiled back at her.

And, to his bewilderment, at him also!

Neither of them had the slightest inkling they were in imminent danger. Attacking them, he thought, would be a sin that no amount of confession would expunge, even should the priest absolve him.

Wordlessly, he signaled his companions to move on, not to stop or bother the young couple. When he passed by them himself, he nodded courteously to her and she bent her head quickly back at him, looked directly into his eyes, acknowledging his presence, sympathizing with him and his friends for being other human beings caught in the drenching rain at midnight on a dark Manhattan street.

He turned to look at them once, remembering the radiance on her face, the love in the boy's eyes, and he dared to feel a bit of hope for himself.

Chapter 59

The situation was hardly as romantic in reality.

Sofie, becoming increasingly agitated, aware at last that manipulating her daughter's future would not be as simple as she had assured herself (and the compliant Albert), and not used to being disobeyed, acted erratically at times, screaming obscenities at the girl, followed by days, weeks, of mutual silence.

Once, Petra came home to find the contents of her record albums thrown in every corner of the bedroom and some in shards on the ground, the objects of her mother's stamped-on fury.

Too shocked to cry, she reassembled the albums, replaced them on the shelf where they belonged, picked up the broken pieces and silently walked through the apartment (past her mother who was sitting in the living room expecting some kind of reaction), to the incinerator shaft and threw them away. Then she returned to her room and did not emerge again until the next morning to go back to the job she hated.

Still, she was not willing to give Dev up, even going to absurd extremes to continue seeing him. Although it was anathema to her, she learned to lie, telling her parents she was attending yet another feast or function at the I. House and would stay in the women's dormitory overnight rather than trying to return to Riverdale so late on the subway (which they had to agree could be dangerous).

Of course, she had no intention whatsoever of actually sleeping there but did sign the register, paid the few dollars charged for the room and then went with Dev to his apartment, knowing her mother was quite capable of phoning the reception desk for confirmation that her daughter was, in fact, on the premises. But there were no phones in the individual rooms, only one for each floor in the hallway, and the receptionist had no way of knowing if anyone was in or out.

And Petra was definitely out.

At other times, she informed them she would be home late from work and having dinner downtown with friends, and instead stole the few precious hours to be with Dev (without bothering to eat) and later took a taxi (which he insisted on paying for), while he followed behind in his own car to insure she reached her house safely, to the amusement of the cabbies.

Often she felt as if she were losing her sanity, trapped in a low-paying, demeaning job she hated, laboring for a spoiled, arrogant boss; going home afterwards to a hysterical, violent mother from whom she could not escape, because her salary kept her dependent!

Inadvertently, Dev helped her mother by becoming increasingly jealous.

He had little choice.

In a few months he would be transferred and in the meantime watched helplessly as Petra struggled to survive in two untenable situations at once. He phoned her at work frequently, met her for lunch when he could get away from the law office where he clerked, but realized he was beginning to lose control of himself, becoming paranoid.

Terrified, he cancelled the planned visit to India for later in the year, already hesitant to leave New York at all without her but knowing a long separation was inevitable when he went to San Francisco.

One afternoon, as the sun gleamed through the floor-to-ceiling windows of the I. House lobby, Dev squeezed into one of the pay telephone booths placed in the corners, dialed the number he needed and observed a young man approach

Petra, begin a conversation with her, take out his wallet, pass something to her and noted she took it and gave him something in return.

He quickly finished the phone call, stormed towards her and exploded. "Do you do that every time I am not in view?" he spat out. "Speak to strange men, flirt with them as if you have no morals? And why were you accepting money from him? Did you give him your phone number, too? What kind of woman are you becoming? Have you no shame at all?"

She stared at him in bewilderment, held out the dollar bill in her hand and answered, her green eyes enormous with confusion.

"He needed change for the phone and asked if I had any. I have no idea what his name is and he never asked for mine. Dev, what is the matter with you? Why are you making me feel as if I have done something wrong when I know I have not?"

A few days later he told her Jerry Roth was telling everyone he had slept with her.

When she confronted the little professor, he was horrified and vehemently denied it. The following weekend, Petra fled into the darkened area of the Waffle Wing in tears as the two men fought, first verbally, but soon the argument escalated into a physical altercation (with Dev, younger, taller and more athletic having the advantage in every area). It was halted by several astonished students who had observed everything.

Jerry had told the truth, she realized, but she loved Dev, and in spite of the change in him, stood by him.

Now there was no safe place for her, besieged at home, demeaned at work, mistrusted by her dearest friend.

He tried to change but could not, desperate to be near her, knowing she was innocent, disgusted with himself for even doubting her at all; still, the jealousy conquered him eventually, no matter how hard he tried to control it.

Worse, he knew she was suffering, shared her confusion and hated himself for adding to it.

Both were miserable with each other or without each other, talked the situation over and agreed to a trial separation for one month, no contact of any sort, no letters, no accidental meetings.

Total nothingness.

But they relented somewhat, aware such a radical split would be intolerably cruel...and chose to permit one phone call a week, which he would initiate, just to insure each one was all right.

After the month was up, they would decide what to do in the future.

Or if they had one.

Chapter 60

The trial separation began immediately.

For both of them, it was a catastrophe.

Dev could not concentrate on his work, saw her face everywhere he went, searched for her on Broadway, at the I. House, aware she would stay away from the Upper West Side entirely, but hoping she had unilaterally broken their agreement and decided to appear anyway.

And if she had, and he found her, he swore he would enfold her and never let her go again!

Loneliness devoured him, and he dared not go to sleep because she was there immediately, laughing with him in his dreams, returning his caresses, murmuring the words lovers share. Waking up was worse, her absence unbearable. He lost his appetite and didn't care about his appearance anymore.

How was it possible, he asked himself, they had become so completely intertwined, so interdependent? How had either of them even survived before they met, he wondered?

But now...?

Distraught, he recognized there was no alternative. Somehow he would have to muddle through and once a week be satisfied with hearing her voice on the telephone.

It was not enough!

He counted the endless days, second by second, minute by minute, hour by hour, obsessed with the slowness of time until at last the excruciating month of isolation was ended and the agreed-on Friday meeting arrived.

Giddy with teenaged joy, he showered and dressed, put on a clean shirt and tie, a grey wool suit, got in his new car, and drove downtown to pick her up.

An hour early.

He walked to the newsstand, bought a paper, couldn't concentrate on reading it, paced in the lobby until she emerged from an elevator, and although trembling uncharacteristically with nervousness, finally drew the first totally exhilarated breath since they had parted.

She was wearing a navy blue silk dress and matching jacket, the sleeves and cuffs of pure white, setting off her skin. As always, he was amused to see that no matter what she wore, cashmeres or cottons, blue jeans or evening gowns, she always looked so clean, her pale skin flawless, a positive side effect attributed to her Northern European genes. She laughed when he commented about it. "Right, the always clean look while being boiled alive after five minutes in the sun!"

He ran forward, led her away from the hundreds of people thronging the lobby to hurry the moment he could hold her in his arms again, know she belonged only to him.

She stared at him, startled at the change just a month had made.

He looked haggard, the skin on his beautiful face somewhat yellowish, the eyes bloodshot, his features appeared thinner, the wool flannel jacket loose around his shoulders, and she began to understand how miserable he must have been, just what this month of estrangement had cost him.

They drove to the Village for dinner, which neither could eat, stumbled miserably through it somehow. He paid the bill and without telling her where they were going drove directly to his new apartment on Riverside Drive.

When he took her in his arms, thankful she was there, all he wanted to do was hold her, gently, tenderly, to care for her forever, emotions devoid of anything except simple gratitude.

"My love, my little doll, I cannot live without you, don't want to live without you. But with you in my arms I can do anything. Anything. Once you said you would marry me. I am asking you again. I love you, love you with all my heart. Will you marry me?"

She sensed what he would say, could read his mind as if it were her own and was not surprised. But she replied, "You know me better than anyone ever has. You are my best friend, my soul, my life, the only happiness I may ever know. You inspire me, humble me."

"So," he said controlling his pain and anger, "you are saying no? Only a month, and you no longer feel about me as I do about you? Our relationship has been so superficial it could not endure a few short weeks' separation?"

"No, no," she whispered, leaning up and kissing him, a kiss he did not return. "I do love you. More than I can even express. Listen, please, and try to understand."

He leaned his head against his hand, looked down at her and saw she was telling the truth: Her eyes were troubled, but there was no subterfuge, no deceit in them, and he knew no woman could look at a man with such an expression on her face if she did not love him.

He felt as if he was dying of grief but whispered, "Go on, then. I will listen."

"In 1950, five years after the war ended, my parents took my brother and me back to Holland, our first trip back after we escaped. Arnhem, my mother's hometown, was still badly damaged. You may remember the Allied armies were ambushed nearby, and half-demolished buildings, broken bricks, huge areas of nothingness were evident everywhere. We visited the Jewish cemetery where a plaque had been placed in memory of my grandfather, the one who saved our lives, gave my mother his life's savings to make sure we made it safely to America, but was then murdered himself in Sobibor."

"Yes, I remember you told me about him. And?"

"Almost every night this past month, while we were apart, I dreamt about him, Dev. He didn't say anything, just looked at me in bewilderment. Then during the day my mother had at me, threatened to throw me out of the house if I continued seeing you. But for once my father stepped in and assured me no matter what I decided, he would always love and shelter me."

"How did your mother react?"

"It stopped her for about five minutes and then she began again."

"We will win her over, my love."

"No, Dev. We won't. She is adamant and determined I will marry Albert."

"And will you? Can he make you happy, Petra?"

"I am certain it would be a huge mistake for me...and definitely for him."

Dev slumped forward with relief. "So you will defy her?"

"Yes. But there's more, Dev. Much more. And I don't know what to do."

"Tell me, then."

"During the same trip, we went to Brussels and met my father's Aunt Betsy. Betsy, the black sheep of the piously Orthodox family, generous, loving, beautiful, who dared to marry outside the faith. When she was just twenty years old she met a handsome Armenian aristocrat in Belgium and fell in love with him. He returned her feelings and asked her to marry him.

"Her parents were scandalized and forbade the marriage. In those days a woman could not wed without her parents' consent until she was thirty years old, the age of female majority! But Tigran loved her deeply and was willing to wait.

"On her thirtieth birthday he proposed again, but this time with a caveat, 'Now or I am leaving you!'

"They married soon afterwards but she never converted to Christianity nor he to Judaism.

"The family ostracized her. Lovely, spontaneous Betsy, whose decade-long sufferings had magnified her warmth and willingness to embrace and forgive everyone. She was my father's aunt but was actually younger, and he loved to tease her by insisting on calling her *Tante* Betsy. But they had been childhood playmates, adored each other, were raised like brother and sister, so he defied the family edict and always stayed in touch with her after her marriage, during the war years and afterwards."

"How come she survived?"

"Through her husband, she claimed Armenian citizenship. Ironically he, a leader in the Armenian Belgian community, sheltered some of the same relatives who disowned her, obtained Armenian passports for them, fed them, hid some in their home and saved their lives. And, oh Dev, the minute I met him, those gentle, sweet eyes, the compassionate smile! I understood immediately why she fell in love with him!"

"Aha! He looked like me!"

"Not even the toes on your feet resembled his!" she answered, without laughing.

"You saw his bare feet?" teased Dev, hoping the serious conversation was ended.

She didn't react to his taunts, her eyes gazed at the ceiling but did not actually see it, tears rimmed around the reddening eyelids, a frown gashed the pallid forehead.

Immediately he stopped, took her in his arms and held her. "All right, doll. The rest. The part you have been avoiding. Tell it, get it out."

"I can't."

"You have to. Now. You are safe here with me."

She closed her eyes, spoke softly with enormous effort, an inward monologue, which he could barely hear.

"Tante Betsy invited us to her vacation home outside of Brussels to spend the day with Tigran and their three grown children. Eve, another cousin, and her husband Ben, both of whom survived by going underground, were also guests. It took years before their story would be revealed; a sentence here and there, an unexpected allusion to obscene events, which I was too young to understand, the studied hardness on my mother's face, which suddenly appeared when Eve's name was mentioned.

"But I was a teenager then, not really sensitive to anything outside of myself and my emerging adulthood, experiencing a re-acquaintance with my birthplace, meeting people who knew me but whom I did not know, trying to reconcile reality with places and things I remembered but might have imagined. Continually absorbing, processing, accepting and rejecting everything around me in a too-short time frame. The impact Eve would eventually have on me would not show for a long time. But it began then, at the lovely, tranquil Belgian country house owned by my newly met relatives, the pitiful handful who had somehow survived the German butchers and their accomplices."

"Do you want to go on?"

"I have to now. But could you get me a glass of water, please?"

He walked carefully to the shelf, filled a tumbler and gave it to her. She drank quickly, then turned to him again, wordlessly, for comfort. He put his arms around her, protecting her.

"Eve was probably in her late thirties when I met her, tall, regular featured, a redhead with huge green eyes and fair skin, who wore expensive clothes and drove her own American imported car (an enormous luxury in early post-war Europe) and talked hysterically and incessantly in Dutch and French. A babbled mixture, which didn't seem to make much sense in either language.

"Ben, thin, blue-eyed, quiet but supportive, was probably a few years older and obviously very mucn in love with her. Once, I overhead him berating her softly about driving more carefully.

"'What can happen to me?' she screamed, 'I can die! And so? I have no reason to live anyway!'

" Then her voice rose to a high-pitched wail, 'I want to die. Please let me die! My children are dead!'

"'Ben gazed at her sadly, tried to console her but she pushed him away and ran into the house. She emerged later, red-eyed but calmer, sat down next to Ben but said very little, in her own world of external mourning aware she was among people who loved her but could not change the circumstances.

'Why don't you adopt a child?' my mother asked later.

'No. No more children. I am afraid.' was the immediate reply.

"The topic was dropped and no one referred to it again, but my parents saw Eve the following year and commented she seemed much better, had adjusted at least outwardly to the loss of her children. And I finally asked my mother to tell me the details. She did, and now I, too, must live with them."

Petra turned her face away.

"Maybe I should have remained ignorant. It would have spared me many sleepless nights, helpless fury. Those children were my cousins, my family! Now, Dev, forever I'll be haunted. No matter how old I grow, how much time elapses, I know I can never forget them!"

"What happened?'

Softly she began again, the whispered horror torn from deep within her soul, the elusive damaged core he constantly probed and desperately wanted to touch.

"When Holland was invaded, Eve and Ben had been married for several years, were the parents of two little boys—Dries, three and Ludi, just a year old. At first the Germans didn't persecute the Jewish population too badly, with the exception of restrictions which were tolerable, they couldn't own cars, then were denied bicycles. Each new rule continued to make life more difficult. But soon the actual intent, to kill the entire community, became evident and many people made contingency plans for survival.

"Ben had a thriving business, adorned his wife with everything she wanted, a huge house, servants, gorgeous clothes and expensive jewelry. Nothing was too good for her or unattainable. Most of the time she didn't even ask, he simply kept gifting her with the best in the world.

"When Dries was born, they hired a young woman to help, and with the birth of Ludi she became a cherished member of the family, mutually in love with the two little boys. As the situation deteriorated for Jews, the attendant and her husband offered to care for the children in their own home until it improved. Eve and Ben thrilled to know Dries and Ludi would be safe with people who knew and loved them, gave the diffident couple money both in gratitude and for the care of the boys and a few days later were warned by members of the resistance to go underground themselves, learned Jews were being rounded up throughout the country, sent first to Westerbork for 'processing' and then on to concentration camps in Poland. Where they were murdered.

"But Ben and Eve moved with the help of the Dutch underground to Friesland, deep in the Northern Dutch countryside with its dikes, endless fields and dark, frozen winters. Each week Ben managed to contact the loving caretakers, inquire about the boys, give them money, a diamond, whatever he could salvage for the well-being of the children and their unselfish rescuers.

"He never saw the boys, was told it would upset the little ones too much but was always assured they were asleep, or at a party or out for a walk. In fact, after the first week there was no direct contact whatsoever but Eve and Ben knew the boys were safe. They also heard the Allies were slowly winning the war.

"As soon as it was actually over, they rushed to retrieve their children, but did not find them with the couple who supposedly had cared for them. The authorities informed them the boys had been turned over to the Germans less than a week after their parents went underground. Subsequently, they had been put on a train to Sobibor, where they were murdered immediately after their arrival at the camp."

Dev shook his head in disbelief but remained silent.

"Can you imagine? Two little toddlers, alone on a train, considered orphans but not orphans at all—one two years old and the other, four—traveling deep into Poland among total strangers, wondering where they were going, why their parents had abandoned them? Probably cold, thirsty, hungry, bewildered and absolutely helpless. I see their faces before me every night, Dev! The children! My family, my cousins!

"Eve learned later, almost as soon as the door was closed behind her, the Germans came for the children. The maid, who received a reward from the Germans for betraying the children, continued to collect Ben's money, wore Eve's jewels. Who was ever going to find out? she figured. Or who cared about a couple of spoiled Jewish brats anyway? Those bastards felt pretty safe until the war was lost. Then they assumed they'd admit what happened and take the consequences which certainly couldn't be that bad! They were right, of course!"

"Oh, my God!" Dev exclaimed, "were those monsters ever prosecuted?"

"Apparently there was some sort of trial and they were found guilty. Not that Eve and Ben cared. What punishment could ever replace their babies? Every second of their own lives they will miss them, regret they were not with them on that horrendous journey into hell, despair at the suffering the little ones must have endured as the cattle car trains transported them, completely alone, to their deaths.

"I tried to discover more about the trial, the proceedings and what punishment was meted out, but the Dutch authorities refused to divulge any information about the case, concerned about guaranteeing the privacy of the perpetrators much more than helping the family of the little victims!

'Without the consent of the criminals themselves, no data will be released.' is their official viewpoint.

"But someday, I will find out anyway. I will inform the world about those two children, give them a real identity and reveal the circumstances which led to their betrayal and deaths—rather than allowing them simply to remain two more names which appear on a list of transported and murdered Jews.

"You see, I am crying again!" she said, facing the beautiful Indian boy who loved her and immediately took her in his arms to comfort her.

"I understand, Petra. I do understand."

"Do you, Dev? Do you realize what is happening in my brain? In my conscience? I am haunted and there is no cure! If I marry you, I betray my family. If I don't marry you, I betray myself!"

"You must live with what has happened and go on with your own life. I hope it will be with me, but if not, I know the reason and respect it. Soon I will go to San Francisco. Until then I will not pressure you further. But do not elope with the milkman, either, please." He laughed thinly, his natural good humor returning, despite the pain in his heart.

"I don't like milk. If he sells champagne I might consider it," she answered, trying to match his attempt at allaying their grief a little.

"I love you, mixed up, silly, wonderful blonde!"

"I love you, marvelous, tolerant, sensitive Indian!"

"We would have made lovely babies."

"Uh, not tonight. I'm busy. I have a heavy date!"

"Hmm, can't be with me. I've lost ten pounds."

"That reminds me. Can we get something to eat somewhere?"

"At two o'clock in the morning? The only places open are bars. In six hours we can have breakfast. Good night!" he mumbled.

She kissed him and fell asleep in his arms.

The next few weeks passed far too quickly, but neither one wanted to spoil them by broaching the subject, until only seven days remained.

Now it was unavoidable.

Chapter 61

"When, Dev?" she finally dared to ask.

He winced but was glad she had brought it up herself.

"Next week. Tuesday. I'm going home for a quick visit and then will fly directly to San Francisco. One of the firm's attorneys is making living arrangements for me until I have time to make my own. No farewells at the airport. Please. Leaving you will be difficult enough as it is."

She agreed, but as the day came closer the slight veneer of courage both had assumed was scratched away and they could no longer hide their unhappiness. Particularly after they mutually, miserably, agreed to release each other from the pledge of marriage made more than a year earlier. Perhaps, they concurred, the prolonged separation would resolve any misgivings in his mind and hers.

"But I will ask you again, you know. Don't think you can get rid of me so easily," he laughed, trying to stay upbeat. "I will phone, I will write, I will deluge you with love letters. The post offices between California and New York will have to hire extra personnel to handle all the extra mail!"

And then he took her in his arms and sobbed, "How can I live without you!"

Chapter 62

As stultifying as the hours at the advertising agency were, with their hysterical insistence on making ordinary things appear extraordinary and their eternal emphasis on and illusions of deeming the unimportant important, they did offer a slight surcease from the volatile tantrums in Riverdale.

Going to the I. House was too painful, and Petra did not have the strength yet to face it. She didn't just miss Dev, she was directionless without him.

Determined to overcome the brainlessness of work, the frustrations at home, she signed up for a Red Cross volunteer nurse's aide class at Columbia Presbyterian Hospital, removing the focus from her (in proper perspective) limited sense of misery to alleviating (if even by just a little bit) the pain and helplessness of patients who were actually suffering.

From the stupidity of Burken's world, she subwayed to the hospital, committed to at least six hours a week in the evening.

The four-week course taught her to bathe and feed patients, anoint their dried skins with cocoa butter, massage stiffened muscles, move them carefully to alleviate or prevent the onset of bedsores, change sheets while patients remained in their beds, renew bandages under the supervision of the registered nurses, offer and remove bedpans, take and chart mandated temperature, pulse and respiration data, and be available to assist the paid medical staff as needed.

She had never been in a hospital before or in contact with serious illness. Thin and frail as she might appear, her health was excellent and her youth enabled her to assist the helpless while gaining unexpected satisfaction in performing the lowly chores expected of her.

The emotions she could no longer lavish on Dev, were transferred to the patients.

From the first day, she and a classmate became friends. BethAnn was tall, beautiful, dark-eyed, with lovely olive skin framed by soft, brown curly hair. She was born in Trinidad and had something exotic, perhaps a black East Indian, Caribbean ancestor in her heritage, in addition to the prevalent white one...and the resulting mix was glorious. The best characteristics of the races in one lovely woman.

Like Petra, she was college degreed and hated the flunky-level job where she labored for a high-school diploma-ed man far less intelligent or sensitive than she was herself.

Eventually both completed the course, took a required examination and earned certificates allowing them on the actual wards. They agreed to always work together, first because they genuinely liked each other, second because they were absolutely terrified! Volunteers could choose the areas where assistance was needed. Everyone always picked the nursery, cuddling the babies so fragile and sweet, trying to bottle-feed them although they understandably often balked at the taste of the rubber nipple, soothing and patting their newborn-ness in a world they could not understand. Most were healthy and beautiful, having only to complete the mandatory, five-day hospital stay to insure no mishap would occur to them or their new mothers. They would then go home with their parents and lead normal lives.

But also among them were the tiny creatures too weak to cry, who shook constantly and were given a special formula containing a slight dose of the drugs with which their addicted mothers had massively infused them. Some babies were physically affected, some obviously already brain damaged, others not yet manifesting the permanent results of the maternally administered poisons.

And soon, perhaps blessedly, some would die.

After cuddling, feeding, changing, rocking, crooning, and singing to dozens of infants, BethAnn and Petra realized there would always be volunteers for the babies.

They wanted more.

"What's the worst ward in the hospital?" BethAnn asked the volunteer coordinator. "Where no one wants to go?"

"Neurological" was the immediate reply. "It's hell on earth!"

"Do they use volunteer help?"

"I'm sure they'd love it if they could get it. But no one ever wants to go there. And you're too young. Neither of you could handle the stress."

"How old are we supposed to be?"

"They need at least college-aged people."

"If you'd bother to look at our files you'd know we have degrees already."

"Oh," she admitted blushing, "I hadn't noticed. You both look so young. But are you sure you want to try this? It's very depressing."

"If we don't want to stay there, will you let us switch?"

The woman agreed and they took the elevator to the neurological section. The main ward consisted of perhaps twenty beds, all filled and doubly reflected on the huge, linoleum floor. Patients, the majority extremely ill, were generally completely silent or groaned softly.

With one very noisy exception.

In a rail-raised bed lay a thin old woman surrounded by a large family. She motioned to them continually to come closer and spoke in staccatoed Italian, shouted something and then gestured frantically towards the two passing volunteers.

Again she repeated something harshly in Italian and made an obscene gesture.

"Can I help you?" Petra asked.

"She don't talk English," a man retorted.

"Will you translate for me then, please?"

"She wanna pee!"

Quickly, BethAnn and Petra hustled the family members away, closed the curtain around the patient and assisted her. As soon as she was finished, the relatives were again around the bed, holding the old woman's hands, speaking softly to her, jostling for a place to be near her, while she continued her spectacular screeching, thrashed her arms, and her eyes white-rolled like a terrified, dying animal.

"Can you help me with Laurie, please?" a nurse asked, hurrying away from the ward and towards the hallway, disappearing through an opened door and into a private room.

In the bed lay a young girl of perhaps eighteen or nineteen. Her auburn hair was cut short in ringlets, magnifying blue eyes staring at the ceiling. A tube was connected to her arm, and she appeared to be neither awake nor asleep, not aware of the women who stood at her bedside. She was obviously in the final trimester of pregnancy, the slow rising and falling of her abdomen the only visible motion.

"Hello, dear," the nurse murmured gently, "we've come to give you some nice clean sheets and you can sleep more comfortably tonight. Now we're going to lift you carefully and not hurt you and the baby. Is that all right?"

There was no reaction from the patient, who allowed her bedclothes to be changed without the slightest struggle, was rolled gently onto the clean ones, remaining totally silent, unseeing, unhearing.

In the hallway, which was now turning evening dark, a young man, thin, mustached, no more than a teenager himself waited, his face mirroring fatigue and worry.

"Thank you, nurse," he whispered. "And you too, ladies," he added to Petra and BethAnn. "When this is over, I swear I'm never going to let her get pregnant again. I just want her to come back to me. Healthy, with or without a baby!" he sobbed and the nurse took him in her arms.

"We're doing our best, Tim. Now, you keep thinking good thoughts!"

"I know. I know. But she just lies there and it's been a month. How long before she can come home again? I love her so much and I don't know how to help her! I'm sorry," he said to the volunteers, "sometimes I feel I can't take any more!"

He went into the room, leaned over the bed and kissed the immobile face of the girl lying there. "Hello, sweetheart. It's me. How are you?"

He picked up a chair and sat down next to her, talking softly, caressing her hand, kissing her forehead.

Back in the hallway, the nurse whispered, "He works all day, then comes here and stays with her. Every night. For the last month he's done it. We're concerned about him, too. He looks exhausted."

"What happened to her?"

"Stroke. It's rare, but occasionally a pregnant woman suddenly develops one. Hers is very serious, but the baby is alive. All we can do is hope."

"Will she survive?" asked BethAnn.

"That's entirely in God's hands," was the answer.

The two young volunteers went back to work, accomplishing the necessary menial chores, allow nurses time to give special care to other patients, and finished the promised shift.

In the hospital elevator, as they prepared to take the subway partially home together, BethAnn asked, "What do you think? Did you find it interesting?"

"Very. And as depressing as we were warned. And you?"

"Same. Do you want to work here again?"

"Absolutely. Yes!"

"Me, too!"

Still dressed in their blue striped uniforms with the nurse's aide caps pinned to their hair, they emerged from the austere, hushed building and suddenly began to sing, grasped each other's hands spontaneously and danced across the silent sidewalks, drunk with happiness.

Drunk and grateful they were alive, healthy, free to leave whenever they chose, so they could return another time to assist in the worst ward in the hospital.

The following week they noticed the old Italian woman's bed was empty.

"Oh, she had an operation and is recuperating at home."

"You mean she's going to be all right?"

"Yes. Unless her relatives kill her with too much pasta and Chianti, she'll completely recover."

Laurie's room was also empty, and BethAnn said, "So, she's had her baby and is home again with Tim?"

"No," replied the nurse, "three days ago Laurie went to heaven."

Petra, shocked, asked, "And her baby, too?"

"The baby is fine. But Laurie had a Caesarian and is now with God," answered the nurse, tight-lipped, picked up a stack of clean sheets and handed them to the girls."Now, please help me prepare the beds for the next patients."

As she lay in her own bed that night, Petra pondered why a young mother with a husband who adored her and a lovely new baby would prematurely have her life snuffed out, while an old woman who had already lived more than eighty years and experienced the birth of her children and grandchildren had survived and totally regained her health.

Something about both situations seemed completely off-balance.

Maybe, she thought, life itself is off-balance.

Chapter 63

Wilson Burken, appropriately dressed in Ivy League grey flannels, white shirt with blue silk tie, and kewpie-doll face adorned with a supercilious, sanctimonious bow-lipped smile, was waiting anxiously (and uncharacteristically early) for her on Monday morning.

In his manicured hands he held his résumé and an application form. "Fill it out for me, will you? All the information you need is right here"...and extended the papers.

"When you're finished, I want you to compose a letter informing the Foreign Press Association of my qualifications. I'll look it over and sign. Then you go to the post office and mail it immediately."

He disappeared into his office.

She glanced at the list of names on the paper. Board member of three (restricted) country clubs, belonged to a yacht club (also restricted), the alumni clubs of his prep school and Harvard University, and, by virtue of having completed one Himalayan climb while in India, made himself eligible to join the Mountaineers.

Nowhere was any charity mentioned, not the Red Cross, the March of Dimes, any refugee organization, and at no time had the great man volunteered even five minutes of his valuable time or a single nickel to help anyone else except himself.

There was no mention of New York's double Metropolitans (Opera and Art), while apparently he also had no interest in Carnegie Hall, the Museum of

Modern Art or the Museum of Natural History...some of the glorious institutions which had (gratis) educated her.

She sneered as she saw the names on the list, unable to hide her disgust at yet another manifestation of his limited view of the world, prophesying while she typed the ordered material that his future would continue to be simply more of the same.

Multiple country clubs, but nothing to reduce the suffering of others. How could a woman love such a person, she wondered, unless of course, she was as limited and would undoubtedly whelp additional images of themselves, a depressing thought so early in the day!

And those phantom children, would they ever learn the family secret, a secret Petra had discovered by accident a few days earlier?

She had attended a party given by BethAnn and met a man who innocently asked where she worked. She told him and he replied he knew the agency well and wanted to know her boss' name. Before telling him she blurted out, "The greatest idiot and biggest windbag ever born!"

"Ahahaha," he replied immediately, "you must work for Wilson!"

"Oops, I probably shouldn't have said what I said."

But he just continued to laugh. "Well, next time he tries to impress you with his pedigree, remember this! He can boast all he wants that he's deeply rooted in high society but his old man was an immigrant and ran a speakeasy on the Lower East Side. For pin money he rented out rooms and hostesses, both by the hour."

At first Petra couldn't believe it.

"Yup. Arrived here with a stuffed pillowcase on his shoulders and ten bucks in his pants pocket. Did well in the wine, women and song business. Married a girl originally from Poland. Wilson changed his name as soon as he was legally old enough and became a church-going Episcopalian at the same time. It broke the old man's heart but what could he do? I don't think they see much of each other anymore."

Would he ever tell his future family? Petra wondered and returned to filling out the demanded application form and its accompanying letter (which her pretentious boss would sign as if he had actually written it).

Later she mailed it, bought a newspaper and glanced through the "help wanted" pages. During his next trip abroad she would find a few hours spare time and do some serious job hunting, determined to escape the agency's glamorous trap.

She could no longer tolerate Wilson Burken...and had never respected him.

Chapter 64

Letters and phone calls arrived from Dev, who directed both to her workplace to insure Sofie could not intercept them. He loved San Francisco but missed Manhattan and Petra.

One Sunday in November, excited and happy, he uncharacteristically called her at home in Riverdale, not willing to save his news until Monday. "I'm coming to New York, but only for two days! I have to do some research at the Columbia Law Library," he sang across the miles apart.

"Do you still love me?" he asked shyly.

With her parents sitting yards away on the couch, she could barely talk to him at all but managed a cool "yes."

"Eavesdroppers?" he asked quickly.

"Right," a platonic response.

"Good. Just listen. A friend of mine has an apartment on Riverside Drive. He's going to be away and will let me use it in the meantime."

She managed another non-committal reply, but the possibility that they could actually be alone together (with some creative explanations to her family) made her cheeks flush.

"I don't have my plane tickets yet or know what day I'll arrive. But I'll call you from the airport as soon as I get in. Probably late next week."

But Dev didn't phone.

Instead, the following afternoon, he suddenly opened her office door, holding an enormous bouquet of golden chrysanthemums and purple irises nestled on a bed of rust-colored oak leaves. When she took it from him, it was so large she could barely see him above it.

"You remembered," she sighed as she cradled them in her arms, overjoyed to see him and aching to embrace him instead of the flowers.

"Yes, my love. The autumn shades. Your favorites. I can never forget anything you tell me. Now, can you get away tonight, make some excuse not to go home?"

Still shaking with elation, she arranged the flowers in a vase, placed them on her desk and phoned her parents, hoping the excitement would not be reflected in her voice.

"One of the secretaries has tickets to a premiere for this evening and instead of going home by myself I'll stay with her in Brooklyn," she informed them.

It was such a logical lie she almost performed it automatically. Premieres occurred all the time, gratis tickets were always available to the agency staff.

And then they were in each other's arms, laughing, crying, overwhelmed with happiness.

"So, mademoiselle, what have you been doing while I was in the wilds of California earning money to feed you and the children?" Dev demanded.

Not commenting, he was shocked at how thin and tired she looked.

She told him the basics, no details of her mother's continued displeasure, Burken's characteristic idiocy and her own sense of confusion. But she couldn't resist telling him about having met Albert. "He insisted, kept phoning until I agreed to have lunch with him."

"And?"

"Nice man. Bored me to death!"

"You're disobeying your parents? Or have you decided to marry him after all?"

This was a subject he knew well. In India, girls were routinely married to men they didn't love, sometimes hadn't even met before the wedding.

"Uh. Should I?"

"Hell NO! So what did you talk about?"

"He asked if there still wasn't just a tiny bit of the old feeling left for him. There wasn't."

"And did he accept it?"

"I told him 'no' but what I didn't say was, before I met you I had no basis for comparison. Now I do."

"So, am I better or is Alfred better?"

"Albert, not Alfred. Neither of you. The mailman is better!"

He grabbed her and began to kiss her passionately. "You still like the mailman better?"

"Hmm. Not as much as before. Do it again."

A pause while he complied.

"Okay. For now, you win."

"I'd better win, you difficult woman! I come all the way from across the country and you taunt me with the many men you have played with in my absence. Just wait until we are married. I will lock you up in my harem of ten thousand beautiful slaves and never let you out!"

"I'll seduce you into setting me free!"

He laughed and said, "You probably could, too!" Then continued, "Despite this foolishness you've become reticent, thoughtful. What else has happened?"

"Nothing specific. Perhaps working at the hospital is affecting me. You're a bit down, too, my friend, despite the attempts at being funny."

"I'm sorry darling," he replied, "I think traveling and constant pressures at the firm are getting to me."

Then suddenly he took her tightly in his arms and moaned, "Petra, please, please don't leave me. I cannot go on without you. We must find a way to be together."

She nodded silently, kissed him and folded into his embrace, the shelter which never failed her. But avoided responding directly to his plea.

"It's been such a marvelous day. Look how beautiful the river is at midnight, with the moonlight reflected in the water. The only thing spoiling it is the ALCOA sign with its neon reds and greens! Someday I'm going to take a canoe, oar it to Trenton and complain to whoever is in charge to demand they take the thing down and toss it in the garbage!"

"Yes, my little revolutionary. You just go ahead and do so! But first we have more important things to do!"

"Damn it, Dev. That's probably the exact answer I'll get from them!"

"Well, love, get used to the ways of the capitalist minority," he replied drawing her expertly back into his arms and onto the topic she was evading. "If you marry me you'll be right in the midst of it!"

It was the first direct allusion he had made in the more than two years she had known him concerning his family's wealth. It certainly didn't surprise her. Common sense made it obvious the average man on the Bombay streets could hardly afford to send his children abroad to study!

"Tell me," she asked, "how do your relatives spend their days?"

"Why the same as here, I guess. We go to work, we come home, we play, eat and drink, love our ladies." He paused, "Enjoy making lots of babies!"

"But what about the women? What do they do while the men are off earning millions of rupees?"

"The women? They do what women all over the world do."

"And what is that?"

"You should know. You're a woman!"

"Oh, so they go to school, they work, or..."

"Not after they are married, of course."

"No? Well what do they do after they are married?"

"Take care of their husband and children. Just as over here."

"You mean cook, clean, wash dirty diapers?"

"Well, no. The cooks, the nursemaids, and the servants do those things."

"So, what is left for the wives to do?"

"They shop for groceries." He stopped himself. "Oh no. Not exactly. They order what they want and the servants purchase it at the markets and bring it home to be prepared."

"Undoubtedly by the cooks. Do they go shopping a lot for other things?"

"Perhaps. Or they might ask the sari makers and jewelers to bring their wares to the house. Maybe later they have their hair dressed and get manicures. Or go to the country club to show off their new acquisitions. Then they have tea with friends. And, like women everywhere, they just gossip."

"Sari fitting and jewelry purchasing every day, I think would take up at most about two hours. And afterwards?"

"Well, by then it is time for the husband to amble home. Later the wife probably manages to keep him entertained. And he, her. I don't think we'll have problems doing the same, I assume."

"Oh."

"Darling," he finally replied in exasperation, "I don't know what they do! Your friends will show you themselves. Besides when our babies are born, life will be much more complicated and busier!"

"Dev?"

"Yes, my love."

"Does your father own a car?"

His answer was accompanied by just the slightest blush. "Uh, yes."

"More than one?"

Again, he agreed.

"How many?"

"Well, usually there are several at our disposal. The next question will be what makes. Am I right?"

She nodded, her mouth suddenly tight and tense.

He sighed, "All right then. A Jaguar. A Bentley or two. Probably a few Rolls Royces...And my favorite little red Austin Healey convertible. So what? Satisfied?"

"Do your parents drive?"

"Good heavens, no! They have a chauffeur. There is one especially for the ladies in the family. My eldest brother usually drives the Jaguar himself, though."

"And I hope he doesn't overwork himself when he does it," mumbled Petra.

He laughed tolerantly, "Now, what is wrong? Are you trying to solve the problems of the world by yourself again?"

"No, but I wondered if your gossipy female relatives did any social work. You know, volunteered at a hospital, for instance. Or went among the poor to help a little. Maybe donated money or food. They seem to live such useless lives. And your country has many people who desperately need assistance."

He stared at her, the expression of shock on his face open and bare. "You don't understand, Petra. Life in India has always been so for them. Not like here in your Western world where philanthropy is a necklace worn ostentatiously by the rich to impress the middle class minorities."

He was very solemn now but continued, "When we marry, you will be expected to perform many social functions. But from our home. Not outside of it!"

She retorted immediately, "If we marry and live in India, the first thing I am going to do is apply at the nearest medical school. And if they won't accept me as a student I'll sign up to do volunteer work!"

The shock was still engraved on his face. "To give dirty, disease ridden children bottles of milk, I suppose?"

"If they need me. Yes. Or put men on bedpans, if that's required!"

He suddenly looked totally defeated. "My dearest love, my darling. A woman of your position cannot. It simply is not possible."

"Then if it isn't, I will do it anyway. God endowed me with a brain, and I think a heart. Evidently when I marry you, I shall have the money to equal both. Oh Dev," she implored, "do you think I could ever enjoy such luxuries, aware babies right outside of my gate were starving to death? Were desperately ill and I had the resources to help but had to ignore their sufferings? My love, try to understand, I would not have rest in my large house, with the chauffeurs, the servants, the saris, the sapphires, unless I helped them!"

But Dev doesn't answer because he knows (although she does not) that they have reached an insurmountable obstacle. He loves her exactly as she is, but if he takes her home with him, she will have to change. And he wonders if he will recognize the woman who must emerge as a result. Not once in their long relationship has he asked himself such a question, and he has no answer.

And what she knows (and he does not) concerns the nights when she is sporadically able to sleep for just a little while, when the battle to stay awake and aware is lost through ordinary exhaustion.

Unexpectedly at first and then more frequently, the face of her grandfather enters her unconsciousness, during the hours she is most vulnerable, alone in the quiet of darkness.

His love for her, evident on his face, is mingled with bewilderment and a command.

Silently he reminds her of an obligation. To whom? To what? He never speaks but stares at her, expecting her to understand.

She relives in dreams the moment in their living room in Scheveningen when he offers a leather briefcase filled with his life savings to Sofie, which will allow her family to escape the Germanic horror he has foreseen.

And Petra senses he feels betrayed.

But soon his face resumes its habitual intelligence and kindliness, while she clearly hears her own brain asking his advice. "What must I do? Tell me, Opa? Where do I belong? Where do my obligations lie? With myself, my own happiness or with my people whom I hardly know?"

Just before she awakens, trembling, she hears him respond, *"Shemai israel, adonoi elohenu, adonoi egod."*

His message has reached her.

Horrified and frightened but unable to do otherwise, she realizes she will obey him.

But not now, not tonight.

She rests against Dev's chest, hears the gentle beating of his heart, the bitterness and confusion temporarily muffled, gazes up at the man she loves while he looks into her eyes and to his amazement sees his own face reflected there.

And she sees hers in his.

Alone again in the nights after Dev returns to San Francisco—he sorrowful, understanding everything—the question mark of their future haunts her.

As she knows it is haunting him.

Chapter 65

"You have no idea how glad I am to see you," the balding, aging but-still-youthful professor told her, his beglassed eyes alive with delight. "I'm bored with lecturing to sleepy sophomores. I've seen every new art exhibit between Greenwich Village and Mt. Sinai Hospital. And much as I love the opera, another clichéd Verdi, Puccini or Bizet, and damn it, I'm going to cancel my subscription!"

"What? No 'Zauberflote' among the over-done?" she taunted him innocently, having just read the music critic's temperate review of its most recent Metropolitan Opera production.

He squinted at her, trying to read her thoughts and moved forward before he lost his nerve. "Yes, as a matter of fact, my tickets are for Saturday evening. Would you like to join me?"

Not a date, no, he hadn't asked her for a date. Just mutual music lovers, friends, absolutely no more. He wondered if she would accept his innocent offer and fall into the trap.

"I can't, Jerry. It's impossible. Thank you for the invitation but you knew before you extended it I would not accept."

"He lied, you know. I never said any of those things about you."

She didn't answer, but he realized she knew he was telling the truth.

"So, are you going to marry him?"

Still no response.

"Does silence imply you don't love him enough or he hasn't asked you?"

She smiled her newly learned all-encompassing Eastern smile, feeling her entire body beginning to recoil.

"Petra, before you make a final decision, consider carefully."

For just an instant he stopped talking; his face flushed vivid red, he took a deep breath and exploded. "God damn it! There were six million of us lost in the kilns. Don't you feel any obligation towards them? No need in your personal way to rectify even a tiny amount of such a loss? How can you, who escaped all the horror, desert us, as if none of it ever happened?"

She had not expected such an emotional attack from the introverted academic and felt her own face burning while his eyes still blazed with anger.

"Are you Jewish?" he demanded.

"Yes," she answered instantly.

He nodded towards her. "That's all I wanted to hear you say. Run away, hide in comparative theology, study everything the world's philosophers have brilliantly and at length written about their own and everyone else's religion. None of it makes a bit of difference. You know in your heart who you are and what you are."

"And you? Do you know as much, as well? Just what do you believe in, Jerry? What makes you so sanctimonious?" she countered.

"Me? I believe in the Ten Commandments but little in organized religion with its mysterious ceremonies and prohibitions. But, I will never marry anyone but a Jew. Fear of the unknown, perhaps. Not daring to hear my wife, my best friend, whom I will trust more than anyone on earth, scream one day during an argument (and we will argue, because all couples do) she hates me and I am nothing but a dirty Jew. The thought of such an outburst from her, perhaps in front of my children, terrifies me. So I will stay safely within the tribe, thank you very much."

He grimaced. "Life is difficult enough for us without having to endure right to the groin attacks from the people we love most in the world!"

"Excuse me, please," Petra announced, desperate to escape from the conversation. "I have to go downtown. Take care, Jerry. See you later."

He watched her hurry from the Waffle Wing unaware that the decision he thought he could influence had already been made.

Unable to completely pretend that neither existed anymore, Dev and Petra made some concessions: to write whenever they needed to and to phone no more than once a month, except if there was an emergency. Most important of all, they promised to remain always and forever friends, no matter what happened after the break-up.

During the surprise visit, Petra, caught unprepared, had borrowed some money from Dev but when she attempted to repay it, he stopped her.

Instead, he tore the ten-dollar bill she held out in half, gave her one piece and placed the other in his own wallet. "Someday when these halves are together again, you and I shall be united. Until then, we must both keep them safe."

He took a plane to California the next afternoon.

Despite his attempts at levity when he returned to San Francisco, Dev was in reality completely broken, unable to eat or sleep, and lost so much weight, his colleagues insisted he seek medical assistance. The physician he consulted immediately prescribed complete bed rest and signed him into a hospital to recuperate from (or adapt to) dehydration, malnutrition and nervous exhaustion.

Dev caught his breath, returned to his practice, immersed himself in work during the day, sought oblivion at night, and when he thought he could not go on for another second, picked up the phone, talked to her, mourned, and found the courage to carry on again.

She fared no better.

Although he went through the days and nights in semi-misery, adjusting to living without her, expunging insistent thoughts of their possible future happiness and memories of their mutual exultation, he was in a city that held no memories, while she continually faced streets they had walked on, passed restaurants where they had eaten, spoke with people who knew him and inquired about him, until she thought she was losing her sanity.

Often, she thought she saw his face when she crossed from one side of Fifth Avenue to another, only to realize, of course, she was mistaken, and grieved silently when she heard someone speaking with the lovely, familiar Indian accent she knew so well.

One day, as the light was changing on Madison Avenue, she walked deliberately into the path of oncoming traffic. She hardly heard the curses from the furious car drivers.

And although mourning was all she could do about the situation with Dev, Wilson Burken finally gave her the opportunity to quit the job she hated.

The "La Boheme" incident, when he had kept her typing and retyping, editing and re-editing one stupid draft after the other of his inanities, became the rule rather than an exception.

Meanwhile, she had to keep up with other duties as well and arrival at the office by 8 a.m. was expected, a one-hour lunch break a rarity, and being able to catch the five o'clock train to Riverdale a mirage.

But the sanctimonious oaf was summoned to Brussels, and as soon as Petra knew he was safely (or unsafely) on the plane, she bolted, hoping to have a benign smile on her face and a letter of resignation in her hand upon his return.

Her life might not be without pain right now; still, she was young and it was not over!

Chapter 66

There were plenty of jobs available but they were basically more typing, dictation and filing, exactly the robotic skills she detested and which could be done better and with more enthusiasm by any high school graduate ...and led nowhere.

Someone informed her that Yeshiva University (ideologically and philosophically totally removed from her own background) had an opening for a copywriter in their public relations department. To her surprise, it occupied several floors in a modern building at Fifth Avenue and 57th Street in the heart of the city, many miles removed from its secluded main campus in upper Manhattan

With few expectations that she would be offered or accept work at the Orthodox Jewish institution, she applied anyway.

The University's promotion manager who initially interviewed her was small, brash, wore glasses and perfectly fit the caricature of the ambitious ad-man. She was too well used to his sort, bravado without much substance, and was not going to be trapped again.

But he gestured to her and she followed him into a small office and was introduced to the man she might actually be working for.

"No," he insisted immediately, "you will be working with me, not for me! I don't need a typist, we have a steno pool. I don't want a secretary to take notes, my tape recorder does it masterfully. I need someone who knows the English language well, can write news releases and promotional material and stand in for me at meetings when I am unavailable. If you're able to do those things, we can begin to talk. Otherwise, it was nice meeting you, thank you for stopping by and good luck in your job search."

Suddenly, the potential position seemed much more interesting.

The man who addressed her was tall, perhaps in his mid-thirties, shirted- and -tied but jacketless, had fair skin; a clear, rounded forehead; regular features, a small mustache, and brown, soft, intelligent eyes.

On his head he wore a yarmulka.

When she informed him immediately that she was not religious, did not keep kosher, didn't even belong to a synagogue and had no intentions of changing, he shook his head, shrugged, and said, "Who cares?"

By the time they had talked for an hour (or perhaps longer because neither of them bothered to look at the clock), they had hired each other, although neither had said so.

He encountered a young woman, ambitious, who understood the classics, loved literature as he did, and had probably endured more than he dared to discover at this initial meeting. He knew, however, she was Jewish, born in Europe and drew his own conclusions.

Her piety or lack of it didn't concern him.

Her intelligence did.

She met a sensitive, brilliant scholar (completing his doctoral dissertation in English literature and teaching several classes at New York University, the reason he needed someone capable and able to fill in for him at the office when necessary), a man of enormous integrity whom she sensed she could rely on as a friend while respecting and learning from him professionally.

When he returned home that evening, his beautiful, Israeli wife (who had recently earned a doctorate in microbiology) inquired about the search for his assistant.

"I think it's over. We're going to make someone an offer tomorrow. I hope she accepts."

She put her arms around him and kissed him. "Me too, Jack. It's asking too much of you, the office, preparing for your classes, compiling the research, both of us working. We need time together to just be young and silly. Particularly now."

"How long, sweetheart, before you're quitting?" he asked softly, holding her carefully, nuzzling his cheek against her radiant, exotic face.

"Another two weeks, I think. I'm fine but am feeling tired. Very tired."

"Then stop, love. Immediately. It's not worth it. If anything ever happened to you..."

"Ah, you are being ridiculous and over-protective. Arab rifles couldn't kill me while I was in the army, so how could a tiny baby?"

She pushed him away and commanded, "Now, come and eat dinner!"

Chapter 67

When Burken returned from Belgium, Petra's letter of resignation was first in the pile of mail on his desk. He looked at it in astonishment, shook his head and mumbled, "Where will I ever get another one? With Dutch and French, who can write like this one does?"

With his eternal arrogance and stupidity, he was still incapable of understanding that she was not "another one" but a human being endowed with unappreciated skills worthy of his respect (and far greater rewards), not simply a flunky who had to kowtow to his self-assumed (but decidedly questionable) superiority!

On her final day at the agency, he presented her with a small bottle of perfume and joked, "So you will smell nice for another boss."

She thanked him and couldn't resist adding, "I won't have a boss. But I am certain my wonderful new colleague will appreciate it."

Then she walked away from him, Brooks Brothered in grey flannels, past the grey walls, the grey office, the grey desk with the grey typewriter shackled to it.

Free, at last, from all of them!

Chapter 68

A glorious summer Sunday.

In the distance above her, she sees bright skies, vivid foliage floating past. Hidden in the dimness of the car, the world is veiled and white before her eyes.

Her brother, home for the occasion and wearing a United States Navy officer's uniform, is driving, stops for a red light while another vehicle glides into the lane next to theirs.

A woman opens the window on the passenger side when she glimpses the bride and calls out, "Good luck to you."

Petra thanks her, surprised her voice is hoarse, a whisper, as if she is not capable of speech.

They arrive at the shul in Riverdale, enter and the rituals begin. Twenty minutes later she and a tall, curly-haired man emerge together and are assisted into the backseat of a waiting, black limousine.

With shock, she realizes he is her husband. She has known him only a few months but moments ago, with state and religious sanctions, they agreed to share their lives. At least, she assumes that is what occurred. The ceremony itself has left no impression on her, no retrievable memory of admonishments delivered, promises made, blessings adjured.

As if, instead of being directly involved with it, she too, were merely a bystander.

The limousine stops before a large, white house in Scarsdale and her father is standing on the steps, blue-suited, watching her and the young man emerge from the back seat. Her mother (adapting finally to the many-years-ago loss of Albert), stands next to him, her mink stole, and retrieved-for-the-occasion-from-the safe-deposit-box-family-diamonds and watered silk dress amusingly similar to those worn by the fat, middle-aged woman who greets them from the doorway.

A grey-haired, thin man, grinning, back-slapping, welcomes them to his home for the reception and repeatedly calls out, "Mazel tov! Mazel tov!" Then he takes Sofie's arm and Sam extends his to Petra's mother-in-law, and the four parents disappear into the garden now decorated with vases of white flowers.

With her new husband, she follows them.

Guests are already enjoying snacks and beverages from trays passed around by bowing, tuxedoed waiters and white-aproned, gauze-capped waitresses.

Suddenly, there are many people pushing towards her, groping for her face, kissing her. She has never before seen the overwhelming majority of them. As each perfumed woman and custom-suited man reaches for her, she is again no longer a participant.

It is all happening, she thinks, but none of it is happening.

They wish her good luck, ask her to visit them after the honeymoon, welcome her into their family, gush over her, and effusively congratulate her husband on landing such a beauty. Automatically she thanks them, assures them they will keep in touch.

Has no idea who they are!

BethAnn, her best friend for so many years, leans over and with a clean handkerchief wipes a lipstick imprint (whose?) from her cheek and hugs her quickly.

"I think I just shocked your new mother-in-law," she notes with a mischievous grin, her eyes dancing with delight.

For the first time, Petra is able to respond genuinely and hugs her gratefully, overjoyed there is at least one person among this enthusiastic crowd of unknown well-wishers whom she recognizes and cherishes.

"How did you do that?" she asks.

"I told her you were the most wonderful person I've ever known and I hoped her family could live up to you!"

The laughter erupts from both their stomachs, gurgling loudly out of their mouths.

BethAnn's husband, carrying their three-month old infant, joins them and kisses Petra, his nearness more familiar than that of her own newly sanctioned husband. She clings to him for an instant, dreading the next stranger's breath in her face and hands on her body.

And yet another lipstick imprint!

Champagne bottles appear, are opened, glasses are filled and overflow into the grass, flashbulbs blind her as she is given the ivory-handled cake cutter her grandfather had presented to Sofie long ago on the day she married Sam (one of the few things the family took with them to America), and is directed towards a four-tiered confection awaiting the surgical incision, while the perpetually jovial man who appears at her side puts an arm around her waist, protectively, possessively, and smiles into the camera.

She stares up at him and realizes she does not know him. Terrified, she understands too late he knows her even less, precisely because he is convinced he DOES know her!

Already, she is afraid to be alone with him.

More people crush around them, congratulate him, comment on his excellent taste, their glorious future together.

The clichés alienate her even more.

She does not want to listen to them, does not believe them, is disgusted by their worn-out insincerity.

Just like some of the wedding guests, she is a stranger among strangers. In spite of all the attention or perhaps because of it, she is desperately lonely.

She wants to go home but suddenly realizes she doesn't know what that means, either.

Or where it is.

Verging on panic, she rushes to an upstairs bedroom (ostensibly to change into the dupioni traveling outfit waiting there, and eager to be away from the celebration and start her life as a married woman).

But actually to find a moment's surcease, a little while alone to breathe and attempt to absorb.

The whalebone stays, sewn into her dress to support the bodice, have made deep-red gashes all around her waist. In anguish, dabbing at the bloody striped wounds with a tissue, she writhes out of the gown, exchanges it for the dupioni and welcomes its sensation of silk, heavy and soft, falling gently and smoothly around her, grateful for immediate, blessed relief from the tortuous, over-stiff virginity of the stained wedding gown, now suspended innocently from a clothes hanger on the bathroom door.

No longer in constant pain, she peers through the curtains at the celebration in the garden below.

It is crowded with people, drinking, eating, feasting, laughing, talking, telling jokes.

"Why are they there? Who are they? Is all the commotion caused by me?" she wonders. "But that cannot be. None of it has a thing to do with me!

And could this almost-entirely-strangers-attended festivity really be my wedding? To whom?"

A few weeks ago, without mentioning it to anyone, she stopped in at the I. House, noticed several students in the little park nearby, walked into the building aware everyone she had known was gone.

Baboo (promoted to an executive position for his firm), Ellen back in Boston without Salmi, Alan absent from everyone's list since Parvati's death.

But in a corner of the immense lobby, several Middle Eastern students were discussing plans for the next Halloween Festival. Two women in saris were huddling over books and a student wearing a yarmulka was tutoring them.

Dev, she thought, oh Dev! After all this time, I still miss you!

She phoned San Francisco the same evening, informed him of the engagement, felt and heard him pause for an instant, then he congratulated her and asked when the wedding date would be. "Be happy, my love. You are right. It is time for you to marry," he said and reminded her that if she needed him he would always be there.

Swallowing the sudden tears, she murmured, "You too, Dev. Be happy, please, please be happy!"

Among the few belongings she takes with her, wherever her future home will be, is a copy of William Shakespeare's works, the same textbook she used as an undergraduate student in college.

A banknote torn carefully in half lies hidden among its pages. Underlined in blue ink, a passage devoid of further clarification:

"Where souls do couch on flowers we'll hand in hand."

She hears a man calling her name.

She does not respond.

He calls again, more insistently.

Quickly, she runs into the bathroom, locks the door against the intruder.

Footsteps ascend the stairs, pause at the empty bedroom and retreat.

Quietly, trying to be unobtrusive, she opens the door, calm now, controlled, intending to descend the stairs, rejoin the party downstairs, but in her own time, at her own tempo.

Directly beneath her, a wine bottle in his hand, is the man with whom she will share her life.

She lies down on the bed, suddenly exhausted, and falls deeply asleep for no more than a few minutes, but immediately the aristocratic old gentleman appears. His face is clear, peaceful, beloved.

He blesses her and vanishes.

She awakens, no longer hesitant, descends the stairs, finds her wedding bouquet and tosses it, her husband takes her arm and leads her outside to the car under a shower of rice, and she rides away with him towards an unnamed hotel on an unnamed island.

Only in childbirth, while she is again asleep, will the beloved old man appear to guard, comfort, and bless her each time her Jewish children are brought into the world.

Part Five
REPRISE

SEATTLE

The news continued to be depressing.

Innocent people were again being attacked by hypnotized fanatics masquerading as true believers, ready to die for one or another amorphous cause, (while the disingenuous instigators remained hidden, eager to seize the spoils for which they would never, ever consent to sacrifice their own lives).

And the puzzling emergence of exotic "new" diseases (the probable result of poisons belched from factories throughout the world or the uncontrolled destruction of forests and pollution of the seas and lakes) impacted all living things, while the lovely, blue paradise bestowed on humanity was being destroyed inch by precious inch for the enrichment of a handful of money-blinded, incredibly selfish families.

Like everyone else Petra adapted, continued the daily routine of waking, showering, swallowing a cup of tea and driving to the college where she taught.

She heard the front door opening.

"Thanks, Mom, I'll get them from school later," her daughter called, and then a clear little voice said, "Hello, Oma. We're waiting for you!"

"I'll be there in a minute, sweetie," her grandmother replied. The two little girls sat down on a chair near the door and began to sing.

"Twinkle, twinkle little starrrrr......"

Petra automatically hummed the Mozart piano variations to the ancient folk song and finished dressing.

She passed the mirror in the bathroom and saw a wide gray streak in her blonde hair, numerous furrows etched deeply into her face, realized they were the price paid for being allowed to live, and did not resent the onset of old age. Indeed, was intensely grateful she had been granted the ability to have life.

"*Met de ouderdom komen moeilijkheden*," a Dutch acquaintance had whined the last time she had visited Scheveningen.

"*Met de ouderdom komt dankbaarheid dat ik mocht leven*," she had retorted instantly, remembering the two little boys, her cousins, betrayed and murdered before they were four years old!

On the rug she suddenly noticed the limp, green half of an ancient ten-dollar bill, which had fluttered out of a book she had just leafed through, and hurriedly replaced it between the pages.

She closed the tattered cover and put the aging text back in the night stand next to her bed.

Where she could easily find it.

Then she went downstairs, passing several photographs of her grown son and daughter with their spouses and children decorating the staircase walls, murmured once again (as was her daily custom), "Thank you, Opa," as she nodded towards the pen and ink sketch of the Dutch Sephardic grandfather who had sacrificed his life to guarantee the continuance of her own, and then heard an insistent, "Oma, hurry up! We're going to be late!"

She rushed outside and then took the two youngest grandchildren to school, before driving herself to work.

For an instant, before getting out of the car, she mused on the past, with its shared years of overwhelming happiness and endless mourning.

Then, as always, she accepted it and looked towards the classroom building where her students waited.

Overjoyed, she was alive!

The End

ACKNOWLEDGEMENTS

I thank my family, particularly, my grandson, who guided me through the vagaries of the computer age: my friends, Shmuel and Gail Elad, Ann Marie Putter, Susan Guralnick (and the Brandeis University National Women's Committee): Dr. Bob Baugher: Zelda Prensky Weiss: my editor, Carole Glickfeld and publisher, Kristen Morris.

But ultimately, without Izaak Abas and Carel Arnold Abas, both late of Arnhem, The Netherlands, this book would not have been possible.

H.M.

2008

AUTHOR NOTES

How can I begin to acknowledge the gifts bestowed on me by New York City? With gratitude I recall among them: free access to the Metropolitan Museum of Art where I spent my childhood gazing at marble art treasures of the Ancient World, as well as the magnificent paintings for which it is renowned: the welcoming, open doors of the Museum of Natural History, wandering with my father, hynotized by the dinosaur skeletons or staring in wonder at the sky in the Planetarium: weekend showings of free movies at the the Museum of Modern Art, followed by a visit to the Picasso "Guernica:" the glorious Metropolitan Opera, avidly listened to on the radio as a child, visited often as a young adult.

And two Manhattan landmarks I cherish for very different reasons: Temple Emanuel and the International House both of which taught me tolerance and understanding.

New York, the most amazing city on earth which I owe a debt I can never repay, and will love forever!

AUTHOR BIOGRAPHY

Born in The Netherlands, Henriette Mendels found the peace and time to complete *"Intermezzo for Solo Viola,"* after retiring from teaching at an American college. With its publication, she fulfilled a promise made many years ago to two little victims of the Holocaust. She has written an anthology of short stories, soon to be published, and is working on several other books. Henriette Mendels lives in Washington State, is a graduate of the University of Maryland and holds an advanced degree from San Diego State University.

ORDER PAGE

To order: visit our website www.tigresspublishing.com
or call 1 800 771 2147.